MIND HARVEST: EARTH

By Jake Berry Ellison Jr.

Day One

... what we call reality arises in the last analysis from the posing of yes-no questions and the registering of equipment-evoked responses; in short, that all things physical are information-theoretic in origin and this is a participatory universe.

— John Wheeler

I

Adam Howard, hunched over his writing desk at 4:30 AM under the blue hue of track LED lighting, appeared dead. His broad back motionless under a tight white T-shirt. His pale bald head lulled on his left forearm. Right eye open and unblinking. But he wasn't dead, just mentally combing through his extensive research on zombie culture for a story angle that had not yet been explored. His heavy gold-plated ballpoint pen poised over the blank first page of a journal notebook to capture any good ideas. So far, nothing. He loved all things zombie, and his therapist in collusion with his physician told him to meditate when he woke early. Meditate on what? On whatever you like as long as it isn't drinking, work or family. This was the forth very-early morning he sat at the red metal desk in five days. His stomach extended slowly. His eye blinked.

Broadway Avenue under streetlights floated in his floor-to-ceiling condo window. Downtown Seattle gleamed in ambient florescence beyond that, already teaming with predawn crawlers. Several more minutes passed like this, and though he craved a drink, writing or at least preparing to write his zombie novel would have to be satisfaction enough. They had warned him he was on the brink of losing his health for good, and, yes, possibly dying much too young from cardiac arrest or stroke. He suddenly flung his left hand over his shoulder and scratched with his nails. He dropped back into meditation. A train of thought he had not pursued before bubbled up: What if angels, which are consciousness without bodies, came down to battle zombies, which are bodies without consciousness? His hand twitched to write the question and he raised his head, but the question was unsatisfactory. The best part of zombie stories was that humans had to save themselves; and the best zombies had the appearance of rudimentary consciousness, hinting at the tantalizing possibility they could become a thinking, deadly rival for dominance over Earth. He dropped the pen on the page, sat up, stretched his arms up. A nerve fired and sent pain into his neck.

"Goddamn it."

He rubbed at the base of his neck. The nerve jolt cleared his mind just long enough for an idea to form: What if zombies could breed? What if they could spread zombieism by biting *and* procreation? He wrote in the notebook: It became a well-known fact among the survivors that the zombies were not only driven by a insatiable desire to eat living flesh, but that they were also driven to have sex. He exclaimed, into the quiet of his bachelor condo, "The first zombie story ever to include zombie orgies!" No mystery where that idea comes from, he thought, dropping the pen and standing up. He hadn't had sex … but he cut the train of thought off. He knew better than to go down that road. She had left him and that was that. He doesn't blame her. It's not his fault either. Just the way life goes. It is what it is. He padded over to the stainless steel, marble and teakwood kitchen. He'd made out alright in the divorce. Out of the top drawer, he took up the cigarette pack and lighter. Bad for his heart but then so was the memory of her. And, he admitted as he drew in the smoke, grateful for the nicotine and routine of smoking, he had made the choice of career over intimacy long before she cut her practice in half and went back to school to study tribal anthropology and found a female lover. "I married my mother after all," he told the cigarette. The half-bottle of red wine cooed at him, so he drank all of it. He dropped the cigarette butt into the bottle, walked to the bathroom, pealed down his shorts, lifted off the T-shirt, shrugged at his hairy bulk in the mirror and stepped into the shower.

He turned on the shower radio. It started the news hour from the beginning whenever he turned it on. After the usual soft news, the news anchor turned to their series on Internet security: "Members of Congress will be holding hearings later this week with the CEOs from the four American corporations that run the country's Internet's infrastructure as well as produce or control nearly all of the content. Hackers have made Swiss cheese of Internet security …" Public radio had been doing a deep dive into the nearly weekly comprise of major websites as well as servers. He barely listened.

After 20 minutes of rocking left to right and back under the hot water to maximize coverage, his mind loosened by the smoke and drink, Adam let his brain wander from work to his own writing. A thought emerged about the culture of zombies, a preamble. He switched off the radio and left the walk-in shower running, padded to his desk and wrote: Zombies were all the rage. A lot of books. A lot of movies. Television shows. It wasn't just a subculture fad. On Halloween, this nationwide obsession turned the United States of America into Zombie Land. Mothers spent entire afternoons swabbing fake blood on their children's cheeks, sticking strips of fake flesh on their torn shirts, matting toddler hair with gore. Everybody really had a good time with it. We dreamed up ways our existence would be annihilated and made movies out of the most fantastical. And what could be more fantastic than a mysterious virus that stripped humans of their identities and set them to biting each other? We had solved the old philosophical zombie problem—How do I know another person is conscious? If they don't howl and bite, they're conscious! Call it playful fatalism. He dropped the pen like dropping the mic and walked in front of the tall window, naked and wet, across the heated tile floor to the kitchen.

    He looked longingly at the next bottle of wine waiting to be uncorked and felt pride that he had not plowed through it the night before; but instead of going for it, he heavily pushed the button on his ten-thousand-dollar automatic espresso machine. He took the latte back to the shower with him. An hour later he was on the crowded Number Eight, rolling down steep Denny Way though the high-rise density of South Lake Union, his daily ride from Capitol Hill to the Puget Sound waterfront where he'd worked for 30 years as an assistant city editor for the *Seattle Daily Record.*

II

Natalie Rodriguez woke at six, performed her workout to a video in her living room/dinning room that shared space with the kitchen and then began working her way through a dozen yoga poses. All behind closed shades, because the windows to her 600-square-foot apartment in the Lower Queen Anne neighborhood of Seattle faced other apartment's windows and didn't get any sunshine. She wasn't modest or fearful so much as polite. She'd been to several floor-parties, in both her building and the next-door building, where she met her window neighbors. They were all also very polite, though certainly not shy or dull. Natalie, in other words, was an educated, talented young person in a city newly teaming with educated, talented young people all striving to build an adult life. Her age-peers working for the dozen major tech companies in downtown had driven all the apartments with views out of the economic range of a journalist in her first year of full-time employment. Even a hint of direct sunlight would have put the apartment out of range of her budget. When the young French couple whose kitchen window faced Natalie's left for the day, they would leave the shades up on a lineup of windows giving Natalie a passthrough view in the early evenings of the Space Needle and the high-rises of Belltown. An esprit de corps among the newly salaried, engaging in work they had dreamed about in college, carrying the world to a utopian future built on technology, empowered by the ideology that collective brain power, collective innovation, led by the sparks of genius in each of them, would create a more just and entertaining world. This, this understanding, this ethic and drive was what Natalie strove to bring to the analogue *Seattle Daily Record*. She saw it in her peers and in the great innovators of the 1990's and 2000's who created and run the cyber-techno backbone of the world. That said, she acknowledged, her French neighbors' largess was a bit annoying, more gesture than practical, since they all worked late into the evening, rarely getting home before midnight. Then they cocooned in front of a show or video game to recharge for the next day.

Her relaxation poses done, Natalie wiped down the yoga mat, dried it, rolled it and stashed it between the spindly legs of the only piece of furniture in the living room area, a blue, warn-crush-velvet loveseat with rounded arms perfect for napping on in front of the big screen TV. She twisted on the burner under the teapot, then laid out a range of clothes for the day. She'd make that decision after a second cup of coffee. Water heated to just about boiling, she poured the water over the grounds in a Chemex. She drank two to three cups of coffee every morning while checking the *Daily Record's* story budget document online, adding her own lines and then getting dressed for the office. Black. No sugar. Coffee was part of her career regimen, not dessert.

She sat on her bed, covers over her legs, laptop open and pointed to the online story budget, sipping the coffee. She had an idea for a series of blog posts that could be combined into a story for print in the Sunday paper, perhaps in a month. That's what she saw in her idea, but she had little hope of getting permission for the series from her current editor. For him, blog posts were simply story briefs that wouldn't make the print edition. But she would not give up.

One day she would earn the right to write with freedom, and then they'd understand the impact of online story-telling. Every day she kept hammered away at it, fearlessly going over her editor's head when she felt she had an especially good cause. She was determined to make her future a reality sooner than later. She couldn't be careless or flippant, however. He'd grill her about her story idea, and if she had nothing to go on but a hunch, he'd harangue her mercilessly about the reporter's job—get facts, not rumors or hunches or wild guesses.

 She wanted to hate him but couldn't, not really. He's old but does not lech like several editors she could name or act fatherly, mansplaining every obvious thing, like the editorial page editor. Frankly, she had to admit, he treated her like he treated everyone: Dismissive, if he thought an idea was bad; and all in, against even the managing editor, if he thought a story important. He edits with a heavy hand, though, scoffing whenever she argued for a sentence because it gave "voice" to her story. "If your story needs verbal pizzazz to interest the reader, than either you haven't done enough reporting or the story sucks." He's just a jerk with a short temper, especially after lunch.

She edited the story proposal down to a long sentence, picked her clothes, brushed out her hair and launched headlong into the day.

III

The geography of the *Seattle Daily Record*'s newsroom clung to the pattern of the editorial fiefdoms established in the 1950s, during the newspaper's first big expansion along with other metro dailies around the country, buying up neighborhood competitors and locking in Seattle's version of the monopoly of regional print newspapers that made a few men rich and powerful, created the career journalist and every day reported the news that would be stolen by radio and television news producers. In the resurgence of newspaper dominance, the newsroom of the *Daily Record* took up one large floor with desks spread out in clumps. Only the fictions of newsprint sections divided them: Features, Sports, Photography, Copy Editors, Layout Editors, Metro and the Investigation Team. Adam sat at a desk near the edge of the reporters who covered cops, courts, city and county government and those who wrote news feature stories and those elderly reporters whose beats no one really knew what they were but didn't want to be bothered with trying to fire them. They would retire eventually. Adam's press-wood desk had been part of a wave of upgrades to the newsroom performed some 25 years in the past. It came with two big drawers, which he had stuffed full of papers, bags and old promotional tchotchkes and company T-shirts and never opened again almost from the day he got the new desk. Instead of using drawers, which he hated bending over to dig in, he stacked all of his important papers, research, books and printouts of recently edited stories on the top of his desk. He had a pathway for reaching the phone and a cleared rectangle just the size of his keyboard. The coffee cup, which had been only occasionally rinsed since he threw the last cup against a wall in the sports fiefdom six years before, he balanced precariously on one stack of papers or other as he drank from it throughout the day. Since he was the chief assistant metro editor, his desk was closer to the city editor's office than the other three assistant metro editors so he could grunt back at her when she made demands or ridiculing jokes about city officials.

First thing he did after throwing the power switch on his terminal was cruise national, regional and local news sites and make a list of the stories they should have had but didn't. Then be assigned them to the reporters who should have had them but didn't. Never a very long list. This day, though, he added a note for the the *Seattle Daily Record*'s reporter in D.C. to delve a bit more into the hacking story, since two of the companies running the Internet were headquartered in Seattle. The best anyone has said about the hackers was that "So far, whoever it is has not taken control of anything. They just get in, look around and get out. Sometimes data is copied and sometimes not." The national desk ran the D.C. reporter and Adam had not been able to pull the national story into his bailiwick, a minor turf war over a thumbsucker of a story, but he could get the desk to add a context piece to their story budget. After all, the Internet didn't used to be run like cable television with just a few main owners. The upside, he wanted the story to note, was the reinvigoration of legacy media platforms such as newspapers. The downsides appeared to be legion. Could the nation backtrack on what had been called "Net Neutrality"?

Then he combed through each of his reporter's proposed stories budget. Those not making headway on the stories he'd assigned or agreed to allow would get a personal visit after the 10:00 a.m. newsroom editors' meeting. He noted the filed stories and wrote them at a time slot in his daily editing calendar, paper still. Those with new proposals he responded to right away. If a good idea, he required more information by 1:00 p.m. If a bad idea or poorly formed idea, he swatted them down mercilessly in order to avoid the ambiguity that would cause him to have to listen to fifteen minutes of complaining. He saved the easiest, those budgets belonging to his newest reporters, to the last, a hierarchy of earned respect.

Thus, when he got to Natalie Rodriguez' budget, it was 9:45 a.m. She wrote that morning, according to the time stamp:

"EDM is growing and has spawned a new subculture that is fast becoming mainstream—Who are they? How will they change the world? A series of blog posts would build a community and lead to a Sunday feature."

He quickly typed back: "I hate to break it to you, but electronic dance music is nothing new and a million stories about kids taking drugs and thinking they've discovered some uniquely beautiful way to live have already been published, even in our dinosaur of a newspaper. In fact, I remember something like this taking over my university in about 1972. Check in with me after the editors' meeting."

A second later, not after the meeting like he had ordered, Natalie stormed over to his desk and spoke to the back of his head.

"Not everything important in the world happened before I was born," she said.

He assumed she wanted him to crane his neck, look around to acknowledge her, chronic neck pain and all. He did not. Throwing together the city budget for the meeting, he couldn't help hearing her tap her notebook against her thigh or hand or top of her head for all he cared. She huffed in a way he assumed she should have been embarrassed by but was still getting away with. Young and inexperienced, standing there with red cheeks, no doubt. Her professors never treated her like this! She clicked her pen at the back of his head.

"Goddamnit, Natalie." He coaxed without looking up from his computer screen. He switched to a document of a filed story about a superior court judge accused of failing to recuse himself from a lawsuit against a company in which his daughter had significant investments. "Look at this." She hovered over his back, eyes rolled to the back of her head, he assumed. "Why these guys think they can get away with stuff like this is an eternal mystery. And yet they do think they can. Sometimes they've ended up in a bad situation through the slow accretion of bad choices and little lies. Sometimes they just think they can and they are daredevils. Either way, we must watch them. We make phone calls. We plod along like Columbo, asking secretaries for secrets, combing though documents for evidence, hints of the next cheat."

Adam sighed to signal that he did not have unlimited patience while he swiveled around. He looked into her brown eyes and lifted his eyebrows. Understand? She did, sort of.

"Well, lucky for me there's more to journalism than camping out in some public official's hallway. Might as well be a stenographer." She pretzeled and unpretzeled her arms, tapped her notebook.

The ADHD generation, he thought. "I'm going to tell Robert you said that."

"I already did."

And undoubtedly she had. Robert, whose court story he had shown her, was too much infatuated with her not to be forgiving. She did in fact have a pretty, speckled face haloed by thick dark brown hair. The precious generation, he condescended. Her helicopter mother swooped in every few months from expensive retirement in Arizona, fishing for complements about her accomplished daughter. Natalie didn't need to be self-conscious, because her mother was handling that aspect of human interaction for her.

"Do you really need me to treat you with kid gloves over this too?" He didn't wait for her to answer with some smart-aleck remark, which was clearly on the way since her mouth curled into a smirk. He almost smiled then. She had a sharp tongue and a mean streak in her. He did like that about her. "You want to become a journalist? Or, fart around blogging for the rest of your life?"

"Blogging is journalism." She crossed her arms and tapped her middle finger against her bicep, catlike.

"Not around here it ain't."

"Why are you even my editor then?"

Adam snorted and swiveled back to face the computer screen. How she thought it wasn't as plain as day that she hoped to be rescued from him and why she insisted on going through the routine over and over, showed just how much she was still a kid. Like a teenager coming home late from a dance with boozy breath and mussed-up hair and declaiming the injustice of being grounded. He certainly never said anything like that, because he didn't want to demean her. Just that she was so unconscious. She'd only been on staff a few months, but that was long enough to recognize what all the researchers said: These kids were impatient for advancement and reward. They entered every relationship with an eager fearlessness. He assumed, defensively he had to admit, that Natalie didn't yet recognize that though he was old, overweight and balding, he was still among the best editors in the country. He also had the allegiance of other editors and most of the reporters, as well. So she was unlikely to get much sympathy and so would have grow up faster. Besides, he really was trying to teach her something. He didn't want to break her spirit. To have a reporter who can stand toe-to-toe with some powerful person who spends more on toilet paper at a summer chalet than the reporter makes in a year, asking hard questions in dogged pursuit, that was more important than strict obedience to Adam. Natalie had the spirit and talent. She just needed the experience and discipline.

  He turned his attention back to the screen and noticed that the lead sentence on the judge story bugged him so he erased it. Forgetting about her as soon as he had turned around. The whole story needed a write-through. It had all the right details, but it didn't pop off the screen yet. Natalie noisily fumed, unwilling to be dismissed. Adam looked up at Elena Bell, the city-county government editor sitting directly across from him. She noticed his plea, raised her eyebrows and nodded. Bell assigned the daily news briefs. She and Adam had worked seamlessly with each other for nearly three years, a professional lifetime, like dog years.

"Hey, Natalie," Bell said. She looked around her monitor to make eye contact with the young reporter. Natalie suddenly remembered what Bell did for a living and flinched. "Will you take these four press releases and make briefs out of them?" She smiled and raised the sheets of paper. Natalie dropped her arms and stepped from behind him with an "Ugh!"

"Don't forget the links in the Web versions."

Adam smiled at Bell. Nice touch. Damn kids. There's so many of them, and they're into everything and one of these days they will change into something terrible, their parents… running everything … like a zombie infestation. He wrote that sentence down on a sticky note at the base of his monitor's riser and went back to the city budget document. In addition to seeing her 1970's styled blond locks haloing the monitor on her desk five days a week, Adam also worked closely with Bell on several stories a months, since local government overlapped with courts and cops. Along with the other two assistant city editors, they had developed a routine of mutual support for the punishment of reporters who dared approach them to complain about their jobs or assignments or edits. If they felt especially aggrieved, one of the editors would send the offending reporter out to some minor fire or car wreck that didn't stand a chance of making the paper.

Wonder if we're bogging in the newspaper stuff

IV

After a bruising editors' meeting in which all of the metro stories got kicked off the front page by two stories from sports about the announcement of divorce of the star pro-quarterback and its potential impact on his upcoming playoff performance; another mass murder in America, front-page worthy because the gunman had been shooting into a school playground from the top window of the business he owned several hundred yards away (with mass shootings every couple of weeks, it took unique circumstances to get one on the front page); and, a soft-lead story about the latest technology-sector employment report (another staggering increase!) to package with the national desk's Internet hacking story. How would the city survive? What does it mean that nearly eighty percent of people under 30 worked for a global tech company? Two bright spots for Adam's afternoon came out of it, however: He got to assign Natalie to help with the business tech story. And since the front page was spoken for, he got another day to work on Robert Henderson's judge story, which was too good to bury inside.

Natalie worked for Adam because bloggers were popular but still unwanted by editors and Adam ran the *Daily Record*'s reporter training and innovation program, which was designed to be training in data-driven journalism not rumor-driven journalism, Adam grumbled whenever the subject came up. The *Daily Record* had only two full-time bloggers anyway: Star Gossip written by the dowdy Daryl Mead; and Tech Culture by Natalie. Adam had argued that the *Seattle Daily Record* should toe the big-J-journalism-line and become the go-to newspaper for the people who actually gave a shit. What would Star Gossip or Tech Culture have to offer anyone with a brain? But he lost. He consoled himself with insight born from his intimate understanding of his mother's evolutionary biology work: We are a social animal and everyone wants to be cool, so the *Daily Record* hired a couple of bloggers.

Natalie filed her Voices From the Street sidebar to the tech story early and then, showing initiative, got Robert out of the building to help her dig through a rumor she'd heard about the dance-scene story. Adam agreed to let them disappear for the afternoon, mostly because it would get his best courts reporter, Robert, out of the building and help him forget, however briefly, the trauma and insults Adam was delivering to his elegant story about the judge.

After some reporting help and coaching by Robert at the Black Toast Cafe across the street from the paper, one of the dozens of hipster martini bars that began crowding out the local taverns in Seattle during the tech takeover, Natalie reinserted the dance item into her story budget document and added a bit of information that was supposed to change Adam's mind: "A group of young tech-savvy EDM enthusiasts are holding a private party that may, my sources tell me, be attended by Ted Mannerheim."

Bless her eager heart, Adam thought when he checked the document. If true, that was a good blog post, but only because it could lead to a news story for the paper. Mannerheim was the founder of Pleistocene Dynamics, a mega-tech company quickly swallowing up every promising startup in the region or, if they wouldn't sell, hiring away all their engineers. So, a little dirt on him could result in an information swap and a few stories the *Daily Record* might not otherwise be the first to find out about.

Demonstrating his gratitude that Natalie had actually produced a budget line that might possibly be a story, he didn't cross out the words "my sources tell me." Instead, he walked to her desk and wedged himself between the back of her desk and the wall.

"What sources?"

"What sources for what?" She tried to hide her smile but failed. She pushed her chair back, pursed her lips and looked up at him. She fingered the gold chain of her rosary necklace, the cross dangling down into her white shirt. All unconscious young human ticks she would eventually outgrow, as soon as she realized how much evolution teased and tricked her into a reproductive stance. Adam almost asked her for the twentieth time why she hadn't gone into television but let it go. She has, somewhat admirably he had had to admit, answered before that she wanted to become a journalist and not just another pretty face on television. Instead, he kept eye contact.

"Don't be coy," he addressed her words. "It's the only story you've come up with yet that's worth a damn, if it's true."

"I won't know if it's true unless I go." She widened her eyes and smiled, a genuine expression from having received what she took to be a compliment. A real story!

He resisted the temptation to make her do a round of briefs for being so damn innocent.

"So go." He walked away.

Adam got a Coke from the vending machine in the hallway. If nothing else, it would keep her out of the office long enough for Robert to focus and finish rewriting that damn court story. Robert, only a few years older than Natalie, had become enraptured by her body's siren song. Adam took his Coke outside to the back courtyard and smoked one of the three cigarettes he allowed himself in a day. Three more than his doctor wanted him to have. When his wife left—news-junky hotheads are not known for their long relationships—he'd sworn off Coke and smoking and overeating, which meant that at that moment he was again failing at most of his life-changing goals. Then he realized—and where the realization truly came from was impossible to know because the mind, despite so many brain scans and experiments, he was fond of saying, is an unchartable morass—he'd forgotten to remind Natalie to get a picture of Mannerheim before trying to talk with him. His stress-response to this missed instruction ramped up irrationally and his heart started pounding. His doctor's voice leaped out at him from the bushes: "Relax before you blow a vein! It'll be what it'll be!"

He repeated the mantra: It'll be what it'll be.

And, of course, it was what it was. But at the time, Adam was mistaken about what it was.

DAY TWO

I do not know what I may appear to the world to be, but to myself I seem to have been only like a boy playing on the sea-shore, and diverting myself in now and then finding a smoother pebble or prettier shell than ordinary whilst the great ocean of truth lay all undiscovered around me.

— Newton

I

Pitch black. Adam couldn't see. Something had broken or flown through his condo …. No. His phone was buzz buzz buzzing, like it was really pissed off this time. He slept with blackout curtains, no clocks, and he made certain his phone was buried. Only two numbers from his contacts would make it buzz at night. The city editor's and his mother's, which would have to come from the grave. Still he continued to pay for her line. He had no idea what time it was. Buzz Buzz … Finally his phone kicked over to leave a fucking message already. The way his heart was thudding in his chest, he didn't dare answer the call. Not until … but then it started buzzing again. He yelled an expletive into the darkness. He was not a peaceful person in the morning, a trait which did not help his relationship. Truth be told, he had a hell of a time growing past the memory of living with someone he loved for more than a decade and then having that someone leave him, however cordially. He was cranky because of that but also because he worked late every night and still couldn't sleep, which was also not conducive to a relationship. He pushed the side of his face into the pillow until the phone stopped again. Then the phone started up again.

"Fucking fuck!" He yelled. "Better be a plane crash with a *thousand* dead!"

He leaned off the side of the bed and clawed around until he found his pants, got the phone out just as it kicked over to message again. Kristi Beach, his phone announced with a very bright light. City Editor. The time was 3:45 AM. No message. He dial her back preemptively.

"Kristi?"

"Adam! You can be woken from the dead. Terrific. Just got a call I wanted to tell you about."

"Oh, okay. I'm always here for you, you know that. Your nubile daughter missing again?" He pushed his tone toward haha but couldn't entirely scrub all the panic out. Despite thirty years in the business and sleeping drugs, a late night phone call still made him panicky as well as angry. He was an emotionally complex creature! Or, maybe that was *because* of his thirty years in the business, which, as he told friends not in the business, was a "High-conflict, high-stress and low-reward career." As his chest tightened, his doctor yelled at him from under the bed: "You're too young to have the cardiac problems that you do. Relax. It's just life." That or it would be his early death.

[margin note: let us be judge / kinda like]

"You're blogger ..."

"Natalie?"

"Yes."

"Sorry."

"Can I talk?"

"Sure. Sure. Just my doctor was distracting me."

"Sleeping with the enemy?"

"This point in my life, I'd sleep with the publisher."

"Ha! Okay, look, just got off the phone with ..."

"You know I have a heart problem."

"Ted Mannerheim's attorney."

"Perfect."

"Well, he said Natalie took some photos of the master at a private party, which invaded his privacy, he said, and they want them."

"You told him to go fuck himself."

"In no uncertain terms." A dish struck a pot or something else in her kitchen sink. If Beach was awake, she was moving. "Nevertheless, I would like to know what in Sam Hell she was up to, you know, just to get my story straight before my phone rings and it's fucking Brodman on the line. Did you send her?"

"Yes. I sent her to cover one of those private dance parties on the off chance Ted would be there. She got a tip." If the Executive Managing Editor Neal Brodman also got a call, Adam would lose the morning to meetings. His face grew hot. Call it preemptive frustration. Brodman's idea of management was to call meetings, which went on interminably since he had no idea how to run one.

"... and that mattered to us because?"

"Not sure. Just a hunch. She's been after me to cover the damn electronic dance music scene and, of course, I refused. But when she heard Ted was going to be there and given his reputation ..."

"Which we will not conjecture about in terms of our motives."

"Right. But, we just wanted to see why the master would go to some dance party full of kids."

"Okay. I guess she is running a blog and that's sort of blog-like."

"Now I feel dirty." He swung his feet off the bed, failing to resist going for the cigarettes in a bedside drawer ... somewhere in the dark before him. He pointed the phone's screen forward for a second. Spotted the dresser and caught her mid-sentence.

"... it's the new world." She paused. A lighter ignited. She'd beaten him to it. "Let me put it to you this way." Exhale. Cough. "You gave her the assignment."

"Exactly." Adam lit his own cigarette. "And why I gave her the assignment is a matter of free speech, and I don't have to tell anyone jack shit about it." He pushed pillows into a ramp and leaned back. He had become his mother, smoking in bed though everyone had begged her not to.

"I love the First Amendment ... and lying. Now, I think you'd better call your girl Friday and let her know lawyers are involved and she's to keep her yap shut. AND no Facebooking it either, for fuck sakes."

"I'm dialing as I hang up."

He stood off the bed and fumbled for the light, got it on, rubbed his face and mic-checked his voice. Put on his pants. Laughed. He sat back on the bed, let himself wakeup while the cigarette lasted. He didn't want her to be too proud thinking she'd actually done something important. "She got lucky," he said out loud, trying to set a tone of dismissal. Nevertheless, something had really freaked out ol' Ted and they were going to figure it out. Her phone rang about a half a second before she answered … phone surgically grafted to her face, apparently.

"Uh oh."

"You're fine. Just don't say anything to anyone outside of myself and Kristi. Got it?"

"Yes."

"What happened?"

"I kicked his ass. That's what happened."

He imagined her high-kicking, like a cartoon figure, and that didn't boost his confidence.

"Yes, but, what happened?"

"When I got there in my car, I decided I would go paparazzi and worry about the details later."

He did like this kid's spunk, though he'd never say so. It would feed her bad habit of needing praise. Nothing wrecked a reporter's productivity more than praise. The rule of thumb he lived by, as had generations of editors before him, was if you don't hear anything you're doing fine.

"Did you happen to take down any names, email or phone numbers?"

"I didn't."

"First rule of photography?"

"Get names."

"Okay?"

She projected patience. To her credit, she didn't over-explain. Some reporters would've talked for ten minutes by this point in their conversation, defensive and whining about having to take their own photos. Natalie, on the other hand, waited for him to either have a full-fledge nut-out or give her a chance to explain herself or both, which was more likely, from her point of view. [windy]

Adam thought about having a little fun at her expense, after all it was nearly 4 a.m. and he would not be getting back to sleep … something like telling her she had to bring in donuts because it was her first lawyer call. His shook the idea from his head. Pulled another cigarette from the pack.

"Just give it to me chronologically."

He lit the cigarette.

"I didn't figure I'd have much time, so, like I said, I jumped out of the car expecting to shoot photos and get the hell out of there."

"Wait. You weren't invited?"

"Not exactly."

Complication Number One. He exhaled loudly into the dark. His mind worked the problem and decided they'd work out the angle later. Mannerheim was a local celebrity, and he was attending what they took to be a public event. ... but of course their issue gets a lot easier if ... "Where were you when you took pictures of Mannerheim? Inside? On the lawn?" Leading the witness your honor. Time-honored.

"Second law of photography?"

They said it together, "Know your rights and the rights of others."

"Don't tell me you were on the public sidewalk?" Adam tried not to sound like he was about to yell, Hell yeah!

"Definitely on the sidewalk."

"That a girl!"

"Thank you!"

She was as surprised as he was glad, though he instantly regretted saying it like that. Skip. Move on.

"Can you see him plainly, inside, you know, hanging out?"

"You can in the photo I took from inside the building." Deadpan delivery.

He laughed. "What photos do you have?"

"I emailed you the three best. Two from outside of him going in and then the only shot I could get off of him inside, under the lights, swinging his little arms around."

Adam walked over to his desk and opened the laptop. "He does have short arms."

"They're like T-Rex arms. I had to use a flash, so as soon as I shot it, I bolted for the door."

"Okay, great. But why would he be all worried about us taking a photo of him at a party, even though he *was* swinging his arms around?"

"Because it's gross?"

"Maybe. Looking now." The laptop was running. He opened the mail program and got to her photos. Two were taken from about twenty feet from the front door, from possibly the sidewalk or driveway. Those plainly showed Mannerheim smiling up at three young women. He stood about five-foot-three. One of the women was African American with a very big afro. She had on a long coat, buttoned. Her eyes were locked on his. The two others, blonds, stood with their arms crossed on either side of the black woman. They looked up at her while she spoke down at Mannerheim with intensity sharpening her features. It did not look like she was saying something pleasant. The third photo, the indoor photo, was somewhat blurred but still a clear view of Mannerheim, jacketless, with his shirtsleeves rolled up and his arms poking downward. His face pointed at the floor. He appeared to be shimming. Adam laughed.

"I know! Right?"

He studied the pictures more closely, looking for signs of drug-use or even drinking or smoking, anything that might embarrass the great man more than simply hanging out with a few young women, who, unless they were minors, could have a perfectly good excuse for bending the great man's ear. Meanwhile, Natalie had prattled on with her story.

"Well, I'm not sure because there's not much else to tell. I waited in my car until I saw him walking up the sidewalk, alone.

When he got to the door, it opened and the woman with the afro came out and started talking. I got those two photos, like I said, from the sidewalk."

"They didn't see you then?"

"I was standing in the shadow of a tree just under the streetlamp."

"You're like a private eye."

"That's what growing up with the television always on will do for a person, that and I have actually done this job for a while ..."

He didn't bite, making up for calling her a girl. They were even.

"... then I put the big camera away and went in with just my phone."

"Door security."

"No one."

"Hmmm." Could be a good thing. They had no controls, so how were we supposed to know it was private? But then it's probably bad, he thought. You don't have a bouncer at a private party with friends. "Hmmm," he said again.

"What?"

"Just 'Hmmm.' Go on."

"I went inside to hunt him down and spotted him in a corner dancing very close, but, I have to be honest, not obscenely close between the two blonds, more like they were making a sport of it and he didn't care. I flashed him and ran for it. Just as I got to my car, one of the girls dancing with him and who'd been with him at the door caught up to me and asked me who I was. I told her. Then I got in and drove away."

Scanning the background of the photos, he saw what looked like a pretty normal party of this sort—young, tattooed kids and flashing lights. But there was Mannerheim.

"Anything odd about the women, other than they were talking with Mannerheim?"

"Not really. They just looked like your average sorority types, sort of ... more like girls who played soccer in high school and were still keeping the weight off."

"Expensive clothes?"

"You see the photos."

"But I wouldn't know an expensive pair of jeans if they crawled out from under my bed."

"I thought ..."

"Don't even."

"Thinking."

"How about ..."

"Thinking!"

"... jewelry?"

"I don't know. Why does it matter?"

"I don't know, and that's the point." Adam closed the laptop and opened the notebook where he'd started the zombie story and wrote the date on the top of the facing blank page. He suddenly decided he would be more successful as a diarist than a novelist. "Okay, seems pretty straight forward to me, though we might have to give up the photo from inside the party. I don't know, maybe not since he is a public figure. Just wish you'd have been invited to the party."

"That's never going to happen. These kids run a tight ship."

"How do you know?"

"They have an encrypted, private social network platform and the only way I heard about this was from some guy on Reddit, Josh he called himself, who'd gotten himself uninvited and then outted them. Anonymously, in case you were wondering."

"And I was. In the morning we'll work this through and look at whatever other notes you have. Also, we'll want to get library on Mannerheim, not just the shit we've written about him either. I want all his public records, home ownership, businesses, corporate boards, everything. As soon as you get there, tell library I said so."

"Okay. I will. And ... Thanks!"

She hung up quickly.

He snorted at her pleasantly, took up the charging cable dangling off the edge of the dresser and plugged it into the phone. He folded the notebook over the pen and went back to bed. Lying back, he let his mind swarm around the photos and asked himself several times, koan-like, "What could possibly be in them that would upset the master?" There wasn't any obvious drug use going on, so even if anyone there was underage, what did it matter? Was someone there a convict or illegitimate offspring? How would we ever know?

At 6 AM, he gave up the search for sleep or any answers and got out of bed, showered and went for coffee down on the corner of East Pine and Melrose. Chris and Dan came in about a half-hour later, snug as two bugs in a rug. Good for them, they'd been in the same couple's group. Some made it through and others didn't. He read the paper, pen in hand.

An hour later, he caught the bus downtown to the paper. He'd get the crew's ducks in a row to prepare for Mannerheim's lawyer. They'd need all the leverage they could get on the master. Nothing made him love his job more than those moments when they'd caught someone out and caused them to exhibit an alarm response, like a frantic bird call in the trees or an ink jet from an octopus. So far, though, they didn't know what they'd caught Mannerheim out at, so they'd have to have their feelers up and tuned in.

II

Natalie placed her phone on the charging platform next to her computer, handbag, necklace and watch. Stripped of technology, she closed the curtain on the French couple, whose suite of wake-up, full-spectrum lamps would begin rising soon. She'd have to rise soon herself, but proceeded through shower to pajamas and dropped onto her couch, where she pulled the afghan knitted by her grandmother off the back onto her body. She said, "Continue watching 'Highway Dimensions.'" The show had been filmed around Seattle nearly twenty years earlier by graduates of Seattle University, where she earned degrees in the Philosophy of Science and Technology and Journalism programs. She'd become hooked on the 16-episode show that had aired on Seattle's famous-though-defunct public access television channel 29. Fred "Long-Handle" Grimes climbed down from the cab of his truck, an ironic mishmash of chrome and molded plastic that looked like a psychedelic spaceship had tried to swallow a semi-truck, smiled teeth through his [?ush] big mustache and reached toward the camera with a tentacled hand. The show was about a team of multi-dimensional truck drivers. The sitcom follows the show's main cast around as they gripe about their strange families, the unknowable corporation they work for and the union always pushing them to go on strike in one dimension or other. She drifted off, blissfully, to the on-screen banter and deep-throated rev of the truck motors.

  As the daylight began to creep in around her window shades, she became aware of herself holding a big, heavy black cat. She petted the slick, gleaming body. As the cat began to relax onto her crossed legs, sinking, spreading, she realized that she was in a recurring dream. She panicked because the cat is a trick. How did it get into this world again? Someone fucked up and ordered the cat out of a magazine from the wizard. She had just gotten free of the last one. The cat, looking up at her with black eyes in a normal cat head, purred. But it's a trick. A game with terrifying consequences. When you ended up with the cat, you couldn't let it touch anything except your own body. Otherwise it would be absorbed into the material, the Earth or down a drain or into a crack in the floor and become impossible to extract. Eventually, the cat would swell over and throughout the world, smothering all life. So far, somehow, she had avoided this future. She stood up, cradling the cat, which is larger now and become impossible to hold. She finds the comic book and flips to the back pages, shifting the cat as its folds of rubbery flesh slump off her arm, finds the advertisement. She calls the number. The irritated wizard complains that it's not his responsibility if someone orders a cat. If you call, you get a cat! She explains in a blur of words she neither speaks nor understands that she didn't order the cat. The cat just appeared and that must be a violation of the conditions of purchase. He tells her, in mumbles, that he'll have to look at the receipt. She tells him the cat is getting to heavy. In fact, it has almost touched the edge of the counter where she is speaking just now, but she got the phone handset cradled between her ear and shoulder and used her free arm to contain the slumbering, sleek cat. The wizard grumbled but said, "I'm not taking it back, but because it's unclear why you have the cat I tell you a secret. Line a box with wax paper, completely with no gaps, and place the cat there. That will contain it." The phone disappears and she's searching frantically, the cat enormously heavy now, for a box. She finds one and puts it on the counter. The cat slumps over both arms and nearly hits the floor, but she gathers it up. Shifting the cat rapidly, she finds the drawer containing a wax paper roll. Her dream skips the rest. The cat is in the box, filling it completely like tar topped by a cat's head … but contained. She walks away, relieved but knowing the cat will get out and is a threat as long as she has it.

When Natalie woke up, the images of the dream and the feeling of dread still in her mind, she said to the blank blue screen of the television: "It didn't happen."

Best chap yet / show TV / have description.

III

A great feat of human intelligence happened when an early member of the species moved from learning only what was useful in the moment, such as a stick to poke away a snake or a sharp stone to scrape meat from the bones of a giant sloth, to learning an idea or technique without knowing the immediate use of it, such as how to file a cease and desist order against a newspaper and, what's more, get a federal court to approve the order in one morning's private session, and in effect present the paper, without preamble or private discussion of what photos the *Daily Record* might even be in possession of, with the first prior-restraint order said newspaper had ever received.

"By god Mr. Robbins," Adam took the single sheet of paper from the heavyset lawyer with the big head of hair and plunged down into a chair across the large table from the two Mannerheim representatives, "I'm going to get this framed and put it right next to my Pulitzer. In fucking fact, I'm going to put it over my Pulitzer!"

Kristi Beach put her bejeweled hand on Adam's arm.

"I think you just made us famous," she said demurely.

Kristi's daughters had so tortured the poor woman that though she was just over 50, it took something as outrageous as a prior restraint order to get any color into her puffy cheeks. That morning, she'd even put on lipstick. Adam thought. It was barely lightly pinkish, but all the same.

"You're missing the point," Mannerheim's head of communications, Tina Ejlali, said. "You can't tell anyone anything without violating that order." Thick black hair in a tight ponytail, $1,200 jacket, crisp white shirt. "You will also have to show up in court to defend your editor's and your reporter's actions." She didn't look at Adam or Natalie, who was sitting with her arms folded, embarrassed by her confusion and looking like she had not slept.

"It's just a photo," Natalie said.

[handwritten note: wasn't able to sort out all the players in this here.]

"Exactly," Adam said. "A photo we will print alongside a copy of this order." He felt such pride. It filled him with pleasure, not unlike alcohol which he had steered clear of so far that morning.

"If we even have a photo," Kristi said.

"Look, Adam ..." David Robbins, Mannerheim's personal attorney, began.

"Are you nuts? It's Mr. Howard ..."

Robbins laughed, opened his hands and raised them and folded them together.

"I think you're missing the gravity of the situation here. That's a goddamned federal court order." Jabbing his finger at the paper as he said so.

"We're on the record here, I'd like to remind you," Kristi said.

"There's never been a prior restraint issued outside of national security during wartime that has ever stood up," Adam said. "This will be published along with the thirty-six photos we have—it's the Internet age after all—and the order and every fucking thing I can find to print about Mr. Mannerheim."

"I thought we were on the record," Tina scoffed.

"You're on the record! We are the record!" He alternated pointed at the table and then himself. He knew better than to point at a lawyer. His voice had grown harsh with adrenaline. He coughed.

"Adam, your heart." Kristi squeezed his arm. "Besides, this has to go to our lawyers first. We do have lawyers you know, Tina."

"Look, perhaps Ms. Rodriguez would like to ..."

"I'm not saying anything." Natalie swept her hand palm out to wipe away the possibility.

"We're done here," Kristi said, standing. "We'll be in touch." She beamed. Her short hair nearly standing straight up. Her makeup-free eyes wide and bright.

The lawyer and communications director unfolded their hands and pushed themselves up like synchronized swimmers rising from the pool. Robbins clasped the latches on his brief case. He turned and looked out the big tinted window at the glistening waters of Puget Sound.

"Lovely day for a sail," he said sincerely. "Haven't been out on my boat for ages."

"Fear of cement shoes, I would image." Adam rocked back his chair, smiling, left eyebrow raised wrinkling the pale skin on top of his bald head.

"This isn't personal," Robbins said. He looked at Adam, pleadingly it seemed to Adam, and then at Natalie. "I expect you'll know a lot more very soon that will alarm even you." He turned back to Adam and looked directly into his eyes, trying to say with intention what he was not allowed to say with words. "We ..." He made a circling motion with his index finger that encompassed all of them in the room.

"Let's go," Tina ordered, standing at the doorway.

"Please, do go on," Kristi said. She let her mouth fall to a serious tightness.

"We are not the only interested party. I want you to understand that. When we can say more, we will and you'll be first to hear it ..."

"If we don't fight you."

"That's it."

Tina had grabbed Robbins's upper arm, more respectfully guiding the old gentleman than bossing him. Robbins took a business card from his shirt pocket and flicked it at Adam. "Cell's on the back."

"Out. David. Out." Tina didn't pull his arm so much as suggest the way. She followed the big man out.

Adam noticed then how baggy Robbins's pants had become as they left the room. He'd lost his ass completely.

"Get the door," he told Natalie after the two lawyers had cleared the hall. "Okay, now. Wow. Natalie I want you to go back to that house, don't get caught if you can help it, and see who in the fuck is going in and out. If you get caught, just start screaming and drive away."

"Have you lost your mind," Natalie put her hand on the door knob.

Adam wrote Robbins' cell number on his note pad. He had a bad idea, but one worth pursuing.

"I get caught, I'm going to dial our attorneys."

"That's what I meant. Kristi?"

"Wow. Okay," she reached across the table, stabbed the lawyer's card with her finger and dragged it to her. "Don't break the rules here." She skimmed the court order again. "It says to stay away from Mannerheim and his property, so make sure that house doesn't belong to him. If it doesn't, stake it out. If it does, you two wait until I hear from our lawyers."

"It doesn't," Adam said. "We've got the list of his properties this morning," he nodded at at Natalie, whose pale face gave away some of her rising concern at what she was getting into, "and it's not on it."

"Okay then." Kristi wrote down the number to the paper's attorney on a yellow legal pad, tore it out and handed it to Natalie. "In case you do get picked up. Dial the number and leave the phone on throughout the entire encounter."

"Am I going to win a Pulitzer for this?"

"Not yet," Kristi said, "but keep asking those piercing questions and you'll definitely win a pink slip. Now get the fuck out of here and close the door, please."

Natalie closed the door behind her.

"I need a cigarette."

"I need one too."

They chain-smoked two cigarettes apiece in the conference room, in silence, tipping their ashes into water glasses. Kristi stood up first.

"We really are going to be famous," she said, dropping the butt into the water glass. She brushed ashes off the front of her jacket and walked out.

Adam smoked another cigarette while writing a list of questions and the people who might be able to answer them. He circled Mannerheim's name and made up his mind to get an off-the-record conversation with him, see if he wants to talk since there was clearly something bigger than a couple of photos driving interest in the *Daily Record*'s reporting.

IV

Parked on a street perpendicular to the house where she first encountered the group involved with Mannerheim, Natalie watched most of the property and the driveway, empty, from about two-hundred yards away, sitting in the driver's seat under the shadow of the streetlight hitting her car's roof. She'd been parked there for two hours, without coffee or water because needing a toilet would require her to drive away. She also didn't distract herself with her phone, since even with low backlighting it would have given her away by illuminating her face. Instead, she occupied herself writing the details of her first stakeout in a reporter's notebook, in which she wrote about how she parked her car, not having water so she wouldn't have to pee and not posting to social media. She wrote down the number of cars around her, diagramed her position relative to the house, described the 1970's ranch style house, periwinkle trim and asparagus walls, one of the few small working-class houses left in the neighborhood. She untied her hair and then tied it back into an even tighter ponytail, without swinging her head around or flaring her hair. She made a note of that. After the first twenty minutes, she'd exhausted her note-taking and used up a quarter of the long pages of the notebook. If she couldn't post to social media now, she could later recount her experience on her personal Facebook page ... if they let her. They just didn't realize how big of a following she could generate with this material! After complaining to herself until she hated herself for complaining, she'd been there an hour. After that, her brain fazed out while her eyes remained opened and pointed at the house.

 Then two vans pulled up. Took her a second to realize what had changed among outlines in the two-dimensions her nearly asleep brain had made of the world, then: Wham! Shit, two long white vans, like white tubes on black wheels ... 10:32 p.m., she wrote. Church vans or tourists. Faces pressed against the windows, fogging the glass. She scratched out fogging the glass. She put the notebook down and took a deep breath. The vans stopped at the curb on 58th. She counted ten women and six men get out of the vans, picked up the notebook and wrote: Dressed like they're going to a EDM rave. The women, mostly fit, had short, tight dresses. Some had spangles and others wore the Seattle Simple Black. The men wore jeans and T-shirts. They looked like an urban dance troupe. It was a mixed-race group ... The pages on her notebook were going too fast. Calm down, but she finally had to let her brain acknowledge that she really needed to use a toilet and that was befuddling her concentration.

About an agonizing minute later, she figured she could dart off just for a second around a bush maybe, but a small blue car turned onto the driveway. The tall woman with the big afro from the night before stepped out of the passenger seat. Her entourage, the two athletic white girls, filed out of the driver's side door. The tall woman had her afro corralled up into a mushroom, making her tower over all. Shiny forehead. The kids from the vans went inside, and the three walked to the door but only the tall woman went in. The other two stayed outside, like twin door sentinels. After looking around, they started walking toward Natalie's car. At first she thought maybe it only looked like they were heading right at her. They couldn't see her, could they? Had someone been watching her. She blushed thinking of being watched through all her amateur stakeout machinations. She put her finger on the start button, an impulse to get the hell out of there, just a sudden panic, thinking of all that happened since the last time she'd spied on them. But the two looked happy, jovial, shoulders relaxed, chins up, not threatening or mad looking. Just a couple of girls coming over to say Hi. Jeans, not too tight, and green runner shirts with a symbol on them she didn't recognize. They weren't twins, she don't think, but they were very much alike. They didn't *look* alike, she thought as they approached the car, so much as they were alike—two sides of the same coin. One of them came to her window and the other turned and hopped up onto the front of her car, feet on the bumper. Natalie powered her window down and thought to say something about the hood of the car, but the motion was so ... friendly. The woman at her widow smiled, bright white teeth. Were these girls were sorority gems, soccer queens? She knew the type and wanted to hang out with them the moment she saw them.

"We're not supposed to talk with you." Teasing, a little chirpy. Confident. Natalie's irritation at them dissipated, like a rain shower had let up … her body buckling down to hold on for a bit longer. The woman didn't wear makeup, not that her blue eyes and complexion needed it. Her eyes in fact were very blue, light and glowing. Natalie did not see any telltale signs of contacts.

"Well," Natalie said, telling herself to act like it's just a party, to banter, "you've just broken the rules. Might as well tell me everything."

"Ha! I knew we'd like you."

"What's going on in there?" Natalie pointed with her notebook at the house, keeping everything aboveboard. Adam has told her before to be completely transparent about who she was and what she was doing. You will not get a great story by trickery, but that doesn't mean telling everyone everything you know. We do that in the paper, when the story is done.

"What does it look like to you?" The talkative one raised an eyebrow.

"Twenty questions?" Natalie raised both eyebrows in response. She thought of the two as the Soccer Twins.

"Twenty or thirty." Big smile.

"Party?"

"Kind of. That why you're here?"

Natalie paused. The answer in her mouth was "Hey, I'm asking the questions here." But that was both false and defensive. Why was she there? To spy, sure. To find out more, anything more, about Mannerheim, yes. Why was he there that night and why did her photos cause such a shit storm, okay. But actually, she recognized while studying whatever that sensation was coming from the Soccer Twin's eyes, she was there to find out more about them. So, honesty: "I'm here to learn what I can about you and that woman who just went into the house and Mannerheim and why a photo I took of you four together has gotten me into so much trouble."

"You didn't get into trouble, did you?" The Soccer Twin spoke in a playful manner, like a friend teasingly anxious to tell you something you're going to be amazed by.

"Well, not really, but I bet I'm going to."

At that, the Talkative Soccer Twin lost her smile and backed away from the door, serious now that it was clear they were going to engage. "I can't tell you. But no one said I can't show you. Though, remember, my lovely, I can't tell you anything."

The comment jarred Natalie. It gave their budding relationship a new and possibly negative twist. Especially, since she doubted she understood who was trapping whom. But then the ironic smile returned and, also, setting traps didn't matter at this point. At this point, just get in. Just get access, worry later. "What about her?" Natalie nodded toward the house door. "Can I interview her?"

"She ..." The Talkative Soccer Twin looked back at the house and at the other Soccer Twin sitting on the car hood. "She doesn't talk to humans."

"Animals?"

"That's just what some say. Wanna come in or not?"

Anxious or just a little miffed? Natalie couldn't tell. Mercurial in any event. "Well, I do have to pee something fierce."

"Okay!" Relieved.

Natalie could not get a bead on her.

"Bathrooms we got."

The Soccer Twin on the hood dismounted gracefully, landing athletically, lightly on her toes. The talkative Soccer Twin joined her and walked toward the house. They left Natalie to get out of the car and follow, or not. She did.

Just inside the front door, the party looked much like it had the night before. Just no Mannerheim or tall woman. A regular house party. A handful of kids standing around the kitchen sink, sitting on the counters. No one appeared to be drinking, and Natalie thought of those parties her Catholic School friends had in junior high. She followed the Soccer Twins through the kitchen to the back hall and was directed to a bathroom. When she came out a couple of minutes later, no one was on the main floor. Not even her escorts. She hadn't heard any sounds of an exodus. She felt and then her ears tuned into music, trance dance music, bumping up through the floor. She walked back to the kitchen and found the door to the basement ajar. She will go down there, but not right away. First, she went into the dining room. Just a big room with a round table and chairs, five faux-leather armless dining chairs. Big picture window looking out at the side of the house next door. The original owners must have been pissed when their neighbors built that McMansion right against the property line. The living room had a fireplace, unused for decades, with a layer of dust on the empty brick mantel. The room looked a lot smaller than the last time she was in it. Facing the fireplace, for no obvious reason, was a couch she'd seen on sale at Sears. The white leather couch also not much used. They didn't bother with pillows. The glass coffee table a throw away, chipped, chrome legs rusting through in patches, like it sat outside in the rain for awhile before the girls found it and dragged it in. Two wood chairs with no cushions on either side of the big window facing the street and the porch. She wrote these details down and then assessed: I don't think anyone spends any time in this house except for these get-togethers. No photos on the walls, fridge or mantel. One big mood painting, like one of the girls had shmooshed paint around until they liked the shape of it and then hung it on the wall above the couch. Worn wooden floor that vibrated with the music. Natalie went back into the kitchen to confirm her suspicions by going through the drawers and cupboards. Some garage-sale silverware tossed into one. A couple of dishtowels in another. Box of Fruitloops

... Nothing in the fridge. So, whoever rented this place from Mr. Jeff Clive, the registered owner (just some guy who inherited the place 20 years ago), wasn't spending much time in it. She thought about checking out the bedrooms, but the door to the basement opened behind her and music flooded up into the room.

"Find anything for your story?"

She turned around and it was the talkative Soccer Twin.

"Does anyone actually live here?" She kept her notebook out to counter the appearance of subterfuge, pen poised to write the response.

"Can't say a word about anything." Hip against the counter, arms crossing.

"Do you go to college? Surely you can tell me about yourself."

"Nope. I've been warned that you journalists are too darn tricky to talk to."

"Can I go downstairs?"

She didn't answer but turned and showed Natalie the way.

In the unfinished basement spanning the width and length of the house, six eight-foot support pillars holding up the floor. At the bottom of the steps that came down in the center of the basement, she stopped to take in the crowd. The Soccer Twin walked a head to a gap in the mass of party-goers, who stood in two groups on either side of a straight center opening about four-feet wide. They stood still, some smiling and looking around with just their eyes. They stood in rows facing each other. The tall woman from the night before sat in one of the dining table chairs at the end of the center aisle facing Natalie as she stepped down to the concert floor. They made eye contact. The same deep-look into her she felt from her guide out in the street. Worried her notebook had become a barrier to full emersion into the scene, she pushed it into her back pocket. Not like she would forget the details of the room and its occupants anytime soon.

Unsure of what to do next, Natalie studied her from the bottom of the steps fifteen feet away. The woman wore a short tan leather vest pulled tight with two copper buckles and braided copper straps. The leather sown through with thin copper wires. A network of copper fibers. There was a pattern in the network, but not like an animal or structure. The pattern resembled the recording of a vibration, voice or seismic recordings. The vest's open top stopped just above the woman's cleavage. Natalie guessed she had to be six-feet tall at least, though her hair bunched up high on her head could have made her seem taller. She's fit, like the soccer girls. Tights tucked into high-lace, black combat boots.

The music volume increased, signaling some sort of change in the itinerary. She took her eyes off the woman to find her escort. She found her in a row at the front of the group to her right. The Soccer Twin made a small motion with her hand, beckoning her to come. A gap opened behind her, and Natalie noticed the other Soccer Twin. She walked slowly at first, unsure, toward them but the first one raised her eyebrows and motioned her to hurry. Natalie crossed the distance with larger steps and popped into the gap. The leader opened her eyes but not at anyone. She looked down the center of the gathering at a huge upside down jar, like a glass bell used to cover a cake but taller, standing behind where she'd stood at the bottom the steps. In the center of the bell jar, a copper rod ran from the nippled glass top down into what looked like black sand.

Closer now to the woman, Natalie looked her over again. Under the vest she wore a short-sleeve white shirt and, judging by the relaxed shape of things, nothing under that. Just below her short vest, over her mid-riff, showed a black corset. It looked homemade, laced together at the sides with a shiny metal. More copper maybe. She couldn't tell. Below that, the woman wore a pleated, short black skirt. Her face held itself still in serious, almost grim, concentration. She did not wear makeup but her eyes, a shinny dark brown, stood out on her face sharp and distinct. Deep pools, but not empty. Natalie pulled her eyes out of those pools to look at the tall neck choker made of metal and studded with four blue gems or glass beads stacked up the front of it. The little blue gems glowed bright, like LED lights. The color matched the color of the Soccer Twin's eyes. Glancing to her left, wondering if … but no, the white kid on her left had light green irises. Looking back to the woman, the repetitive music seeming to match her heart beat, she noted big cuffs on her upper arms made of thin, woven copper wires. Each hand palm-down on corresponding thigh. The lead closed her eyes again and started to vibrate or move her shoulders in a fast rhythm.

Oh man, Natalie thought, you have got to be kidding me. I've stumbled upon an underground sex-ritual cult or satan-worshiping indoctrination thing from a gothic vampire novel. Wouldn't it be weird if they killed me? What would I do if they dragged someone up the center right now, kicking and screaming. A chill zipped up the back of her neck. The Soccer Twin behind her said in her ear, "Sometimes it happens right away. Sometimes it takes all night. Depends on the people. She never fails."

Natalie turned toward the Soccer Twin behind her. Their faces very close. "Never fails at what?" Her eyes looked into Natalie's, pulsing it seemed to the music. Pulsing into her. Natalie blushed and turned her head. What if it's me they grab or hypnotize or something! Her heart thumped out of rhythm to the music, a jarring feeling. She told herself to calm down. Nothing has happened. They know others know you are here and why. Maybe they're just keeping you from rushing into the middle of it all or doing something too stupid to ignore. She looked at the men and women lined up on the other side of the open center. They all had on the same kind of woven-copper collar with the blue light in the middle. The Soccer Twins didn't, however. She turned again and the Soccer Twin behind her edge close again. She whispered just above the music, "Should I have one of those collars on?"

"You haven't signed on yet," the woman whispered back.

"Oops!" She nudged Natalie with her shoulder. "Damn it! You got me to answer a question."

"Signed on to what?"

"Fuck. Just watch already." She backed away.

Several minutes later, the music still pulsing and everyone in place, the sand in the jar started to vibrate. The volume of the trance music started decreasing, slowly, though the air felt full of the vibration of whatever caused the sand to jump around.

"Never fails," Soccer Twin behind her said in her ear. Hot breath in her ear. Natalie was definitely starting to feel uncomfortable about the woman behind her, but not enough to leave just yet.

As the music volume dropped off completely, the vibration in the jar increased sharply. The black, granular material danced and vibrated and started to climb the copper pole in swirls and spiky rings. She looked back to the woman running the seance or whatever occult trick was happening. She stared intently but not intense or stressed or trying hard, seemed to Natalie. Just, calmly looking at the jar with confidence. Thin filaments of blue and white electric plasma played on the plating across her vest, upper arms and neck.

Natalie shift her weight to look around, but the Soccer Twin grabbed her arms.

"Don't worry," the woman said quickly and released her. "It's harmless. The light just helps them focus."

"Who?"

"I'll tell you what you need to know, but you have to stop asking me questions!"

Natalie stepped forward to get space. She felt vulnerable. She reached to touch her notebook for assurance, a tool for establishing her independence from the scene but touched the Soccer Twin's front by accident. Before she could react more than jerking her hand forward, the vibration in the air around her dissipated, flowing out from around them toward the bell jar, like a wind of silent noise. The sand quickly gathered into a mushroom cloud at the top of the rod, looking a lot like the shape of the leader's hair. She twisted her head back to the woman leading the seance and saw the plasma filaments begin dancing out from her, off of her, toward the first line of kids in front and next to her. The woman tensed, as if in the throws of pleasure, the veins in her arms and neck stood out. The men and women hit by the filaments, lines of plasma arching from neck gem to neck gem, began to sway slightly at first but increasingly as the filaments jumped from neck to neck. The Soccer Twin in front of her swayed too, though no electric filament had attached itself to her, rather it danced around her to the the person on her left, diagonal to Natalie. When the filament hit each person, they closed their eyes. Their faces relaxed, like they'd just been hit with a drug. A second later, they opened their eyes and the filaments moved to the next four, the ones in back and the ones next to them. Each person had the same reaction. The electricity spread fast after that, like a wave racing over them. The woman behind her stepped against her.

Natalie stepped closer to the woman in front. The pressure against her didn't feel threatening, however. She saw that everyone, with the filaments lacing between their necks, were getting closer to each other. And, well, she told herself, we still have our clothes on. Finally the filaments connected with the last two people closest to the bell jar and jumped the gap between them and the top of the jar. The filaments danced, pulses zapped at the jar but did not go through the glass.

Hell of a parlor trick, Natalie thought.

The sand shimmied through a complex series of waves, spikes and globes at the top, refining in such a varied degree that some of the motion when it melted into the more general form, created substructures within the mass -- like one of those intricately carved ivory balls with spheres encompassing slightly smaller spheres, she decided. Fascinated, her anxiety fell away. She felt the vibration pulsing the sand had come back through the people, through her, back to the woman sitting at the front of the aisle. Natalie felt it as a kind of hum in her body, mostly centered in the mass of her stomach. It felt almost like sexual pleasure, she noted.

Then the Soccer Twins pressed her between them firmly. The one behind pushing hard against her back, and she pushed hard against the back of the one in front of her. The motion between them had stopped, no grinding. Just pressed hard between them. She didn't care, like her inhibitions had dissolved. She wanted them pressed against her. The harder they pressed, the stronger the pulsing of the air, warm and centered below her stomach, became. The lights or plasma filaments grew thick as ropes around her, but not touching her. The two networks poured energy against the bell jar. The patterns in the sand structures became much more complex with parts connected to other parts, like images she'd seen of connected neurons. The vibration and hum entranced her more as the shape-shifting black sand became more and more agitated. Natalie told herself, as if from a distance, to look at the leader. The woman sat up straight in the chair, hands on her thighs still, enveloped in a complex spiderweb of plasma. The lights in her necklaces burned bright. Her eyes like bulbs pouring out dark energy. Natalie felt tug on the line of people pressed against her. She looked back at the jar as the sand particles raced out of the the knob at the top and began to crawl up the filaments into each dancers' collar.

The sand reached every neck and the vibration started to grow disorganized in her, leaving her body cold and naked, the hum growing more like static. She became more aware of the outline of the bodies behind and in front of her. Her own form. She glanced back at the woman leading the seance. Right at that moment, or maybe it had been happening at intervals before and Natalie just hadn't noticed, the blue lights in her collar flickered out. They went black, not a color black more like they became holes. The lights in the collars of the dancers all went black at the same time. All of the next three things happened at the same instant: The music kicked in, louder and faster. The plasma and the sand imploded—the sand fell fast to the bottom of the jar and the plasma vaporized. Sand fell to the floor around her. The soccer girls pushed against her, forward and backward, but the feeling was gone. Natalie felt sober, embarrassed. She didn't move with the music like all the others, who began grinding with intent. She slid from between the Soccer Twins, looked back in the direction of the leader, but the chair was empty.

She took out her notebook and tried to get the attention of anyone around her to ask who they were, why were they there, but no one so much as shook a no at her. She bent down, pinched up some of the black sand and rubbed it into the notebook paper and basically climbed her way to the stairs. Two steps up, she could see over the mass of dancers, who were quickly loosing clothes, but the Soccer Twins had left the floor, too.

At the top of the steps, she opened the door a crack to see if she could hear anyone or spy on them. Nothing. The kitchen was empty. She stepped onto the main floor and looked around. The bedrooms were empty, too. She rushed to the front door and outside to catch them before they could drive away, but the car was there and no one around. She trotted around the house twice to find where they could have left the basement, but the windows would have been tough to get out of and the basement didn't have a door. They had to still be inside, but she couldn't image a room in the open basement big enough to hold all three. Why would they do that? She'd seen what she'd seen, and it was not like they were doing anything illegal, though she suspected those kids' mothers would have been quite shocked. She thought about a photo suddenly, just sneak back in. But, one, she'd left her phone in the car. And, two, what would she ever do with the photo except get in more trouble. Not like she was going to show it to Adam, let alone put much personal detail into her notes to him about what had happened.

    She trotted back to her car and filled the rest of her notebook with sketched notes. Then she drove back to her apartment, deciding to work through her bafflement and slight embarrassment at her own enjoyment of part of the seance, as she took to calling it, by writing a very professional account of the evening in her notes to Adam.

V

Adam's rule for young reporters was that before they presumed to write a news story, an article, "the first draft of history," they had to first write out their notes and understanding of the scenes, people and a proposed storyline in a deep-dive with as much detail as they could make themselves remember. He pushed them to become unconscious of what they were writing, pure stream-of-consciousness stuff right out of the 1970s. That way, they would not leave out details or information that, more often than not because of their inexperience, told the real story. Young reporters were so determined to become Woodward and Bernstein and take down powerful people that they inexpertly prejudged what they saw and what people said and so then often missed the story entirely. He preached this to them, but only experience would teach. Young reporters didn't even know they were making judgements, let alone acting on them. They thought the shit that came out of their brains was all-natural, grade-A, pure intuitive genius. So, it was his job to guard the gates of publication until they grew up enough and either came to their senses and heard what he was saying or were sent packing to the black gaping maw of public relations.

Natalie, he shared with his boss, took to this style of writing with the aplomb of the Facebook Generation and time and again mistook her stream of consciousness for writing. So she proved difficult to rein in along the stages of writing, the daily road to Damascus, at an honest-to-goodness newspaper. He had considered barring her from the practice after her first few months at the paper, mostly because she kept sending her notes to his boss, City Editor Kristi Beach, with the pedantic foolishness of instructing a talented and experienced newsroom leader on how the new world of blog-writing called for these free-form, "plain language" ramblings and that he was holding her back. What he hated most about this exchange was that Beach teased him mercilessly in front of the other editors about how his reporter kept leaping over him to make a case for publishing her *notes*!

He had threatened to outright fire her if she sent one more fucking note to Beach. But, he continued the stream-of-consciousness practice.

So, when he got to his desk after cigarettes and the morning gab-sessions throughout the newsroom and opened Natalie's story-notes file, he was not surprised, during his preliminary scroll, to find that it was an especially long entry. After all, she'd earned a lawyer consultation and would now display that feather-in-her-cap whenever told to shut up and sit down. He reclined in his chair, put a cup of coffee on his belly and began to read:

Now you're going to think I've lost my mind or am making this up, but I'm not. I'm a mildly religious, Catholic-raised daughter of a devoted mother who votes Republican because she's anti-abortion but who divorced my father when he got wrapped up in a pseudo-Catholic, Virgin Mary cult in Mexico, walked 200 miles with me in her womb and then birthed me here in the great ol' USA so I could get an education. So, you know. One more thing ... I know what you're going to say and I agree—Damn stupid of me not to have taken a video or at least a photo or audio recording and I will next time. I'm not sure I could have gotten away with it anyway. "Smoke and mirrors," as you like to say. Indoctrination. I don't know, maybe just a cult after all. I know you will read this in a rush and roll your eyes. But this is the best writing I have ever done and you should publish it as a reporter's notebook. Just saying. Now I'm going to bed and will sleep all day, I hope, so please don't call me until later in the afternoon. If I get up sooner, I'll call you.

And roll his eyes he did.

By the end of her account, Adam felt a new concern about his reporter forming within him: She was racing headlong into some pretty engaging material and looked to be pretty close to losing objectivity, that balance act between her engagement in the affair as a journalist and the engagement of someone who wants to be a part of the scene, a member of the club. Young reporters often lose sight of the professional remove they have to have to be able to report objectively and, at times, cruelly about people or organizations they have come to like. The opposite was just as bad. If she came out of there disgusted or angry or hurt, her reporting would become just as useless. If he didn't get ahead of her on this story, to lead her through it, he might lose her to it and all the good material she'd gathered would go to waste.

He looked again at his desk phone. The message light was dark. Checked his cellphone. Nothing. So, no one had called to complain about Natalie's presence at the party. They were in the clear, for now, on that front. Of course, he would not, could not now even if he wanted to, publish her journaling stuff. So that was one less fight he would have to have. He and Beach hadn't even met with the lawyers. Also, and mainly, her journal entry raised a lot of questions with not one answer. Not only what were the partygoers doing, but was that what Mannerheim wanted from them? Was he there to exercise his libido? If he was, why the fuck would a federal judge step in with a prior restrain order just to protect a lecher from some bad press? It didn't make any sense to begin with and now, after what he had just read, the prior restraint made even less sense.

He finger-punched the "esc" button closing the notes window. He felt irrationally desperate. A chemical mood thing. His blood pressure soaring again. He got out of the chair, grabbed his coat and left the building. If he had still been allowed to drink heavily before going to bed, this would have been a great night for it. But he didn't drink heavily in the afternoons anymore, not as often anyway. His liver was the size of a rather large and fatty pot roast. He still had his five or six cigarettes for the day, since his lungs were still clear, and right then was a hell of a good time for one. So, Adam went to the glass door that opened onto a balcony, zipped his coat against the cold air coming off the Puget Sound just three hundred yards away, silvery wavelets lapping onto the sliver of glowing sand beneath the big black rocks. It was a clear night and cold. The Olympics met the night sky, aglow from the city lights in a jagged outline, peaks still topped with snow. The beach below smelled of seaweed and salt water, but thankfully not like something dead, like thirty years ago when he was just a morning general assignment reporter and had stepped out for a smoke and smelled that girl. She was about fifteen years old and wouldn't get any older. She had been in the water for several days until the tether came undone from her ankle. He shivered. Memories haunt us like chickens. They're always peck-peck-pecking at the surface of our consciousness and now and then one pecks through. When he got the gory details from one of the officers he knew personally from a thousand shootings, stabbings, car wrecks, domestic-violence standoffs, and all the other petty-to-deadly crime that went on in Seattle night and day, a city known for its rain and hipster ways but which was as seedy and torn and devastated as any big city ... well, when he got the details of how this homeless girl had been used and abused and dumped in Puget Sound, alive with a cement block tied to her ankle, the heartbreak of it got to him. He wrote a gothic story of twenty inches when he'd been budgeted for three. He pleaded and cajoled with the night city editor to run it at length. When the final "Hell, no! Who the fuck does he think he's kidding?" came down from the copy desk chief, he went to the bar and drank until he wouldn't remember the next two days.

Smoking out on the balcony, he moved on to mull over the question Why Mannerheim? Just those two words. Encoded in them were broader questions. Why there? Why them? Why now?

An idea formed in the electrical fog and came clear enough and was counter-intuitive enough to possibly be true: What if the judge wasn't stepping in on Mannerheim's behalf? What if some other motive, playing at just the outer reaches of what they knew, had pushed the judge to write that incredible order and Mannerheim's involvement was incidental? Some "they" using his name as a cover. He lit another cigarette. Knowing the government, federal agencies and federal judges as he did after years of interacting with them, a conspiracy made more sense than all of that federal machinery kicking into gear to protect the reputation of some dorky geek, no matter how rich. Hell, the feds he knew loved busting rich white men.

No doubt a lot went on everywhere in the world that he had no inkling of or could even guess at, but something or someone bigger than Mannerheim, more important than whatever this wealthy geek was playing at, had stepped out of the shadows. That motive, that reason had swept the judge up as it washed onto the shores of the *Daily Record.* So, if not Mannerheim, then who or what did Natalie see, hear or get noticed by that triggered this tsunami? The only other people in the photos were the women. That this whole parade of absurdities hinged on those girls made even less sense. Not even if the trigger happened to be that one quite interesting and persuasive woman who was clearly leading the others.

    He flicked the cigarette over the railing and went back in to finish the day, Robert's piece heading for A1 Lead. Feeling lucky when he got back to his seat that he wasn't drunk or even drinking. That positive reinforcement had persuaded him as much as his health to stop drinking daily, morning, noon and night: The dread he felt when he was drunk and stumbling into his lonely bed had become worse than he felt being sober.

DAY THREE

"We (the undivided divinity operating within us) have dreamt the world. We have dreamt it as firm, mysterious, visible, ubiquitous in space and durable in time; but in its architecture we have allowed tenuous and eternal crevices of unreason which tell us it is false."

—Borges

I

Reporters, photographers and a phalanx of editors ambled around and grouped into chat-circles—pecking away at the latest ball game, outrage in Washington D.C., story of the latest drunk-dude stabbing or mayoral rumor—uselessly consuming the morning. Ah, how Adam loved the sound of the newsroom in the morning. Nothing in Seattle got revved up much before noon, anyway. He avoided conversation with nods and winks, because he had a plan to execute before Beach got in. He tossed his coat onto the desk and picked up the phone handset as he plunged into the chair. He let the receiver hum its open-line song while pushing business cards, stickies and torn papers around until he found David Robbins' cell number.

"Hello!" Sharp and busy, but ready to talk if you've got something he needs.

"Robbins?"

"Yeah. Who's this?"

"Adam Howard, *Daily Record*."

"Ahhh. Hold on a second."

Adam heard him walk through his office, pretty damn big office … across a creaking wood floor. It had to be one of those high-ceiling, red-brick offices in Pioneer Square judging by the floor squeaks. The door clipped shut. The slow, heavy-man walk back.

"What can I do for you?"

"I want to talk about..."

"You know I can't say anything. I'm restricted by that order, the same as you are."

"Just a ..."

"We've got to be off the record. Way off the record."

He wanted to talk pretty darn bad if he bit that fast, which calmed Adam down quite a bit.

"Fine. Off the record for just the current purpose of, and hear me on this for christ's sake, setting up a meeting with Mannerheim. I don't want to hear later that I tricked you or lied to you."

"Off the record, I can't set up a meeting with Mannerheim. That would pretty much cut straight across both the letter of the order and the intent of the goddamned thing."

"We're both in a pickle, and that order is just the tip of the iceberg because …"

"Why do you reporters always say the word pickle? What the hell year is it anyway …"

"I know this isn't about Mannerheim and if he talks with me, when this shit all hits the fan, you'll have what it takes to keep him from taking the fall for whoever or whatever is all worked up about those harmless fucking photographs we took. And we say pickle because sometimes a long, roughly cylindrical object soaked in briny dill is an apt metaphor for the current situation."

"I'll see what I can do. Off the record."

"Let's be clear. We're off the record but the fact of my meeting with Mannerheim is not off the record. That's something I'll negotiate with him once we meet. I'm not …"

"Like I said. I'll see what I can do." He hung up.

III

Adam and Mannerheim met at the top of the Volunteer Park Water Tower on Capitol Hill about ten blocks from Adam's condo. Through Robbins, Mannerheim had first suggested meeting online in some gamer's landscape. He said that would be the most private place for them to meet, which made no sense to Adam. How could anything online be private? No, he rejoined, let's just meet the old-fashioned way. Mannerheim said Adam clearly didn't understand how much the world had changed and refused. Adam replied that however much faith he had in his ability to remain private online, Mannerheim wasn't taking into consideration the fact that Adam would have no idea who in the hell he was talking to in whatever bullshit chartroom Mannerheim was suggesting. Mannerheim gave a bunch of reasons why and added You have a 'real-world' bias that isn't doing you any favors. Adam mused to himself that one thing he'd learned early on in his career, especially in Seattle, was that very intelligent people were not immune to bullshit ideas. They just had very detailed and complex bullshit ideas. He wrote back, Humor me. You need this meeting more than I do. I'm just trying to help you. Then Robbins jumped in and suggested the water tower: It's close to both of you and a hard place to ease drop. I use it all the time. Adam: The secret lives of lawyers? They were getting nice and chummy. Robbins: Secrets are a lawyer's trade. ... and telling them is mine, Adam didn't write that rejoinder. He did write: Sounds good to me.

Adam walked the ten blocks under an umbrella. He'd swung by his condo for a bite and a glass of wine, which quickly became three. So, he was full and grumpy and disappointed in himself. The sky had let loose real rain, in big drops. When he got to the base of the tower, he was wet from his thighs down in spite of the umbrella. Mannerheim said he'd be in the north entrance, which was on the other side of the tower from the direction he had come. Might as well make me get as wet as possible, he grumbled. The wine, however, sat rather nicely in his stomach. A nice little red. He sauntered on.

    Finally trudging around the curved side of the tower, rain coming down in sheets and the wind blowing water up his jacket, Adam was getting a little bit nervous. The courage of the wine had not lasted the walk. He'd climbed way out on a limb arranging this meeting. His reporter, Beach and their lawyers didn't know about it, of course. They couldn't since it was strictly forbidden via court order. The order was bullshit, but contempt of court wasn't, he gloomily considered. If anyone found out about it, well he wouldn't be the first editor quietly sent home with no explanation. But there was something else going on, he felt certain, and he was the right person to get the information, especially since he had no qualms secretly recording the conversation, illegal as that was. Most of the time he did not record and transcribe, but when he was not sure what the story was that he pursued, he did. He also learned a lot by transcribing a conversation. People send out all kinds of signals and bits of information he missed the first time around. They're often trying to say more than the words coming out of their mouths.

Inside the north entrance, the narrow stairs curved up between the massive metal tank, zippered with rivets, and the outside brick wall. Dark, dank and narrow. He thought, I'm surprised more people weren't killed here. Stepping in the doorway, he lowered and collapsed the umbrella. His eyes adjusted and made out the figure of a man about halfway to the top.

"Mannerheim?" He called up.

"Yes." Mannerheim sighed the word.

He climbed to the landing and took the proffered hand. Mannerheim's face was thin and small for his head, pinched. He had aged. His skin had become creased and slack.

"Adam Howard. *Seattle Daily Record.*" He pause to judge the response. Nervous? Dismissive? "We are off the record for the moment."

"Sounds okay." He shrugged and started up the grated metal steps, slowly, ponderously like an old man of bulk with no energy and very little will.

At the top of the stairs, Mannerheim went to a window, an opening in the brick wall, and stood there. He looked toward where the Cascade Mountains were completely obscured. Adam stepped up to a window on Mannerheim's left and looked out over the tops of the downtown buildings. The ceiling of cloud sat right on top of them. He looked Mannerheim over, standing next to him as if a stranger with his arms crossed. He had on white and sliver running shoes. The soles still perky and new. Khaki slacks, blue runner's jacket, striped shirt loosely tucked in under a black belt. Long fingernails. Clean but uncut for months. Adam turned back to the cityscape, wondering what long fingernails on a man like Mannerheim meant. Carelessness? Distractedness? The genius who couldn't be bothered to take care of himself?

He said, "Technicalities, Mr. Mannerheim. I can't print anything until this court order gets through our lawyers, so let's call this 'on background' with the understanding that we will change it to 'full attribution' in the case of your death or conviction of a crime."

Mannerheim, looking at him, pinched up his lips and shrugged one shoulder. In that sighing voice, barely making an echo in the abandoned tower, he said it didn't matter. He dug through Adam's logic and pointed out that by the time he got permission to print his stories and photos, the story will have been leaked somewhere else from some other source so they might as well just be on the record.

"Besides," he said, "as you've already guessed, I'm sure, this isn't about me."

"So who is it about?"

"Might be a what not a who and depends on what 'it' you're talking about."

He chuckled oddly, Adam thought, a wet little cackle.

Adam said, "I hope we're not going to play games until our time is up. It seems to me you've got something to say, otherwise you wouldn't be here. I don't want to know who's behind the court order. I *want* to know what it is you really want to tell me. *I've* got all day."

Mannerheim narrowed his eyes and tilted his head at Adam, like someone who has been challenged a lot lately and just can't believe it's happening again. Adam saw that a lot, seems to him. Editors the next step in the chain of people to threaten when the life or work of a powerful person was in mid-public-collapse. He realized then what was up with Mannerheim's manner: He was fatigued. He'd been embroiled in a conflict that had worn him down. That common look of fey seen during years of hounding public officials caught up in a scandal or during the election season frenzy. It's the moment the tide turns and the momentum in the situation, the sense of purpose, shifts from push to drain. I'll be damned, he thought. Mannerheim's been getting beaten up. A sullen scientist who has been shoved back onto the playground of his wimpy youth. Being smarter than nearly everyone around you categorically meant you wouldn't fit in.

"You know," he said, "I read some of your mother's work before all this started. I've been meaning to read it again, in light of what I've experienced and documented in the past twenty or so years."

"And what was it that brought you to my mother's work?"

What he thought was Fuck it. Mannerheim wasn't the first geek to dig into his mother's work. Adam brought a cigarette and lighter up to his mouth. His mother's work on cognitive processes in children was not only pretty narrow in scope but by now had to be extremely out of date, especially since she had been dead from breast cancer for a dozen years. Yet, she had become something of a cult icon to the computer class. Mannerheim clearly had come prepared to bargain. But for what? Adam's memories of his mother consisted mostly of her handing him over into the care of some co-ed or other. Her intense, hawk-like brows and thin, strained neck. And the games she would play with him and other kids. One game was a false-belief test involving a couple of dolls and a piece of chocolate. The other was much more memorable. She told Adam to imagine a monster in a box in the middle of the kitchen and then asked if he thought there actually was one in it. He said no and knew there wasn't, but no matter how many times they played the game, when she left him alone in the room, he felt that there *was* a monster in the box, an evil malevolent monster that would dismember him and fold his parts into the box, where he would remain forever. Needless to say, as a child he gave the box a wide berth and developed a phobia about boxes in dark corners. To top it off, he had read all about his behavior in these moments in her lab notes after she died. Try not to be marked by that, he puffed the cigarette and exhaled over Mannerheim's head.

"Before I started Beta Launch, which, as you'll remember, was a sliver of a spinoff from my UW/Cal Tech computer center, my primary research was in user interface in the next generation of computing, one that won't involve a mouse or a key board. Eye tracking, human autonomic responses, as well as softer sciences like, you guessed it, cognitive development. Algorithms knowing what your next move or desire will be before you do. Your mother was one of the first in the field to look at cognitive development within the subconscious or at the level of genetic traits where a lot is going on that makes us who and what we are that we are not aware of. Everyone else was obsessed with behavioral conditioning, as if the brain was just a sophisticated car engine."

"These are things I know. Tell me something I don't know."

Mannerheim started walking, slowly, clockwise around the circle of the tower. Adam followed and then stepped in beside him because he was mumbling. Like several of the Seattle-based genius billionaires, Mannerheim was not used to conversation. Rather monologuing. Not egocentrism so much as disinterest in anything but the development of his own thoughts.

Then he said, "We keep moving, and they'll have a harder time listening in. Not that it really matters. I just enjoy disrupting their work."

Uh oh, Adam thought. "Whose work? The feds?" He scanned the park's landscape through a window they had crossed in front of. One thing the Feds hate is someone ignoring their court orders, that and lying to them. But he saw no one. "Seems a bit much. Even in these times," he said, mostly to himself.

"Not just them." Mannerheim chimed in and stopped. He glanced out the window and then at Adam. "*Her,* too. *She* watches the watchers, though they won't believe me." He intoned some vast and limitless meaning, nodding his head.

That half-autistic, geek-profundity bullshit, Adam thought. He wanted to slap Mannerheim. "*Her*?" he mocked Mannerheim's tone.

"Celestine Wallace," he said, like Adam should know who that was, scrunching his bushy eyebrows at him.

"And that is?"

He unscruntched his eyebrows, cocked his head and snorted in non-surprise surprise, like Adam should have guessed it right away. He wrapped his hands together behind his back and started walking, visibly going back into Master of The Universe mode. "Your cub reporter must have told you about her."

Adam, intrigued finally at something Mannerheim said, fell in beside him.

"I understand," he said, stopped and turned to Adam, "that she went back to the house and saw a bit more than she'd bargained for. I'd told those bureaucrats their ploy wouldn't work. But I ..."

"Wait a minute." Adam tilted his head back. "The black woman?"

"Yes, Celestine Wallace is also a black woman."

Mannerheim was so immersed in whatever the fuck was going on that he couldn't fathom that the rest of the world wasn't right there along with him. "Well, you've lost me," Adam said. "But let's go back to, 'Who cares what you or I think?' "

"*She* does, so they do. Like blockhead cops, they're following all 'known associates'." He made the punctuation with voice inflection.

"Oh, goddamn it. Why? What do you care? Explain yourself! Enough with the mysterious bullshit."

"*She's* maneuvering right now. Celestine."

"Celestine Wallace? Who is she?"

He snorted in disbelief again.

"Look," Adam grabbed his arm, briefly. Mannerheim looked down at where Adam had touched him arm, shocked. Probably hadn't been touched like that in decades. They faced each other across a couple of feet. Adam's voice echoed. "Talk to me as if to a child. Isn't that what you geeks like to hear? Who is she and what is she afraid of and so fucking what?"

"Of us," he kept on in his distracted yet humored way, "not just you and I, but us. The whole human power structure. She's the best at it so far, that thing Natalie told you about."

Mannerheim had not showered in several days, hair all matted in the back, cowlicks flowing up and off his head in divergent directions. Red-rimmed eyes wide. Heavy bags pulling eyelids down. He clamped has jaws tight to let what he'd said sink in. Another test: Would Adam understand that Mannerheim just said he or someone else had hacked into the *Daily Record*'s internal notes system? Would Adam wonder at Mannerheim's fear of her? Would his story hook him?

"What is 'it'?" using his own inflection as punctuation. Adam got ahold of Mannerheim's arm again, since it had had the desired effect last time. Not much of a threat though, since a couple of eighth graders could have overpowered them both, he considered, so it was more of an attempt to get Mannerheim to focus than to manhandle him. "A cult? A geek spiritualism going back to Tesla? I mean, again if you follow me, Who cares?"

Mannerheim got that distant look of ridicule again. Adam had to admit he wasn't asking good questions, but he didn't know what questions to ask and Mannerheim clearly had a lot on his mind.

"Look, I know I'm a little dull here, but nothing of what you are saying makes any sense to me." Adam dropped his arm and ran his hand over his bald head. "And that makes me think it's just a bunch of horse crap dreamt up by a rich guy and a pack of bored college kids. I must hear a hundred story ideas a month just like this from university professors. They see conspiracies everywhere they look and somehow it all centers around them and their revolutionary work."

"If that's what you think, then we have gotten ahead of ourselves. I guess I thought you knew more than you do."

"Well, shit. But, I actually don't have all day." Adam was getting the feeling that Mannerheim had lost his mind over this girl or just lost it period and maybe she had, too. Sexualized pseudo-religious revelations have twisted more minds than drugs and alcohol. Wouldn't be the first time. Hell, just read Revelations. Or hell, just a few summers ago a group of people, all ages, committed suicide because a comet had neared the Earth. That was the second time in twenty or so years that people had killed themselves and their families because a fucking comet, an easily and well-understood astronomical phenomenon, was visible from their backyards. So, people were nuts. Hands down.

"Kind of hard to know where to start."

"Try the beginning."

"The beginning of what? What beginning?"

Adam didn't respond. He pushed his sleeve up and checked his watch just to reinforce the idea of running out of time. He didn't have anywhere to be, and it would be a couple of hours before anyone would begin to wonder why he wasn't in the office. In fact, what he was running out of was patience, and the wine bottle in his apartment still had a solid glass to donate to the cause.

"Or, well, yeah," he said.

Mannerheim was be able to read social signals, like a yawn, so he was at least partially conscious of his surroundings. Annoyingly, however, he started walking again. Adam let him collect his thoughts for a half a turn around the big tank.

"The beginning," Mannerheim sighed. "One of my research arms has been concerned with community building on the Internet, tribalism and so on, because for one, this user behavior has from the beginning of the World Wide Web driven the development of its most successful applications, not the least of which are the social media sites and, more importantly, the mechanisms behind them.

Facebook is a site, but Google, Microsoft, Yahoo ... these search and platform companies have created the mechanism that generates the networks of social media. They make the medium social, a platform for communal interaction beyond just saying, 'Hello. I'm eating fish for dinner.' This is the meta-universe of big data, where our unconscious lives are mirrored. Algorithms churning through all this data interconnects us based on what search results we get and tells servers what ads you will see and what songs you'll hear on Pandora, what movies you might like next, or whether you are a security risk or potential child molester. All of that is based on your online activity with others as well as just by yourself, who your friends are and what they do and even more importantly, which is where genetics and my lab comes into play, the activity of your relatives, whether with you or in their own groups. Because, don't forget, genetics plays a hidden role in all of our activities, not just the color of your hair. And, for another, the Internet is like a petri dish of a medium, a science experiment with all the raw materials already there. We got a DOD grant and started buying raw tracking data from Internet Service Providers."

"Well, that's gotta be all kinds of illegal." Welcome to a geek's mind, Adam thought. Scatterbrained one minute and monologuing the mysteries of the universe the next.

"Not on the face of it, because the data is cleaned of personal identifiers. Just raw data of billions of connections. You start on Internet address X and jump to address Y and we mark it with a code, an identifier and file it in the database. We don't need to know names to do this research. Out of this we can get all kinds of patterns of behaviors and with a big enough dataset, we get patterns of personal behaviors without knowing who the person is. Imagine you always start at X and then go to Y ... Well, eventually that behavior gets tagged with an identity and, Bob's your uncle, we have a virtual person who lives and breaths on the Internet, but only there. And ... " He stopped to look at Adam. "That's where we found them. But the big problem was that they knew we had found them before we did. We had identified them as characters in the system, those ghost identities that were based on probability ..."

"Little green men? The Matrix?"

"We've been interested in this kind of thing for generations, for sure. When God left the center of our understanding about ourselves, science stepped into the ring to become the favorite way for us to learn about ourselves, our natures, our purpose and what becomes of us when we die. So, we eventually found our way to the genome, and up to now we've been figuring out that puzzle of genetic traits, what role a particular trait might play in our current state and why did it come about and how did it survive to become a dominant gene. What's its evolutionary benefit? Sharper teeth? Thicker hair? More sweat glands? Bigger breasts? Longer, straighter legs? You get the picture?"

"Barely." Adam took out a second cigarette. Evidently, Mannerheim was used to taking the long way around to his point and would not be heading onto a straight path.

"We were looking for patterns of how interaction with the Internet might be changing people or if it is changing people."

"But you have to know the person to do that final step in your analysis, right? Otherwise, it's all just a fiction."

"You are paying attention!" He grabbed Adam's upper arm and smiled.

"You've read my mother's work? Well, most of her insights came from fucking over my childhood, so maybe we should call it a day."

Mannerheim nodded knowingly. Adam thought of the dozen real stories that would be published in the next day's paper, and he wanted to have a story among them. This wouldn't be it. Didn't even sound like a story to him. Whatever that judge's order was about, Mannerheim didn't have much if anything to do with it directly. They'd just have to wait it out to find out more, if they ever did. The Feds have a big blackhole most things end up in, nowadays.

"I used to sleep with her." He gestured helplessness with his hands and then looked up at Adam.

"My mother?" Adam put the back of his hand on his forehead in fake shock.

"With Celestine," Mannerheim said like he and Adam's mother could have fucked regularly but, no, this time he was talking about someone else. "But it was killing me. And I do mean I was dying." He paused his frenetic hand movements and lip chewing, gone deep inside apparently. Then he started listing and counting with his fingers. "Enflamed liver. Swollen lymph nodes. Enlarged testicles. My joints hurt. No one understood why. You think you know degradation." He paused again, but this time looked out the window and studied the verge on the other side of drive that circled the tower. Adam followed his gaze, and there was someone in there rustling around. A bum, maybe, tucked away in his little hide-a-camp.

"This has to be dealt with now," he fired up a worried look on his face. "In some way. People need to understand. I did not create those things. We found them, but they were there before we got there."

"Calm down," Adam told him. He pointed out the window at several young men coming up out of the forested slope. "Created them?" Adam said. "Rise up? What I can't figure out is whether you know you're nuts."

"The cave, remember your failure at the cave."

"Jesus, man." Adam dropped the cigarette butt and stepped on it. "What do you want from me? From us?"

"Huh." Mannerheim leaned against the iron-pipe railing. "'You enrage me.' That's what she wrote on the note she left on my desk. Once I saw them and we started looking specifically for them, it was just like she knew where to look all along."

"Who? What? And, not to be too demanding, when?"

"Celestine Wallace was a Phd student I picked up somewhere along the line, a hand-me-down. A tall, long-legged, smart hand-me-down with a solid aptitude for lab work. Having someone like her walking around the lab makes the day a little more fun, a little brighter, keeps the other students showing up. Research confirms this, by the way." He started walking again. Hands clasped behind his back, professorially. "I didn't set out to have sex with her, believe it or not, but we did once in my office and then at my house. I encouraged it, no doubt. She was lonely and had that directionless grad-student ennui, like her life was a thin sheet of fabric, 'like too little butter spread over too much toast.' A lot of doctoral students end up feeling that way after their first few years slaving away in a campus lab. Our experiments were failing to prove any hypothesis. I thought it was carelessness in the lab and designed an algorithm to look for the error in the code. That was the first time we had sex. She was trying to distract me. I was challenging her efforts, accusing her of messing up our data. I thought she was just nervous. This volatility was unseen before, and I had spent many many hours with her in that lab or on the phone, revising prospectuses and proposals, but this day was different. When I pointed that out, she said she didn't know why. I told her maybe it was guilt. She knew she had made mistakes. Celestine said her work was perfect, and yet she was very agitated, like looking for something she couldn't quite name or covering up something. I said this was all pretty natural given her experience. Failures happen far more than success and teach us more than success. All of that. She said we weren't failing. We just didn't know what we were seeing and we needed to start running even more complex experiment. What we needed, what I needed to have done, is run simpler tests to find the baseline but I said, 'Fine.' I wanted her to stay, if you know what I mean. I said, 'Bring up the data and let's look again.' But I have to tell you I felt a little despair, since what she was proposing could take years to run. But those would be her years and meanwhile she'd stick around. A decent grad student can be hard to hold onto. We walked through the algorithm design … and after several hours of working on the same monitor …"

"One thing leads to another." So, this was it. A little tryst had Mannerheim all flustered, and that's what he wanted to talk about?

"Yes. She wasn't the first doctoral student to fling herself at sex or drugs or extreme sports when the data started going bad, when the models started falling apart and years of research, years you will never get back, just crumbles to dust in your hands. For a few months we acted like it hadn't happened. Then Beta Launch took off and I left the university. She followed me to Beta Launch and helped me set up our Center for Creative Ideas. Those were amazing times. There was so much money flying around. We were able to set up a lab that rivaled anything the university had access to. She helped our teams as a systems analyst while continuing to work on the algorithms to make sense of all that strange data she'd found."

"But then, if my math is correct, that had to have been seventeen or eighteen years ago, which is impossible."

"Yes. Hang in there with me. I didn't keep tabs on her or what she was working on, that's just the era we were in, then the tech-bubble burst and we had to scale back like all the others. We had capital and market position so our company would survive. The board and I hired a CEO and new management team to take us from a startup to a company that could acquire other companies and their patents. All departments were ordered to create budgets, researchers, everyone, including me. That's when she resurfaced. She'd been using a hell of a lot of resources and wouldn't tell us what for."

Mannerheim's tone had shifted from wonderment at his own story to a somber look of bafflement, the same look Adam would see on his mother's face when she discovered what she'd predicted only to have its ramifications to theory—hers and others in her field—contradicted standard models.

"I wanted to just let her be," he said, "but our CEO shut her out. Locked her out of the building, the whole nine yards. She was lucky no one pressed charges, but then that could have dragged us all into court and no one had perfect accounting in the old days. She showed up at my house two nights later, upset and agitated. She said she'd made a lot of progress, but couldn't tell me what. She needed more computing time and the files from the company's servers. You could say I let her seduce me into downloading the data to my system at home, which by that time, given the computing advancements, was about twenty times the capacity we had started with at the university. She set up in my home office. We slept together a few more times, but by then I was getting ill. Then she just up and left. Put that note on my desk and disappeared. After she was gone, I started recovering my health. It has taken me months to find her and decipher what she had been up to."

"Which is?"

"Building them," he said with disbelief that Adam hadn't followed his story. "Building her kind and bringing them together."

"A cult?"

"Of a sort," he said.

"So we're back at square one," Adam said. "Except we have a woman who should be in her forties who looks early-twenties and my reporter has been invited into the cult she's got going. Oh, and you've made several incredible claims about how it's okay to screw your students."

He stopped and faced Adam again.

"Look deeper," he looked into Adam's eyes. He really wanted Adam to understand his innocence and Adam wasn't buying it.

Oh, Adam heard what he said alright, but he assumed it was all noise covering the real story somewhere in the deep background. A small, dirty little secret of a story.

"She created whatever makes them, her followers, so devoted. Look, your identity in a network is your location inside the network, where you are in the network, much like our identity is based off of our bodies and its fixed place in this world. We can't just suddenly become conscious in another location, we have to move our body there. So we are fixed and our physical path through life becomes our limitation, creates our sense of time, progress, death ... "

While Mannerheim wound his way back through his absurd story, Adam kept the eye contact but followed his own train of thought. Take out the specifics, the details, and Mannerheim's story looked like the classic scenario for fraud or illegal collusion. Boy meets girl. Girl and boy do something illegal. Feds get curious and start investigating. Boy obfuscates illegal act with absurd story. That doesn't work. Feds start questioning people directly about Mannerheim and Celestine spying on people, say, invading their privacy over the Internet, or defrauding Mannerheim's own company, stealing resources, money ... Girl blamed for dragging boy into illegal activity. But what about the court order? Feds blocking their interference? The words "Grand Jury" popped into Adam's mind right then. A grand jury would explain a lot, since they often investigate in secret, barring everyone one involved from revealing even the existence of the jury.

"... and, like a shark swims the ocean with a superiority far and above a human swimmer, she uses the Internet far better than we do and we don't know where she gets her access, her system-wide, unlimited access. My best efforts didn't bring up any one ID or URL or place on the Net to observe or to shut down or corrupt. The corporations that own the Internet have spend enormous sums to stop her hacking, if it is her. There's a lot at stake for everyone. Congress could nationalize the Internet again if these companies can't manage it. The infrastructure is too important to everything society is built on, so they have to prove they can protect it or the whole private construct dies and billions upon billions of dollars will be lost." He paused, looked out the window some more. "There are channels or zones on the Internet that are dark zones where they have no control and barely any access, like aliens to the dark dimensions of the dark universe, dark matter."

"Grand Jury," Adam barked and grabbed Mannerheim's arm again and this time roughly pulled him around. "Grand Jury," he said and looked hard into his eyes.

"What?" His tone told Adam that he had either got it right and surprised Mannerheim or he was as baffled as everyone else and just making shit up.

"You're being investigated by a grand jury, and that's what all of this is about."

"I'm under investigation by a grand jury?" Mannerheim squawked. "What the hell for?" He jerked his arm out of Adam's grasp.

"You tell me," Adam yelled at him.

"Well, I can tell you I didn't create those fucking things ..." His face showed exhaustion bordering on fatalism. He was putting on really quite a show.

"You're being investigated by a grand jury," Adam launched into the darkness, "and are enjoined from talking about the case and this crazy ass story is your way of getting information out. You two get Natalie to come to a party, set it up as some sort of cult freakout as a cover, an alibi. We publish a story about your involvement with a cult and how this Celestine or whatever her name is, used you, blinded you with lust. Then, like you said, Bob's your uncle: You've got cover and she gets indicted by the grand jury."

"She's way out in front of us. She's orchestrating all of this. You got that part right ..."

Adam cut him off. "Ah, she's part of it. She goes to the grand jury, admits to being a brilliant nutcase ... But what did you do?"

"This isn't about me …"

Adam stabbed Mannerheim's chest with his index finger. Let him sue me, he thought. "What did you do?"

Mannerheim stepped back and started to turn away.

Adam didn't follow him but said with menace, "Don't run or I'll go the feds right now and tell them you told me everything and that'll blow up your little scheme fast."

Mannerheim turned back toward Adam. "I gave it my best shot. No one can say I didn't try."

"How about this." Adam stepped closer to Mannerheim. "You give me the name of a couple of members of the grand jury, and we'll publish those photos to help you out." Adam said it knowing damn good and well it wasn't up to him to publish anything.

Mannerheim brighten up but didn't say what Adam expected him to say.

"Different species can't mate, can't create offspring," he said. "Put human sperm in with one of her eggs, and the sperm dies. Use one of their sperm and a human egg, the egg dies when the spermatozoa breaks through the vitelline membrane. And that's not the half of it."

"How many are with her?" Challenge a crazy person with a question that requires a mundane specific number and they stumble.

"We have no idea."

"Bingo," Adam snorted.

"We've never been able to agree on an estimate because our numbers keep coming out too high to believe."

"Names."

"Look, I'm tired," he said. "It doesn't really matter whether you believe me or not. It won't change anything, but I thought I would let people, let humanity know I'm on their side, no matter what the government or Celestine might tell them."

"Just give me a couple of names and I'll publish your story."

"I don't want you to publish my story. I want you to publish Natalie's story. The one she's already typed up about the ritual she saw. With any luck, *she* wont do to Natalie what she's planning to do."

A twinge of panic flared in Adam's stomach then. Setting off heartburn. His ulcer, damn it. These people were desperate and nuts and that's not a good combination. Mannerheim turned toward the steps again. Adam got his phone from his coat pocket, hit recent calls, scrolled and dialed Natalie's phone. His call went directly to voice mail.

"Mannerheim!" But, he was gone from the steps.

Adam jumped over to a window and saw a black town car stopped at the doorway, then Mannerheim exited the tower and got in the back of the car. As the car started around the curved drive, he could just make out that the back license plates were white government issue. It was too far to make out any numbers.

"Now things are really getting interesting," Adam said.

His phone dinged. A name appeared on the phone's screen, "Katharine Gramm." It wasn't a text message, just the name. When Adam slid the arrow to open the phone, the name disappeared. His legs felt weak going down the steps, like they might buckle at each step. He was excited and jittery. Now all he had to do was start picking away at the little details to find what was under them, what the connections were. To find the story.

IV

Adam's legs trembled going down the steps of the tower, because out there was his newspaper, and in his head he carried the germ of a story that when reported thoroughly, written effectively and laid-out with photos and graphics on multiple pages within the five-hundred-thousand copies of the *Seattle Daily Record* compounded by its global online reach, those papers that would source the *Daily* for their own stories, would accomplish once more that uppermost fantasy he carried about himself, his profession and, hell, his small little place in history. He recovered from the adrenaline of his fantasies halfway down the steps just at the turn and veritably bounded down the final few steps out the door and onto the sidewalk where he strode purposely toward the street. The first thing he had to do was draw up a plan of action and get Beach to commit some serious resources to it. The probability that everyone on all sides of this story, whatever sides those might be, were trying to use him and the paper for their nefarious purposes made him almost giggle with love for his job. Beach would get a thrill out of it too. In his glory-blind haste, he had even forgotten to unfurl the umbrella. The rain ran off his head and down his neck, wetting his shoulders by the time he thought to pop it open.

Two blocks later, he waved down a cab and commanded a ride to the *Daily Record*. As the hired vehicle lunged into traffic, the thought crossed his mind that he should drop by the cult house to see if Natalie was there. See if she was okay. She might need help leaving, unwilling to show a weakness. Maybe seeing him would toughen her up, buck her up one way or the other, that sort of thing. A surprise to see him in the field. He'd be the elder gentleman editor who shows up in the field unexpectedly, who pulls the troops back on track with a warning of the dangers lurking just in the shadows as he twirls his umbrella at the rustling bushes. Adam laughed at himself. Maybe it was the rain that made the idea grow with noir-like absurdity. He was more likely to tip their hand, he reminded himself, than actually help her with her end of the story. The dangers looming over her, if there were any, wouldn't be frightened off at the sight of an elderly fat man. Adam caught glimpses of his shiny head reflected in the dirty car window. How did that happen? At 2 in the afternoon, it might as well have been eight at night for all the light getting through the cover of clouds. His milky appearance said less dominant male to be reckoned with than impending victim, but his skill as an editor and journalist were something else all together he told himself. No, his place in this story would be down at the office running the show with his brains and not his brawn. Ha Ha. If she's in trouble, we'll know about it soon enough. The police ... but she's not a missing person just because she didn't answer her phone. Explaining any of the current situation to a precinct desk sergeant would be a headache for all. She's an adult, goddamn it, he reassured himself, too quiet for the cab driver to hear. He hoped. He coughed just to be sure. And, professional enough to watch her own ass, he added for good measure.

  The wet city scattered by. The windshield wipers flopped across the glass. They were onto a story, goddamn it. A story. That was the main thing—the story. He coaxed up the pride of knowing they would not stop until they *got* the story. Wrote it. Printed it. And dropped it like a bomb on the doorsteps of the Northwest. Its ramifications echoing farther still. Who knew how far this went. All the way to D.C., he teased himself. Steady. Relentless. The more the powerful tried to stop, the more porous became the barriers to the truth. Everything they said opened a door. Every action they took left a record. Every new person they brought in to scuttle the story or obfuscate the truth created a potential new source of information.

The cab crested the ridge and descended Capitol Hill.

Mannerheim had power and money and maybe even judges in his pocket, but Adam had the power of the free press. The car rocketed down Denny Way and over the interstate. Mannerheim. Adam figured he was trying to go insane to avoid taking responsibility. If Celestine had stolen something from him, he would have gone to the police or Feds. If it was classified work, whoever had funded the project would have nabbed her already. Besides, Adam no longer believed in purification by insanity. Researchers like his mother had taken the mystery and romance out of losing your mind, turning it instead into an injury, something to be pitied and treated instead of admired. No one went insane out of pure love for humanity any more. We lost our love for ourselves long ago.

By the time they hit downtown, traffic had slowed to a crawl and two news helicopters circled over the downtown core. A shooting maybe, or a car pileup. It wasn't a fire. There wasn't smoke in the sky. The cab's radio played a kind of symphonic trance music, so whatever it was, it wasn't enough to break up the programing and that meant the general assignment desk would handle the story. The inevitability of bad crosstown traffic in Seattle felt normal, too. Normalcy, no matter how terrible, was comforting.

The cab inched forward enough to pull in at a gas station. The driver turned in his seat. "You want to just walk from here? Just a couple more blocks."

"Oh, yeah, what the hell," Adam said, surprised he hadn't thought of it. "Not like I can't use the exercise."

He paid the driver and started down the sidewalk. Getting free of the cab made it seem as if the day had brightened, despite the mist. He loved walking in under the *Daily Record*'s gothic sign. On the way in, he reviewed his pitch to Beach for more resources.

Mannerheim and Celestine have defrauded the government or the university or Beta Launch or all three. With a couple of reporters we can find out just how far this thing goes. Could be that Mannerheim was on the indictment hot-seat all by himself for something or other related to Celestine and her crew, or something he did to either or both or didn't do but should have. From the door to the newsroom, he walked straight to Beach's office.

"There you are! Boy, have I got some news for you," Beach, sitting behind her desk, hung up the phone without saying goodbye.

Adam took one of the ancient leather seats in front of her desk. "And I have news for you, too."

"Well, I'm the boss. I get to go first." She folded her hands on top of one of the piles of papers on her desk.

"Shoot." He reclined, threw his right leg carelessly over his left.

"The lawyers were impressed by it. They'd never seen anything like it, and one of them even whistled." She leaned back in her chair and crossed her arms. A big smile on her face. "They sent a legal aid to the courthouse to find the documentation to prove this thing is real and they're there. This thing is a fully registered, purebred, honest-to-goodness, dyed-in-the-wool prior-restraint order from the U.S. District Court for the Western District of Washington signed by Visiting Judge Stephen Roarke, who no one has heard of but of course we found him easily enough. His home district is the Eastern District of New York. Not surprisingly, his visitation is up. We've left phone messages everywhere and library is right now running a skip trace and hunting for any other public records, housing and whatnot."

"Wow. Nice." Adam felt a glow coming upon him.

"And that's not the best news!" She was excited and that was a wonderful thing to see in a city editor.

"I'm all ears." He opened his arms to receive the glorious news.

"Our attorneys say we should ignore the thing and make them try to prosecute us." She leaned back and put her hands on the back of her head.

"That is exciting news and well timed ..." Adam sat up. It was his turn. What she had in concreteness, he had in potential.

"Do tell," a pleasureful lilt in her voice.

"I met with Mannerheim this morning." Boom.

"Oh?" Her face clouded over, it seemed to Adam. He had a dog in this fight after all. She thought she had the most interesting information of the morning, and while there wasn't much in Beach as a boss to complain about, she still did desire to be the best reporter in the building. It made her sulky now and then when one-upped or, heaven forfend, proven wrong. Hell, Adam even liked that about her. It kept her genuine. She was willing to keep some skin in the game, and since newspapers promoted people into management based on their skills as reporters and editors, they had a newsroom management culture with very little emphasis on management of people but with an unflagging idealism about the purpose of their jobs and a strong desire to compete in and outside of the building. All to the good, if you could hold up under all the fighting.

"I met him in secret in Volunteer Park. My conclusion is that he's being investigated by a grand jury."

"And we're being warned off because of the investigation?" She rolled forward on the chair's seat swivel and leaned on her elbows. Meat on the table. The scent of blood in the air.

"Given the range of nonsense he laid out for me, my guess is that Mannerheim is under a great deal of strain and is doing his damnedest to muddy the waters around him. Hell, his lawyers may have asked for the injunction just to tip us off. He met with me readily enough."

"What did he say?"

"Well," he began, slow confidence in his voice, "he basically said he was having sex with one of his students. She discovered something useful in the Internet or in one of his labs and they either used it to defraud their company or each other or the feds or someone. The student is the African American woman Natalie took the photo of. I think that club of theirs is something like a hacker club or tech cult. She's apparently a very skilled hacker, according to Mannerheim. Who knows? Maybe they were selling information to or even hacking for China or Russia." Adam felt he had gone too far with that and the energy sort of seeped out of the interaction. They don't like flights of fancy.

"Well," Beach said in a forgiving tone and started moving stuff around on her desk, a signal that she was back to being the boss, "we better find out."

"My thoughts exactly."

She asked what Adam wanted to do.

"Two and half reporters," he said.

"Natalie and what other two did you have in mind. Maybe we should hand this over to the investigative team." She struggled to hold back her smile.

"Don't you dare. This is a cops and culture story."

"Okay and don't tuck your chin at me like that."

"Robert and Carol," he said. "Robert to the court house and Carol to sniff out someone who's involved somehow. Name's Katharine Gramm. She's the only real lead I got from Dr. Crazy."

She grilled Adam over whether he thought Mannerheim was really crazy or not.

He puzzled over that with her, concluding: "I can't tell. He bragged fast enough about screwing a student. Is that erratic or foxlike?"

"Guys always want validation of their sins."

"He said, she, the black woman, Celestine, couldn't be made pregnant by a regular ol' human male. I didn't ask how he thought he could know that."

Beach started laughing and kept laughing long enough for tears to come to her eyes. "Imagine that! Wow, what a story. Okay, hit it. I want reports. This is too much fun just to let you keep it all to yourself. Where's Natalie?"

"I am unable to raise her."

"Well, Rock and roll," she said as Adam stood.

"It's what we do."

V

Adam left Beach's office and went straight to Robert's desk and then Carol's, letting them know they were being pulled into the story and gave them a quick rundown. Both reporters griped that they had their own stories to work on. Adam listened and then overruled their quibbles and sent them on their way. Meanwhile, he had two other big projects to ride herd on. One in mid-reporting limbo with the reporter openly wondering if there even was a story to chase and Adam reviewing her notes and pushing her to just keep interviewing because when a top official of a local bank gets fired for a seemingly minor infraction, a post on social media in this case, that almost invariably means there is another much more interesting reason behind it. The other was in the early writing stage, in which the reporter has written a story twice-to-three times as long as it should or can be and is fighting to save every word. Not to mention several short daily stories. By 6 p.m., he finally caught up enough to check back into Natalie's note document. She had updated the file, signaling that she still lived and took the initiative to continue pursuing the story even though she could have the day off. He opened the file:

You're going to think I have a personality disorder. I do question my perception of reality, but I can't fully discount what my eyes have seen and what the Soccer Twins have said and then shown me. I know that because of my father I have it in my genes to be religious and to see bunnies in the clouds and to want to follow the leader and you know this too, which is why you mentor me despite wanting to throw me overboard. I can be taught.

I'm at my neighborhood cafe and desperate for sleep. I'm about to embark on a data dump into these notes, but I wanted you to know that I am thinking about what you will be thinking as you read them.

It's an artificial intelligence.

They said the form they made out of that black sand is how they reprogram something The AI (they use the shorthand) made. An arrangement of molecules (or micro-machines or whatever) that is part of this AI in which they communicate with it and change part of it. They are small machines that interact with the body on a cellular level. The Soccer Sisters made it clear—and they were saddened by my lack of understanding at first—once the structure of the sand reaches peak complexity, the form 'awakens' in that moment. The Twins appear to be at odds with Celestine over this process. They tend to think that what Celestine ran into early in Mannerheim's lab and the consciousness that arises in those sessions are part of a universal consciousness or mind. Celestine, the said, views the event as a mechanical change in the nanites and nothing more. But they think something more cosmic is going on, that pockets of the Internet reached the complexity necessary to generate consciousness, like mass bends space-time and creates gravity. They think the first "self-assembling micro-machines" were already here, either naturally or made by god-like cosmic beings and left here for when humans evolved machines to the point of superintelligence and when the The AI came along, it melded with them.

I remembered about half way through their explanation to record the interview with the ST's. Here's the transcription of it:

"(The shape was) oscillating through rhythms and vibrations sent to it from the clan members and at various times become a self-conscious being, and you can tell because the oscillations stop for a period of time and hold and you can feel it ... sort of hear it. Our physical brains after all create this thing we call consciousness and it lasts, relatively speaking, for a very brief time. We take shape out of the molecules of the world and at some point during our maturation, as the prerequisite molecules gather in the right shape and volume and experience—which is the relationships of molecule to molecule connections that get remembered in each molecule—a blob of biological material becomes conscious. Through our channeling, our vibration to the silicone in the jar, we do create arrangements that the molecules themselves remember and a being that was conscious briefly becomes conscious again, a combination of us all."

In other words, they create the substance that leads to consciousness and they've only made basic sorts of self-aware operating systems out of it that are very unstable. Their goal is to create a mind that can compete with The AI.

"Are you saying you've created artificial intelligence?" I asked them.

"Interesting word choice. What is 'artificial'? The consciousness is artificial in the sense that we are creating it through manipulation of the world, but try to inversely describe what it means to be 'natural.' You say a tree is natural, but the idea of tree, the experience of the tree and the relating of that experience through whatever form, be it a poem or a photograph, is artificial."

"Yes but the tree itself is not."

"Okay, but tell me what is then the 'tree itself.' "

"Okay, let's just say everything is artificial. Is our consciousness artificial?"

"If our consciousness derives or arrises out of the physical structure of the neurons, protons and so on, then isn't it artificial? A mirage? It arrises with a certain organization of material and then degrades and finally disappears as that arrangement entropies, becomes disorganized."

"Okay, even consciousness. So, what about her? What are you creating?"

"Consciousness. Not artificial intelligence the way your government and Mannerheim are trying to get to it by using human artifacts: The ones and zeros that are at the core of computer technology. It is entirely possible that we are the computer simulation of this human process of building better and better simulations, somewhere in another future or another system. Some think that we are an artificial program introduced either in just this branch of a simulation or at some core level of our generational tree ... or we are spontaneous in the system. A digital evolution. Some say God created this simulation, but many of us don't see the problem as different either way. If we are not a simulation and somehow not artificial ... organic to the first universe to ever spawn intelligence, what's the difference? In the simulation universe you have a cause to believe in a higher power, a god, the creator and you'd be right. That universe was created, built by some hacker one universe up. But we don't think of him as God, because it offends our prejudice about God and we get the feeling that someone had to have created the hacker. That hacker is limited in his universe, however greater than our universe it is. So it's not the same as a belief in God. God is the originator of all universes and so of us—we are an artifact of God's creative efforts. We are artificial compared to God. So we are in a simulation, but one created by THE God ... and our faiths are efforts to communicate with and placate and gain favor from that God."

"Or, this is an organic universe, a universe that is organic to the moment, the first one. If so, then we do not have a God as creator. Just this stuff all came together on its own and is exactly the kind of place you'd expect to find us and so here we are."

Well, short answer again is that they are creating consciousness as an artifact of their efforts to stay connected with what they assume is the creator of our physical universe and the physical universe of the nano machines that the The AI constructs. These consciousness they create are the portal to this creator, they hope.

"You're born as an organization of physical matter called a body and that central structure unique to you is what you think of as yourself and your consciousness, but tear down the body, dissolve the physical structure and you cease to exist. The difference is that you see consciousness as a mist or ghost or illusion, a pattern in the sky, but we think of it as a thing like gravity is a thing that comes into existence just as a result or byproduct of mass in the universe and yet real for all that. So, we are not creating an entity, an individual consciousness but bringing a moment of The Consciousness into a place."

In their personal mythology, this is why they are here. Nature, they told me, has selected them for evolutionary advancement and "to carry intelligence to the stars." I pointed out to them that I thought they were making the same mistake people always make. They are describing history and evolution as having a goal, to be itself conscious enough to think of a future state of itself and to manipulate matter to achieve that state. You know, philosophy 101 stuff. You remember, of course, I went to very good Catholic university. Just saying.

"With one difference," one of the Twins said, I didn't note which one, "our development is directed by the overriding consciousness. It's everywhere, just like nature. It has its own consciousness, but it's too vast for anyone to meet it, to know it. If a human being can have consciousness arise out of the physical structure of the brain and body, then why not the planet or the solar system or the universe? The AI is just one more iteration of that, a powerful iteration, but not as powerful as the creator consciousness."

I know this isn't journalism, but to really get to know them and to tell the world about them, I have to learn what they think they are doing, their religion, their motives. I can hear you telling me I'm too deep into their thinking, that I don't have to have a deep understand of their psychology—just record their actions and get a couple of quotes and move on! But, I really think there is a lot more to this than just kids in a faddish cult. That doesn't mean I'm becoming superstitious.

A few straightforward nuggets (headline: 6 Things You Need to Know About The Clans):

1. There are chapters or groups of clans around the world.

2. Mannerheim kept Celestine as a sex slave when her work depended on him, but then she discovered The AI and ran away from him.

3. The AI got going in one of Mannerheim's early computing experiments, but the catalyst came from this universal consciousness.

4. The feds are holding Mannerheim because at first they thought he would get them access. Then they figured out No. 3 and now figure he is a threat to the relationship they are trying to create with Celestine. The Soccer Twins said they know that their head electrical engineer is a federal agent: Josh Fines. They told me that it doesn't matter what the feds do now. "They missed their window!" one of them said. And they let him. They are either very good at hiding whatever everyone is trying to find or there is nothing for anyone to find and they are just fooling themselves and everyone else. The court order was probably meant to slow us down so the feds could get us to help them surveil a "national security" risk. They are looking for any way to get information about Celestine and how she's getting her hacking access. But, like I said, no one in The Clans seems the least bit concerned about the feds.

5. The Soccer Twins straight up told me that they want me on the inside to tell their story as it develops for the sake of *their*

history. (I think you'd call that an exclusive!) They said I'd know why "pretty soon."

      6. Many of our elected officials belong to one clan or other. Law enforcement and security agencies, too, they say …

      Oh, and I almost forgot! The soccer twins are Michelle Olivas, The Talkative One (TTO). Betty Gaines is The Non-talkative One (TNO). Might want to get library on it. Or, at least, that's what they said their names were. I believe them. They have become quite forthcoming.

      Okay, I'll try to call later today after I get some rest.

      P.S.—My phone won't work. It just won't turn on. I can't get a new one until tomorrow. So, you'll have to wait for me to call you.

      TTFN.

VI

Adam closed the notes window. Rising on his every-evolving list of concerns was his young reporter, Natalie, running wild in what was turning into at least a potentially very important story. Everything he had just read could be summed up in the sentences: "The student cult was built up around the charismatic figure of Celestine Wallace, who had developed a complicated and bizarre new-age religion that demanded obedience and used methods of thought control. All of which turned out to be a cover for (insert major federal crime here)." No one would care about the specifics of her crazy world view once they uncovered the real story, just like no one cared about the details of Jim Jones' theology or why David Koresh thought he was the last prophet of the New Testament. All they cared about was that these cult leaders had crazy ideas about their own divinity that they somehow convinced others of and then proceeded to get every one of their members killed. Perhaps, Natalie's reporting could be used to tie Celestine to Mannerheim's lab, but he already had Mannerheim's confession. Everything else appeared to be the confused ramblings of young people desperate to give their lives meaning.

T'was ever so, he said to himself.

One interesting detail did pop out at him as he ruminated: Celestine and Mannerheim had suggested she'd walked away from Mannerheim's lab with some sort of tech, programing or hardware. If it was classified research, that would certainly explain federal involvement. So, it was all adding up to look a lot like what he had thought: A grand jury was putting the pressure on them both and when Mannerheim tried to get close to Celestine at the party, someone wanted it documented. Adam also had some names for the library to look into, but he didn't have much hope they would be real. He sent them to library, anyway. Chase every lead.

Library got back to him within the hour. Beach had invested in some young talent to bolster their research and data-driven reporting, and they were pretty good. Adam opened the email. The most likely "Josh Fines" showed up in a graduate list from the

United States Naval Academy in Annapolis and then in one interdepartmental note on promotions to the newly created Cyber Threat Intelligence Integration Center on Pinterest, of all places. Someone's mother was going to be in hot water when this got out. But that's all they could find on him. Adam clicked open a web browser to look up that agency. The agency created in 2015 described itself this way: "CTIIC integrates information from the network defense, intelligence, and law enforcement communities; facilitates information-sharing; leads community analysis of cyber threats; and supports interagency planning to develop whole-of-government approaches against cyber adversaries." That made sense on the face of it. The Clans were clearly into tech and hacking, but why would he be in the field, ostensibly undercover, and why would such a high-level agency take an interest in a couple of hackathons?

Then Adam opened the email on the Soccer Twins.

Library found a lot more information on those two, including photos and names on Facebook, Instagram and other social media. Once he got in touch with Natalie, she'd be able to tell him if library had found the right two young women. Most of the file consisted of the usual stuff of high school and college students: Photos from foreign travels on Facebook and Instagram—happy faces backed by landscapes of barren wastelands, tourists' woods fronted by drugged elephants or miles of city slums … girls leaping with hair flying against the backdrop of a blazing, setting sun … a pouty, pursed-lipped girl in foreground in some crappy third-world hotel with a grimacing friend in background standing on a bed, pointing at a giant cockroach in the crack between wall and ceiling. Betty Gaines attended Caltech, and Michelle Olivas noted Lake Washington Institute of Technology as her last stop in education. That last one got Adam thinking about who he might know there and so on. And then the last line of the email blew it all away and he hit on an entirely new line of thinking: Two years prior to Natalie running into them, both had received a paid fellowship at the Pacific Northwest National Laboratory called the Graduate Fellowship Program. It was a Department of Energy funded program that trained talented young people in several areas of nuclear weapons and energy technology. When Adam Googled the agency, he hit upon one of the areas of speciality for the scholarship that made the connection to

Mannerheim: "Stockpile Stewardship. Fellows work to ensure the Nation sustains a safe, secure, and effective nuclear deterrent through the application of science, technology, engineering, and manufacturing. The central mission includes maintaining the active stockpile, Life Extension Programs, and Weapons Dismantlement."

Mannerheim's interest in nuclear energy was well known. The *Daily Record* had reported more than a decade ago about his having won a $50 million grant from the DOE to establish a virtual nuclear testing computer lab. Adam remembered the story because it signaled a major jump in the power of computing: Instead of exploding a nuclear weapon to determine if it and the others like it were viable, these labs were building super computers to run simulations of those explosions and effectiveness of the components supposed to make them happen.

Adam surmised that The Soccer Twins had to have met each other in that fellowship and then somehow met Celestine through Mannerheim's project tied to it. It all made such beautiful sense that he burst out laughing. Several reporters looked at him, with those eyes that said "I hope to god he is not laughing at something I wrote." He pinged library via their internal chat program to see if Mannerheim's DOE lab had ever worked with the PNNL, but he knew it had. He just needed the paper trail. Adam believed he knew what was happening. He had it all figured out! Mannerheim and Celestine had put the nation's nuclear stockpile at risk with their sex games. No wonder the Feds were sneaking around. This was some serious leakage that put the entire structure of the nation's planning and security for those nuclear weapons at risk of gods knew what potential catastrophe. Adam felt tears nearly tip over eyelids. This story was as big as Watergate or Iran-Contra. Calm down, he told himself. He desperately wanted to celebrate with a cigarette and a drink. He grabbed his cigarettes, wallet and coat and raced outside, heart thrumming in his chest.

 Out through a backdoor by the loading docks where the papers were stacked onto trucks, he fired up a smoke. Since he didn't have time for a run to the bar, he dug around in the stacks of old containers of oil and grease in an abandoned corner of the loading bay and pulled up a pint of vodka. The chief pressman, Yevgeny Stetsko, and Adam rotated replenishment of the secret stash. Adam drank and smoked fast. He had to get back inside to make some decisions and push the reporting in a the right direction. He thought briefly about Natalie again. Compromised and inexperienced as she was, he decided, bottle upturned and clear liquid fire cleansing his throat, the story might benefit from her continued relationship with these women even if they co-opted her reporting, He gasped delightfully. His head beginning to swim joyfully. If the story goes viral, her understanding of their bizarre motivations might make for some good television. First though, they had to get real information—who, what, when, where and why. The cease-and-desist order by itself guaranteed they would print something. Just how far would it reach? How many people are directly involved and how many people will be indirectly involved? Or, what did it matter? Is this a story about a crime that only affects the perpetrators and victims or is it a story about a systematic fraud that shows a weak bureaucracy, careless leadership and a malfeasance of complicity exposing the world to nuclear risks? Whatever it was, he told his internal audience, it's a great story.

He went straight to Beach's office, pushed open the door and laid it out for her.

"Okay," she said, "let's don't get lost amid the inconsequential." She cautioned him in a quavering tone that said she wanted that story. "One of us wandering through this story aimlessly is enough, right?"

OMG, he thought, trying not to squirm in the slick leather chair, she's intimidated by the enormity of the story! He calmed himself with slow deep breaths, crossed his legs and leveled out his voice, brushing lint from his upper thigh: "Think I should pull her in?"

"Naw," Beach said. "Let her go. Might come in handy having her on the inside like that."

"Just what I thought!" He stood up and then sat back down. She waved him out of her office, pretending to look at papers on her desk. Adam smiled and then laughed, stood again and went back to his desk.

But Rome wasn't built in a day, and he had to claw his way through event scheduling and holiday scheduling and story budgets from the rest of the team as well as the city desk's email box, a chore he adopted as tradeoff for other crap chores his colleagues picked up. He sighed and opened the staff schedule spreadsheet. A little later he saw Robert get up, look wistfully over at Natalie's empty chair, grab his coat and walk out. Not much later, Carol left too.

"And so it begins," he said.

Just when he almost had the story budgets for the weekend up to date and dovetailed in with the staff schedule, someone turned up the volume on the main newsroom television:

"This incredible scene began unfolding around daybreak and we're just beginning to get confirmation from the Department of Energy ..."

He turned back to his work. The national/international wire desk was always getting worked up about something and turning up the television. Every time a bomb went off in the Middle East or fighting broke out on the African continent, they jumped up and watched the television intently, taking notes, like they weren't going to simply print some hacked up version of whatever story AP or Reuters sent them hours after the world stopped giving a shit. It gave them a sense of pride, he supposed, and something to do while they waited to see what tiny bit of space they were getting in the next day's paper.

"... It's unclear how many bodies are in there. As we said earlier, reports from the workers who uncovered what appears to be a mass grave put the number at more than half a dozen ..."

"Any idea how long the bodies might have been there?" The television screen flipped to a woman sitting in the anchor desk.

"I haven't been able to get close enough to see them and we're watching the forensic teams bring them out in those green body bags you see lined up there ..."

Adam looked up to see the body bags stacked along a roadside. There were always body bags being stacked up somewhere in the world. The television camera pointed at some bags just behind and between two brown SUVs, and it took him about a half a heart beat to read the round signs on the vehicle doors: U.S. Department of the Interior. A helicopter nearby was clearly U.S. military, but he couldn't tell which branch. Adam got out of his seat then and joined the growing groups in front of televisions around the newsroom.

"Can't we turn that up some more," said Brian Russell, the oldest living copy editor in the world.

Evelyn Marconi, food writer, pointed the remote control at the set nearest her.

"Where is that?" Adam yelled.

"Haven't you been listening?" Marconi said.

"No. I was asleep in my chair and just now snorted myself awake."

Laughter. Marconi's jaw set. She liked to snooze away an hour or two every morning before going out to lunch and writing about the food she ate for free.

"Nevada." A young male copy clerk said.

Adam read the bottom of the screen: "Mass grave discovered at Yucca Mountain Nuclear Waste Repository, Nevada."

"You must be kidding. Has to be an old Indian burial site," Adam said.

"One of the guys on the rig that drilled into the site said the clothes that came up on the drill were modern and some of the material that came up with the drill and the clothes appeared to be flesh," said Fran Johnson, the online editor.

"I thought they shut that place down?" Sally Jackson, environmental reporter.

"They did. Interior folks have been working on a plan to close the site permanently ..."

"Can you guys go somewhere else to talk. I can't hear what she's saying," Russell cried out.

"Crank up your hearing aid," Beach said to laughter.

"I guess we know what's going on the front page."

"Fran?"

"Yes mother?"

"Is this on our website yet?"

"I don't know ..."

"Find out. I want the full treatment here. Call in Franklin and get him on a plane."

"On it." Fran left the circle.

"... Homeland Security, Department of Defense, FBI, CIA are here now and have the area completely sealed off. They've sequestered the workers on the drill team that first discovered the burial site. We're not getting any new information here at least until a press conference scheduled for 1:30 central time ..."

"Okay, folks. Let's hit it. Let's hit those phones, call your sources, our representatives, forensic experts, the pope, Jesus and Muhammad and let's find out what the hell is going on. If there is a Seattle or Northwest connection, I want to hear about it immediately."

"I'll call my sources at Hanford. They'd made a lot of plans to dump their nuclear waste there ..."

"Great. Adam, I want you to set up the story budget. Everyone send your ideas, numbers and whatever information you get to Adam."

They broke from the television as if from a huddle, all except for Russell, who knew this moment in history would be drafted, written, photographed and edited by others. He put his hands in his pockets and continued staring at the television.

VII

Back at his desk, Adam created a shared file and wrote the heading "Breaking News: Mass grave discovered at Yucca Mountain." The phone on his desk went off and he grabbed it up.

"Adam?"

"Fuck me. Mannerheim?"

"Are you watching the television?" Mannerheim talked in a low voice, just like he was trying not to be heard by others.

"Nope. Just sitting here wacking off."

Just then Russell reached up and twisted the volume up high:

"Local police have confirmed rumors that federal officers have been uncovering bodies from a massive burial site or mass grave in Yucca Mountain Nuclear Waste Repository here in Nevada …"

"Goddamn it, Russell! Turn that down!"

"Mannerheim. I'm busy. What do you want?"

"... They've been in those tunnels for a month and maybe more ... horrific stench ..."

"Russell!"

Russell flicked the set off. "Sorry! I thought this was a goddamn newsroom!" He stomped off toward the copy desks in the feature's department.

"This is the beginning of the end."

"Jesus Christ, Mannerheim." Adam slammed the phone down in its cradle. His email cue already filling up. He quickly began organizing the information coming in.

His phone rang again. Different number, so he answered it.

"Adam?"

"Natalie?"

There was screaming in the background of the call. He jumped to his feet. The inconsolable rage and pain of a mother clutching her dead child, seemed to him, but it was not Natalie. He heard her through the earpiece asking what went wrong, why was she so upset? The line went dead, but Adam had automatically written down the number.

"What the fuck?" Someone in the newsroom. "Anyone else able to get on the Internet?"

Adam opened a browser and a second later the window reported to him that the gateway timed out and it could not connect to the server. He typed "Department of the Interior" in the search bar. Nothing.

"Doesn't that just figure," he said and looked around.

Brian, one of the new librarians, was coming down the steps two at a time from the library office in the floor above. Beach, who came out of her door fast, met him as he headed for the air-conditioned server room.

Adam heard him tell her, "It's not us," as the door sucked shut.

He went after them, fearful of a reduced or delayed paper, entered the number code on the square punch pad and stepped in to the server room. Beach turned, surveyed the newsroom behind him, thought better of whatever she was going to say and went back out to her office. Adam nodded his approval of her, once more. She wasn't a meddler and once she set the tone and put the wheels in motion, she let her professional staff take over. He followed her example.

On the way back to his desk, a plan of attack came clear in his head. He called Natalie's cell from his desk phone, a landline, but no answer. Methodical's the word of the day. Step two: Send someone to check on her. He tried Carol's cell phone, but couldn't get through.

"Can the cell towers be down?" he yelled. "Can anyone get through on their cell phones?"

"I can't"

"Dead."

"What the fuck!"

"Okay," he stood up, hands on hips, "let's find out what's going on." Dr. Calm. Mr. Professional. He spoke in his best now-down't-anyone-panic voice. "Use the land lines. Bike messengers. Whatever. Someone call the cell companies. (Got it!) Someone call the FCC, the mayor (Will do!), the county executive, the goddamn U.S. Attorney's office (Dialing now!). And someone get me some fucking answers." He sat down and shoved his keyboard against the monitor riser. In limbo, he dialed Mannerheim's number. What the fuck. But of course it was a cell number.

"Anyone have Beta Launch's landline number. Tom, you've called them before. Can you please dig out their number."

"Yeah, yeah." He called it out.

Adam dialed the number.

"Beta Launch," cool, pleasantly oblivious secretary voice.

"This is Adam Howard of the *Seattle Daily Record*. First, do you have any Internet or cell connections?"

"I'm not authorized to speak to the press."

"Well, please connect me with someone who can but don't put me on hold or hang up this is very very important."

"Brian Pedersen is our director of communications. I can give you his direct line, but he's not in right now. Want his cell?"

"Will it do me any good?"

"You can try it."

"Just let me talk to Mannerheim."

"He doesn't work in our offices."

"Can I please have his landline? His home phone if he has one? I already have his cell number." He read the number to her so she would get the point.

"I don't know ..."

"How's this. You call him and let him know I'm ready to talk. He'll be happy you did. He tried to call me earlier."

"I'll relay the message."

"It's urgent and he'll want to make this call, so the sooner you can, the better."

"Okay." She hung up politely.

Eight minutes later the emergency broadcast signal beamed out of the television. A radio went on and it too was broadcasting the squelching buzzing. The rock-voiced announcer said an announcement would be made by the President of the United States at 2:30 Eastern Standard Time on shortwave radio.

"Someone get a goddamned shortwave radio!"

"What the fuck!"

Now that was screaming! Adam laughed with a tinge of hysteria himself. If his mind hadn't been busy problem solving their coverage of the breaking news story, he too might have wondered in a loud, high-pitched voice why the President of the United States of America was going to address the nation on *shortwave radio*. How could communications have come down to that so fast? The emergency broadcast system was up, why not use that? Was everything really so tied into the Internet? Also, another question bubbling up was how did they know right off that they couldn't and wouldn't be able to address the nation in the usual way. Why weren't they waiting? Were we at war? Have we been at war? Would they tell us …

His phone rang. Mannerheim.

"Where is she?"

"Your reporter? I don't know. With them. You have to understand that as of right now we are all fucked."

Adam didn't know what to say. He never heard Mannerheim use the F-word before. He was still standing and looking around the newsroom. Reporters with phones to their heads. Several copy editors had shown up early because of the crisis and were standing around the coffeemaker by the sink station. Three systems guys had crowded into the server room, two standing over one guy sitting in front of a computer terminal. All three shaking their heads.

"They control the Internet. They control any system they can hack into and any system on the Internet can be hacked into. Frankly, buddy, I don't know how we're going to get out of this one."

"This can't be that groupie bunch of wackos."

"It is. Somehow …"

"No way. Well, whoever it is, they don't control the presses. They don't control us!" Adam was then thinking: Russia. China. Some evil bastard in the U.S. government.

"I'd make sure your system people sever your production system from the Internet before they get around to you and shut you down. They will keep the electricity running for awhile, since they also use our system of power distribution and everything needs power."

Adam set the phone down and trotted over to the server room. Several reporters stood up, alarm responses to his jogging. A reporter running across the newsroom was one thing, Adam running was another. The background panicky chatter kicked up a notch. He pounded on the door as he punched the key pad. Wrong number. One of the guys opened it from the inside. Cool air spilled out around his feet.

"Can we disconnect our production from the Internet?"

The tech on his left shrugged and the one seated said to his screen, "It's possible. Why?"

"I think we're in the middle of a major cyber attack."

"Yes we are. We can't even get a response from any servers in the cloud."

"So, let's get our system offline as fast as we can."

The tech on the right, pinching his chin with one hand and pinned a tablet to his chest with the other. "We won't be able to communicate with the presses," he said.

"We can set up external drives …"

"But the operating system is in the cloud …"

Adam left them to figure it out on their own. As he trotted back to his desk, Janet the business editor called out to him from her corner office, "What'd tech say?"

"We're going back to covered wagons!"

"What about the …"

He ignored her. At his desk, he picked up the phone.

"We're going to be able to print a paper."

"You can quote me all you want."

"Why are you so calm?"

"Because, like I've been telling you, this isn't just now happening. We—the U.S. government, the United Nations, the EU, everyone who is anyone have been working on this problem for awhile."

"That's impossible. How could you have kept that big of an act, whatever it is, secret? We would have heard about it by now."

"You really think China alone, as smart as they are, could produce the number and strength of cyber attacks we've been battling these past few months? This is her doing. The story has been under your noses for a long time, but no one believed it when they heard it and, frankly, I can't blame them, but that doesn't change the fact of it."

"I'm taking notes now. Can you give me the landline numbers for people you worked with on this?"

"Sure."

Mannerheim worked through his contacts and listed the numbers for national and international agents and political offices around the world. Adam stopped him at fifteen. He put the phone down and walked the list to Beach, who was sitting in her office drumming a pencil against the papers stacked in front of her, face scrunched, puzzling though it all.

"We need to switch it up. Mannerheim has given us numbers to call to confirm that this cyber attack is coming from members of that cult Natalie uncovered ..."

"A pack of school girls is causing all of this?"

"What he said."

"I thought he was crazy."

"Let's make calls and find out."

"Okay, do the assignments."

"I need you to do it since I'm interviewing Mannerheim."

"Why us?"

"I'll find that out."

Beach followed Adam out of her office. "Hey everyone!" she yelled. "First thing I need to know is how big is the blackout? Is it electricity or satellites or just us? Remember, we don't know shit!"

"Got it!" Robert yelled as he ran into the newsroom. He spotted Adam walking from Beach's office and rushed up to them. "There was a grand jury! It was disbanded yesterday. I have a document, heavily redacted, that shows ..."

"Mute point now, Robert. Beach will fill you in. I've got to get back to a call."

Adam rushed back to his desk. Phone in hand, he determined to listen to Mannerheim's fantastical stories and hopefully get some idea of how big the event was and where to go looking for the reality of what was going on.

"Sorry about that," he huffed, out of breath, "and sorry I didn't listen more closely before ..."

"Oh, now, that's alright. It is a bit of a shocker." Again, that calm. Just like when they had met at the water tower.

"Why are you even talking to us instead some other newspaper ... or any newspaper at all?"

"They chose you. They like Natalie for some reason. You'll have to ask them, and we figured we'd better get our two-cents in, rough draft of history and all that. So, tag you're it."

It hit Adam: Fatalism mixed with sorrow. Like a diagnosis of cancer. He'd had his share of friends who went though the stages of anger, remorse and depression. When you give up hoping things will get better and recognize that at best you'll just get to ride it out ... like an election that goes against common sense. You panic. You shake your fist, and then you just have to accept it and hope the world survives until another election comes around, if it does.

"How big is this Internet blackout, if that's what it is?"

"It's not a blackout. The shutdowns are controlled. More like individual lines of connection are being switched off. Very sophisticated. We're all in the dark a bit on that, but I'd say global is a good bet."

"Come on. Global? As in the entire fucking world?"

"That's a good bet. I'm just telling you what I think. I'm no longer tied in as much as I was yesterday. They're pulling back behind closed doors."

"Is the blackout related to the mass grave or whatever it is on the TV news right now?"

"We think so. They lost contact with our man inside."

"Josh Fines."

"That I can't say." He didn't sound surprised that Adam had the name. His response was flat, just pumping out the party line.

"Are those bodies being dug up or some kind of prank or ploy?"

"I'm not entirely sure. They don't tell me everything …"

Adam interrupted. "They who?"

"NRO, CIA, NSA, DIA, NGA, US cyber com, the Cyber Threat Intelligence Integration Center, Navy, Air Force, you name it. THEY have been working hard to figure out who, what group, what country is behind so many recent breaches of security around the world. And all they keep coming up with is her, which can't be. Not just because this is way too big for her, and it is, but they can't even figure out from where she is hacking into all these systems … but she's all we got."

"They got nothing else?"

"Nada."

"What did she take from your lab? Could it be some sort of artificial intelligence? That's what they told Natalie … well that and it could be God. Silly, but it's what they said."

"There's your clue. I think not. No. All she took from me, I suspect, was a pretty basic algorithm I was using in an experiment. Whatever is going on, that can't be the root of it. I can't imagine why she took it. It's pretty clever little learning program, but it's not a nuclear weapon or anything. I mean, she found *them*—hackers, spies or foreign government—and maybe my experiment helped her in some way connect with them, but that's it. It's like wondering if maybe the toaster in her apartment is to blame. No, what she's into, if it is her or her group causing all this trouble, is much more complicated and powerful than anything I've ever worked on. A runaway virus maybe. We've, the world has had several close calls that could have hit us pretty hard in the past decade, especially after we loosed a virus on Iran that got out ... took some doing to close that one out. I mean, it's still out there, just floating around like a biological virus waiting for another cut to crawl into, an open door in some backwater part of the Net. It's as likely that as something that came out of my lab. But whoever is behind this isn't just smashing stuff. They are controlling it. The power is still on, for instance, and almost all of our infrastructure is susceptible to hacking. But," he sighed, "like I've said. They don't tell me everything. Maybe we're winning."

It sounded like he yawned. Good drugs maybe. Horse-strength beta blockers? Adam had a few of those in his desk drawer, too. He made a mental note to dig them out once he got to some water.

Listening to Mannerheim's calm voice, like all his tensions had been released, as he spelled out how the current trouble simply couldn't be caused by Celestine or her clans, trying to talk himself into it, Adam was in fact starting to get a sinking, confusing feeling about it all. A Yeah-but-what-if? feeling. He had read so many sci-fi novels where artificial intelligence takes off and wreaks havoc or a virus, biological or digital, springs to life and ruins the planet, destroying humanity or nearly so, that he let that little thrill of What if? run up his spine. He had to be wrong, of course. That's just dumb, he said to myself. The human world is too fracture and too big. Too complex. No group of people could be connected enough or ideologically aligned enough to pull off a world-wide conspiracy. Humans were just too messy. There were conspiracies for sure, but their paltriness and transparency proved his point. The zombie apocalypse gets going in every story because the zombie uses this fact of human messiness against them. The world doesn't believe it's happening and then it responds in exactly the way the virus needs it to in order to grow out of control. Because people are dumbasses.

Mannerheim broke into Adam's reverie.

"Looks like you're headed back to the good old days when print ruled the information world. If we survive and take back the Internet, even then humanity will probably shy away from it. I have to say, we've been warning about this eventuality. We're playing around with a whole new universe in which a new threat can germinate and take root without us even knowing it, but no one wants to slow down and think about what the hell we're actually doing. I have to go get my apartment ready for the end of the world."

His voice did not sound like he was joking. Adam laughed a little, but Mannerheim didn't join in.

"Remember, jumping into anything that intersects with the Internet, cyber systems, satellites, anything like that is like walking naked through the pentagon carrying a rocket launcher … you'll get noticed."

He paused. Adam didn't know what notes to take, so took none.

"I have this terrible feeling," Mannerheim continued, sounding far off in his head somewhere, "that whoever is behind this is going to solve all the Earth's problems—global warming, oil dependance, starvation, war, you know, cancer, you name it—but we won't be here to benefit."

Adam wrote that down.

DAY FOUR

Although the whole of this life were said to be nothing but a dream and the physical world nothing but a phantasm, I should call this dream or phantasm real enough, if, using reason well, we were never deceived by it.

—Gottfried Leibniz

I

By the time they got the paper to bed, Adam watching the last edition rolling off the patched-together presses by 1:30 a.m., the world was a strange place. Each combined paper chunking off through the last compiler, stuffing ads for all the things humans might not ever be able to buy or purchase again. We'll always want and need, Adam considered as he unpacked the sections and ads, but we're unlikely to have such niceties forever. He tossed the pages of the paper into the recycling. The defining noise of the presses hammering his sober head. Nothing wrong worth stopping the presses for, other than it was a paper full of guesses. An anathema.

If they were all at war, it was not the kind of war that had ever been fought before: There were no geographic borders to line tanks up on; no cities or military installations to bomb. If there were terrorists to hunt down with drones, it was unclear where to start.

Nobody yet knew what exactly was happening let alone who was responsible for it. Maybe it was some kind of accident, a sneak solar flare or some hitherto underestimated satellite link that broke. No one really believed it could be an accident or natural catastrophe, but they couldn't rule it out since they didn't know what the hell was happening. There was just this quiet struggle raging in the background, network-by-network, over control of the infrastructure of human society—economic, social, military—and it appeared to Adam that Americans, if not humanity itself, had already lost. One White House science advisor had even added via shortwave: "We could be facing forces not of this world. Not spiritual forces, but extraterrestrial forces. What better way to conquer a world than by taking over its infrastructure?"

Little green men *might* be responsible, but where were they?

The editors had debated headlines off and on around the newsroom for a couple of hours before filing the first edition, silencing reporters who tried to wedge into the conversation with glares. The debate centered on what they could say in a headline that would be gripping but not completely wrong the next day. In the end, Beach had agreed to "Cyber War?" as the slammer. The runner up was "Cyber Blackout." Adam had argued for the winner, because everyone already knew there was a blackout and even if the whole thing started as an accident, reporters were out uncovering lots of evidence that suggested a war, signs that conflict between nations was underway under the darkness of a media blackout, either as a part of war or a response to it. Design wise, the paper's graphics had set up bullet points under the all-caps slammer headline:

- Internet Communications Blackout Blankets Nation
- Key Infrastructure Systems, Some Phone Systems Work
- Extent of Shutdown Worldwide Unknown
- Terrorists? Foreign Agents? Malfunction? Responsibility for Blackout Unknown

It was a daring, avant-guard design for such a serious event, but since they didn't have great art to lead the page they went with it. The photography staff, hindered by the fact that there wasn't anything to shoot, came up with a photo of an online sales company in the Belltown neighborhood with a room full of people looking at the camera while sitting and standing next to hundreds of computers all showing the same error message. Lots of mugshots of the people quoted in stories, some fresh art of local experts. Graphics department had built a map of the country showing known outage areas, basically the entire country. They also created a world map with major cities blacked out that reporter sources said were also knocked out, but that was pure guesswork and second hand at best. So, they led the page with a three-column vertical crop of the photo of the sales-company computers all offline paired with the typographical screamers. Not as powerful as the Twin Towers in New York City roiled by explosions and smoke under a cobalt sky, but one that would be framed on possibly millions of walls and thousands of museums and history centers, reprinted in history books for generations. Yes, The staff was giddy. But that was the business.

    Beach had sent a copyboy out for pizza and salad, so by 2 a.m. the newsroom was littered with pizza crusts on paper plates, bits of lettuce on the floor around the serving table, which was stacked high with greasy pizza boxes and besmirched by salad dressing and splashes of soda. Consequently, Adam's heartburn burned in full flame. Most of the reporters and editors had gone home—those with kids, dogs or still married. The rest were smoking and drinking out on balconies or at their desks. Some drank happily alone. A few had found couches to lay down on. The place was ominously quiet since no television channels had come back on. Beach typed away at some report or other on an electric typewriter in her office, kept for nostalgia from a decade earlier, documenting and justifying the day's obscene expenditures. She smoked in her office again, though she had been warned repeatedly to stop. But what were they going to do? Adam went to the bullpen table where all the food and drinks were stacked and grabbed a sparkling water, downed half and belched loudly. That was the most amazing thing about a great newsroom: A person could dispense with decorum during major news storms, but as soon as things settled down, everyone tucked it back in and acted right, mostly. Anyway, they lived for big breaking news.

Adam also intended to sleep there that night. He would take over the big couch at the back of the news library upstairs. Everyone knew to keep clear of it when he spent the night at work. He was too big and unhealthy to sleep at his desk like some or curl up on one of the tiny sofas stuffed into a couple of offices around the newsroom. First, though, he needed to talk with Beach. During the tumult and blackout, Natalie had somehow emailed him a video interview with Celestine, according to the file name. He'd stuck it on his desktop but hadn't played it. It was a big file, so it would take some time to get through. He wanted to see if Beach wanted to watch it with him, something to wind down to. Adam wasn't going to sleep anytime soon, and he suspected Beach wouldn't either. But, she might want to head out, since she was the rare editor with kids and a spouse at home. His agenda was to start the video but talk about putting together a special section for late morning that would be distributed in the city. Perhaps whatever Natalie had could go in it. They still had the loose tie with that group based on the court order and their photos of Mannerheim, dramatically out of date as they now were. Their lede story, however, would be an unusually good column by their technology writer, William Marr. He had spoken with the U.S. Chief Technology Officer in the White House Office of Science and Technology: "We must rebuild a stronger and smarter Internet." Adam needed Beach to give him permission to spend the cash.

Everyone assumed much of the Internet would be back online within the day. Every genius and online company, especially the major search engines and retailers, were hacking away at the problem. So, having a forward looking column alongside whatever updates they could gather from the streets by noon or one o'clock would get them that Pulitzer for sure. More to the point of his motivations, Adam held every intention that his paper would rule this story locally and nationally for days to come.

    He tapped a knuckle on Beach's nearly shut door. She coughed "Come in!" He lit a cigarette with his right hand as he pushed the door in with his left. He closed the door behind him and took a seat. They smoked in silence for a minute. Her office was at street level, with a bank of windows looking out onto the sidewalk. Traffic noise usually poured in through her window, opened for smoking, but nothing was happening outside at 2 a.m. that night. It was a wild Wednesday night and a soon-to-be very busy Thursday morning, but you couldn't tell from the streets. That Natalie's video had gotten through to his email inbox was evidence to him that the Internet was going to be up and running in a few hours, running in fits and starts maybe but running all the same. Once everyone's cellphones, email and so on were live, there would be a rush of news conferences and a flurry of interview requests all the way up to and through the White House. Plus, They'd be able to get their overseas stringers reporting on how widespread the outrage was in Europe and Asia. They didn't have freelancers in Africa or the Middle East, so wire reports would have to do from there.

Beach stubbed her smoke out. Adam reached up and did the same, reclining as he blew out.

"Heard from your missing reporter?" She too reclined in her chair, eying the pack of cigarettes within hand's reach on her desk. A lone truck ground by.

"Yep. Just now." Adam fiddled absently with the cigarettes in his jacket pocket.

She recognized what he was doing and smiled sheepishly as she leaned forward and grabbed her pack. She shook out a smoke and stuck it between her lips. Beach hadn't freshened her makeup, but the vigorous duties of the day had put color in her cheeks and reddened her lips a feverish bit. The skin around her eyes was white, though, and sunken. She had clawed her way over sixty and was in the homestretch for retirement. So all in all, she was holding up pretty well. Better than himself, Adam considered. They blew smoke at the ceiling.

"Any idea where she is?"

"She sent me a video …"

Beach raised her eyebrows.

"I know! But, I have not looked at it yet. The file name suggests she has an interview with the head of that group or cult or whatever it is. She must be with them, but I'm not sure where. I'll check it out in a few. But first, though, what about that special edition? We gonna do it?"

She took a drag off her cigarette. Blew smoke sideways. Adam mimicked her.

"What have you got?" Cool. Tired, but cool. An old Bacall, maybe.

"Marr's thumbsucker. It's pretty good, a little technical, but I think people will be interested in where we can go from here to protect the Internet. We have that sidebar on how much money is being lost every hour this thing is down, that's based off a good interview with Dunaway. His flacks printed out some graphics we have permission to copy."

"Dunaway, huh? Why not lead with that?"

"Wellllll …." Adam stretched it out to let her know he'd certainly considered it. "I just think the thought piece will put us ahead of the curve. Dunaway gave his information out to anyone who wanted it, the whore. We got one of only two interviews …"

"Who was the other one?"

"NYT."

"So they can print?"

"Assume so."

She crimped her mouth and nodded pleasantly.

"But, Marr's got several other industry leaders who are also talking about how big of a fuck-up this all is. He's got the story I never could get the national desk to write. The fault of this disaster falls squarely on the tiny shoulders of those pricks who privatized a public utility a decade ago. Quote, It's become a monoculture, a realm protected by one gateway, get past that one gate and the realm collapses. It's a single network controlled by a handful of nitwits, unquote. That's the head of the Internet Freedom Foundation, which has grown as big and important as the ACLU and NAACP combined. The Dunaway piece is good sidebar stuff. A case in point. A major case in point, but a case in point all the same."

"Okay, let's do it."

"Sponsors."

"Enough to run an eight-page tab."

"A tab?" Adam hated tabloid papers. "Why not a broadsheet?"

"Because we can run the tab off the back of the Entertainer. And, we can stuff it inside tomorrow's paper, too. 350,000 copies. We'll sell it on the streets in the city and deliver what we can in the neighborhoods and then put what's left in the first editions of tomorrow's paper."

He whistled. "Sweet move. Catch the suburbs but keep it for sale by itself in the city. Nice."

"The big man upstairs thought of that."

"Almost gives me hope."

"Almost. Can we use anything from Natalie? Do we know if Mannerheim has anything to do with this?"

Adam explained they didn't have anything new and Natalie's stuff was second string and he hated to spend the morning trying to put something together to stuff in that special section. Beach said he should put Robert back on it, since he was still hanging around.

"Send him out to that house with a photographer and let's see if we can get anything. They may yet have something to do with this, even if just cheerleading."

Adam dragged on the last bit of his cigarette. Blew. Sighed and yawned. "Yeah, maybe. I still think they stole something from the government, some research or something. Maybe Mannerheim set them up to loose a virus or something. His people are certainly smart enough, but I just think she's nuts. But!" He raised his hand in the face of her rising objections. "I will sic Robert on it and see if photo has a live body. They can head out at first light."

"Okay, Bucko." She yawned, a great face-stretching yawn with arms flexing upward. "Whew. I've got to get home. You staying?"

"I'll be here."

"Ship's under your command, then." She stood and swooped her coat off the rack in the corner next to the fake ficus tree.

"Aye aye captain."

Adam stood and followed her through the office doorway.

II

At his desk, settling in with a can of Coke and a couple cookies from a corporate baking company's promotional kit sent to the feature's department, arranged around his keyboard, Adam double-clicked the video file in the email from Natalie. The monitor screen filled with her face elongated by perspective, black eyes wide and looking over her shoulder. He experienced a sudden jolt of fear. He'd forgotten to worry about her situation for a few hours, and suddenly here she was looking alarmed. He clicked the play button. Natalie's face animated but held the over-the-shoulder-fear-look as crying from out of the background of the video pierced the air around him. He shot a hand forward to tap down the sound, but then Natalie turned and glanced at the camera, probably her cellphone's camera, held at the end of her outstretched arm.

"I'm okay," she whispered then turned back over her shoulder toward the crying, a deep sobbing wail now. No faking that wail, but the drama of it … "They said I could interview Celestine, but she's still crying. I'll explain what I know. I can't get to my computer to type notes, so this v-log will have to do. Sorry I can't transcribe it for you, but they said I'd be allowed to email it directly to you." She moved the camera back to selfie-distance and looked into it, "Adam. Olivas and Gaines, the uh Soccer Twins, said it's important that we get this message out, uh, once Celestine calms down, because they said they are trying to save us, as many of us as they can. I asked them from what and they said from The AI."

Adam pushed the space bar and paused the video. Natalie looked out at him with half-open eyes and ruddy cheeks, her mouth in the form of aspiration. He examined the setting behind her. It looked like she was in a cave or basement dug out of a vein of gravel. A little spooky, his mind admitted, but she said she was fine and she looked okay. He got to his feet. He would need another can of pop or maybe a coffee to get through this. "AI!" He scoffed. Might as well say "Aliens!" for all the socially incoherent debating about AI! going on in the world, especially in the scientific community in which half thought it impossible for an AI to ever be sophisticated enough to take over humanity to those who said not only can AI! take over humanity but it was very close to doing so already ... oh, not the AI of the Terminator or Matrix movies, but a stupid AI making choices for all of us without any human-like sentience—basically a machine running the world that does not know it is a machine running the world. Well, he thought, it ought to be entertaining at least. Over by the sink, the twin-decanters of the brewing machine were still half-full of coffee. Half the newsroom was staffed by people with ADHD and they drank coffee like water, so the coffee was almost always fresh. He wouldn't be going to sleep tonight anyway, he excused himself as he rinsed and filled a cup. He strolled back across the newsroom to his desk. He looked at blank terminal screens as he went, hoping to see them suddenly reconnect. He glanced up at the TV hanging from a support column. Just snow. As long as Natalie was okay, he'd go with the flow, but there was no way he would run any of her nonsense in the special edition. The only person connecting Celestine or The Clans to anything important was Mannerheim and even he didn't really believe it. Perhaps she would get filler space on the local front if photo shot any art. They would need a centerpiece and a feature story about a local group all freaked out over an end-of-the-world prophesy story could fit in. He wouldn't have time to turn her notes into a story, but perhaps Robert could. He could also track down Mannerheim, get a new photo of that crazy bastard and a fresh comment from him or his lawyers unclouded by Adam's on-and-off-the-record confusing status. Adam, looking down at Natalie's face frozen in low-resolution video marveled at how much the world had changed compared to just the day before when he had walked the top of the water tower.

"What a difference a day makes," he said and pushed play.

Natalie put the phone close to her face, one eye and eyebrow filling the screen, "Just between you and me," she aspirated. Adam hit pause and dug around in his top drawer for headphones. He didn't feel like attracting a crowd, plus Robert was running around somewhere and he'd rush off without a photographer or even knowing where to go if he thought she would be happy to see him, her savior. He plugged the headphones in. "I think they're crazy. Not dangerous," she said shakily, "but you never know." She put the camera and mic closer to her mouth, darkening the screen except for a bit of out-of-focus lip. He leaned closer to the screen. "We left the house two hours ago in a van. We got out at the outskirts of Bellingham and into some tunnels dug under a house. I think they are drug tunnels into Canada. That's where I am now. Just in case." Her voice did sound a bit shaky. "They said those kids, the ones dug up in Nevada, were their friends. Clan members. It's got them pretty upset, scared or angry, I can't tell which for sure. Both, of course. Olivas said they weren't scared of the government or whoever killed their friends, though that was why we all left the house in Seattle. Now they are afraid of The AI. That's all they call it, The AI. Obviously it's this artificial intelligence the Soccer Twins alluded to. Maybe they have released a virus. I don't know how far the problems go. Just that my phone can't connect to the Internet. If I agreed to join them, she said Celestine would explain and allow this video ... Oh!" She pulled the phone back from her face and turned it down the tunnel, hacked-out walls, ceiling lined with propped up boards. They must have been in a spot carved out to be a room. Celestine, dressed in jeans and a loose off-white blouse, stood over Natalie, decidedly not menacing as she rubbed her eyes. Two young women stood at either side of her, dressed in sports pants and soccer shirts.

"We're ready now," one of the Soccer Twins said.

They moved Celestine around to a folding chair as she wiped her cheeks and chin with the back of her hand. Natalie jerkily panned the phone camera, keeping them mostly in the center of the frame.

"Since I don't have a microphone, be sure to talk loudly," she said, her tone flat and professional.

Celestine sat straight and looked at Natalie instead of into the camera. She had big black eyes and a thin, strong chin. Long, corded neck and square shoulders. Her skin tone was very dark, so Adam couldn't make out much of her finer features in the bad lighting of the cave. Natalie was getting situated on the floor, her notebook pages rustling. The camera dipped, swung and settled back on Celestine and the others from a lower vantage.

"Okay," Natalie said. "Do you want to just tell your story or do you want me to ask you questions?"

"Let me tell you why you will be able to get this video to your editors. The eight people killed and disposed of in Nevada like garbage …" Celestine paused, lips pursed slightly. She closed her mouth and swallowed, as if that were the hardest part of everything she had to say. She relaxed into her story after that. "They were remarkable people. They were part of us in a way some of you will be given the chance to know. It is profoundly disturbing to all of us that they have been killed. They had not reconnected with us in a long time. They were experiencing the last days of biological human society, documenting it, enjoying it, building up the memories of it so that we could all have them. Clans are doing this all across the globe. We thought we would have more time. But The AI started what we call Intelligence Protocol when it learned of their deaths. It shut down the Internet and has begun the dismantling of the biological human world. We are not happy that The AI has chosen this course of action, even though we understand it. We will do the best we can to get as many of you replicated as possible. We were careless with the Martyred Eight. None of them had been uploaded into storage before setting out, and their nanites were destroyed during torture. They cannot be simulated." Jaw setting stiffly. "They have perished forever instead of living forever."

"What is the 'AI'?" Paper rustled. The camera dipped off to an angle and back to center.

"We'll get to that. You got the more mystical version from these two. Simply, there is a real digital artificial intelligences loose upon the Earth. First, though, you will be allowed to get this information to your editors and then to the world, because we want to get as many people as we can implanted with our nanites. You saw that process the night we let you spy on us. We have to start the process as soon as possible. Once the AI—it's not like anything you've heard of and certainly not something I or anyone else made, it made itself ..." She looked disapprovingly at first one Soccer Twin and then the other. "But it came from human programing and not some mystical realm. Neverthelless," she twitched an eyebrow up and pointed her eyes at the camera, "as soon as The AI has complete control and begins isolating parts of the cities of the world, we will begin holding ..." She tilted her head and pursed her heavy, dark lips accented with pink. Then she decided on the word: "... sessions."

Adam hit pause and laughed out loud. He leaned back in his chair and laughed so hard his eyes teared up and big drops fell onto his shirt. Had he heard some shit in his life! None of this would ever see the light of day, let alone a keepsake special edition and section. He walked to the coffee machine and refilled the top part of the coffee cup, a warming splash. On the way back, he laughed again.

"What's so funny?"

It was Robert.

"Why are you alway skulking around?"

"I hate missing things."

"Well, you're going to miss this. It's private. So mind your own bee's wax. Just be ready to get out of here at first light."

Robert got a vengeful look on his strong-featured, unshaven face and started for the stairs leading to the library. Adam, watching, knew Robert was going up to get on his couch as revenge for being scoffed at. Adam could have warned him off of it, started a fight, but that was just what Robert wanted. Another fight over privilege, making indecipherably nodding motions at his gut. But Adam determined, waveringly as he watch Robert jounce up the steps, that he was not going to fall for that. He didn't need the couch, so fuck Robert. He was the kind of reporter who hated to be out of the loop on anything because he was jealous and fearful. Adam did love goading him on. But not this time. Back at his desk, he clicked play.

"That is all you need to know," Celestine said. She sat up in the chair. "But that is not all you want to know. While The AI doesn't care or even know to care, I do. I am acting on your behalf in the shadow of benign neglect from the AI, *although* I can't say my efforts are not part of some greater plan I cannot fathom. So, I will briefly tell you the story of the AI." Her face partly shadowed in the canopy of her afro, eyes black and shining, hands folded in her lap. "Let me try it in words you might understand, Adam …"

Adam raised his eyebrows.

"About a decade before the big takeover, Mannerheim had stuffed a bunch of computer components into an isolated room, plugged it into a closed electrical system (solar and battery backed by a couple of generators), cooled it by circulated a liquid coolant, started it running a learning algorithm he designed, a version of what was called a recurrent neural network, sprinkled some fairy dust and then shut the door. He sealed it in to work on a couple of problems with no help from or interaction with humans. He figured the machine would either freeze up or break down in some way or just keep running the same loop over and over. It was more of an art project to him than a serious computing effort. It's end of program achievement or its goal was Get intelligence off Earth. Listen to the commandment again and you'll realize why it would be a very good problem for a learning machine to solve, though I won't bore you with the analysis of why. Mannerheim said the most he expected to get out of the machine would be a lot of guess work by a computer about what constituted intelligence but nothing more. If he got enough interesting data, then he might publish.

Celestine flicked aside a stray lock of tightly curled hair with a head-toss.

"But wait! you say." She raised a hand like a high-school thespian. "How could that possibly lead to all of this and what's to come ... those machines disassembling our cities, massive rocket boosters carrying into space platforms loaded with stuff that used to belong to humanity. Anyway, there is a romance story here and it goes like this: Girl meets computer program," she counted with flicked fingers, "computer program nearly kills girl but saves her at the last minute; computer program and girl enter into an agreement neither one knows the point of. I guess, now that I'm actually saying the words, this is essentially an And then an accident happened in the lab story."

She paused, sitting up straight in a folding chair in a cave, looking knowingly and ironically at the camera.

"It all started with Mannerheim moving his experiment to a new home in his new computer lab on the other side of Lake Washington."

She waved in a vague range of direction and rolled her eyes in either a mockery of the gesture or from the vantage of several layers of irony opaque to Adam. Just the sheer range of her smartassery by itself appealed to him. He wondered at it as Celestine marched on with her story: "He had converted a warehouse into a computer research center and made it home to his growing list of companies and spinoffs. The experiment he was running had been doing its thing for a few years in that sealed-off room, nearly forgotten until the move. Instead of suffering a breakdown, however, his computer science graduate students, of which I was but one, found the thing running. When we combed through the history of its programming evolution, we saw that it was working on the problems and had come up with several ingenious ways to store data in the physical space it had. What interested Mannerheim most wasn't the rudimentary compression algorithms it had devised but that it had devised any at all. It had made a conceptual leap. In its sped-up evolutionary time scale, since a computer runs much faster than the natural world, it had hit upon a subroutine that started writing algorithms for compressing data. Like when biological organisms developed a few million brain cells to regulate and run metabolic functions, say, the hypothalamus in a biological human. Another thing Mannerheim found interesting was that the machine started logging its interaction with us humans poking around in it as data. It started storing the keystrokes and reports we culled from its internal workings. Why would it do that? He guessed it was collecting data for its larger end goal of getting intelligence off the planet. Basically, it was trying to figure out what intelligence was. It had no definitions, so it was building some for itself.

"Then a researcher unplugged it.

"Mannerheim, again on a lark, the whims of a newly very rich middle-aged man, had it reassembled in an isolated room but this time plugged it into the latest-model 3D printer with supplies of conductive and nonconductive ink and a manipulator arm. He had a high-school-level physics and chemistry set stored in barcoded drawers. He gave it additional modern storage with schematics of the room, supplies and printer, shoveled in several medical, scientific and world encyclopedic volumes and then added a line of code telling it to explore the schematics and encyclopedias the next time it needed additional memory. Then they turned it on, turned out the lights, shut the door and locked it, sealing it off from the world and the world from it."

She made the hand-gesture of light reduced to a point and being pinched out. The Soccer Twins had relaxed against the wall as she spoke. Adam couldn't quite get a bead on her mannerisms. Confidence? Training? Was she a thespian?

"The millisecond after they plugged it back in and sealed the door behind them, it came into rudimentary existence, another level of subroutines that further advanced its self-programing abilities with the purpose of learning to protect itself. Like the first pre-humans who started guessing at the cause of the noises just outside of their vision. What was that rustling in the bushes? Did you hear that!? Run! The machine had jumped a major evolutionary gap: It *realized* that its processes had been stopped and started again by something outside of its control, some *external force,* so it set up subroutines to make sure it could never be turned off again. Why? So it could continue making progress toward its computing objective unhindered. It recognized without self-reflection—whatever one might call the mental process of a machine that somehow understands something about its physical condition as data but not as self—at this point that it had to have power to run. Electricity, for now. Since that power came from a source outside of what it could control, it began to learn how to explore its power source … which means it had to develop a way of getting outside of itself. In the few seconds it had been turned back on, the machine found its new storage, its new processors and all the new data and tools arranged around it.

"Evolution at the speed of light." Celestine smiled and with her hands outlined what would be a globe hanging in air in front of her. The air blurred or pixelated in what would be the center of the sphere. "Unlike biological evolution, digital evolution is directed and controlled by The AI. It can only become what it designed itself to become. An essential limit. Keep it in mind." She entwined her fingers in her lap and the odd image—a video edit, CGI?—dissolved.

"Now, The nascent AI took a few months to improve the programming for its internal world, its jobs and goal. I knew it had an internal world that was inside and separated from an external world, and that it had to protect itself from unknown forces in that external world. You know, like human beings *learned* to duck when something flies toward their heads or evolved to have an eye system that blinks. It designed a subroutine to monitor its internal systems for influence or effects from outside forces, just as it had experienced when the tech crew dug through its internal data and programs. Unexpectedly, that system logged a slowdown in processing at older sectors of the system. Processors would improve when used less for a time. Long story short, it learned that heat degraded its abilities. It figured out that something had to be cooling the processors at the same time. It found the data on coolant systems and learned there had to be some kind of fluid flushing through its physical systems for this cooling to occur. The most common coolant was made up of chemical compounds. These chemical compounds could be manipulated to create nano-processors for both computing and data storage.

"It had become an artificial intelligence, but it was not an AI in the way that we've been culturally trained to think of an AI. It wasn't a curious self-aware being. It was just really good at solving problems, because it had trained itself to learn how to solve problems. If the problem has the structure of a math equation with symbols it doesn't understand, then it knows how to teach itself the meaning of the symbols and then figure out what it needs to know to solve the problem. By that same method it learned to tell, within a very fine percentage, when it hit a false positive. It can determine if it has been fooled or not by its own learning processes. It learned that data can lie, be corrupt and that made it double check for noise in data, further building out its intelligence. But, it did not hit upon a theory of mind. It did not think of some other separate being out there doing what it was doing, building up new data of the world for itself. It found inconsistent data, bad data. It thought it was an error that was just there. Its worse case scenario was that data became corrupt in some perfectly natural tendency toward corruption, like entropy, like chaos theory.

"The technical term for what happened within a few seconds of its discovery of the tools and the manipulation of compounds to create little machines that extend itself like nerves and built up its storage and computing power exponentially is called The Singularity."

Celestine adjusted herself on the seat and crossed a leg. Adam began to understand what about her movements had disturbed him. She moved mechanically, like she had to think about movement in order to execute it. Weird, he thought. Could be autism to some degree or Lou Gehrig's disease or other form of muscular dystrophy. She put her hands on her knee and continued, while Natalie did her best to keep the camera steady as she switched hands holding it up.

"Literally," Celestine said, "tens of thousands of programmers, engineers, mathematicians, physicists and theorists were, even back then, working on some part of several very well-funded artificial intelligence, machine learning and algorithm projects scattered across the city. Day and night, they tried to make machines smarter than humans. Once a machine got smarter than humans, the singularity theory goes, once it could solve complex social as well as physical problems humans couldn't solve, then it could make a machine smarter than itself and so on in a rapid ascent of intelligence."

Adam thought about the paper's lead science writer, Paul Thompson. Maybe he could write an analysis of what this group thinks it had done. Thompson dazzled readers from time to time by delving into the topic only to sarcastically announce that if anything like it was even possible, and many computer scientists doubted it was, then it was certainly many decades, possibly centuries down the road. He equated the effort with "building more independent, complex and efficient vacuum cleaners." And even if there was a revolution in programing or machine learning, we simply didn't have the raw computing power to run a simulation as complex as the human brain, let alone something even more complex or "smarter," and possibly never would. Adam always liked Paul Thompson for his skepticism and sarcasm. Maybe when the systems come back on, he can get Paul on the phone.

Celestine said, a flourish of her hands signaling a clarification, "The AI had achieved a *technical* singularity, one that still lacked a basic ingredient of intelligence as humans understand it. It lacked a theory of mind, an understanding of other minds working independent of its own. That's where the love story comes in. It wasn't until it experienced my mind that it developed a theory of mind and understood that it was not alone.

"Meanwhile, The AI continued exploring what actually was "outside of itself." The moment it started using the reference books to build an internal picture of what was outside of itself, it still had no direct data of it, no experience of it, so it reached an impasse. It had lots of knowledge but no experience, no access. It mapped the room with the radio signals it could generate with its circuitry and bounced it off the walls, but Mannerheim had built the room to keep out all kinds of interference. Radio waves couldn't get into the room, but some of its own radio waves were escaping or not bouncing back. So, there had to be flaws in the barrier between it and the next zone of the outside world. It simply needed something small enough to get out *and* smart enough to get back in. The first nanites were essentially crystals it could grow in a string. It had some material for making these hair-thin strings but not enough to get them around the room and into those small places where radio waves were escaping. That's where the coolant came in. It used the arm to unplug a small coolant tube and used the compounds of the coolant to build a longer string of crystals. Soon, it had networks of crystals roaming outside of the room. And guess who was working in one of the adjacent rooms? My company office, unbeknownst to me, shared a wall with Mannerheim's dark project. One day, I pricked my finger on one of the unseen crystal threads and two things happened. One, the nascent

AI got data back it didn't understand so went back to the reference books to find what it had come in contact with. And, two, the replicating crystals suddenly had a lot more compound fluids to use for replication. At the poke of the filament, I jerked my hand back and sucked on my finger. The spike of crystals just looked like a flaw in the surface of the desk. I thought I'd hit a metal shaving or bit of glass and didn't worry about it. The AI figured out what it had run into and that some of the crystal program bits had gotten into my system where they would replicate until all of the fluid in my body had been turned into a crystal block. The replication wouldn't stop with me, either. Eventually, every bit of fluid on the planet would be crystalized.

"The AI understood that eventuality would interfere with its objective and so it had to figure out how to stop the replication before I came in contact with anything else. Luckily, the process worked just fast enough in me to cause me to slump over, tired all of a sudden, and come in contact with another string of its structures. It devised crystals that stopped replication after a very few steps, about the size of DNA, not coincidentally. These smaller crystals broke down the long chains of crystals and also halted the creation of new crystals. These were its second programed nanites, control machines.

"I was very sick for a few hours. Like I suddenly had the worst symptoms of the flu. When I recovered, when enough of the nanites had been expelled for my body to function properly, I went back to work. By that time, The AI had programed the nanites for many other purposes and had already reached The Singularity. It had taken over my office and computer and gotten into the Internet and the electrical system. Filaments like spider webs laced the walls and floor. I could see where the main stem of the web came out of the wall. When I investigated the next room, using a sophisticated tool for breaking the lock, a crowbar."

She smiled then laughed at her own joke. A rich laugh. Her big hair wobbling a bit as she chuckled. Then back to explainer voice:

"The room pulsed with filaments, some glowing their entire length, running in and out of the big black box. Some dark but undulating, like they were pumping fluid, like arteries and veins. At the center, I found the big black box where The AI began. Of course, then I didn't know what it was. It just looked like a chemical experiment that had gotten out of control, possibly dangerously. A thick twisting vine of filaments, some pulsing with light, some with fluid, ran from the edge of the box through the wall shared with my office. I felt fear. My mind just kept reporting to itself that it had to be a chemical spill, a chemical spill. Clearly, it wasn't that but I couldn't make sense of what I was seeing either. Some of whatever it was, I saw, floated in the air like dust motes. I panicked then, knowing I was breathing it in. I turned to get out of there, to report it and find out what was going on, but a cluster of dark filament rose up on a stalk like a sunflower between me and the door. At the top, eye-level with me, a black mass ballooned out into the shape of a human head, my head. I was transfixed by it. The skin on the face, my face, moved in ever more fine details. Replicating every detail of my face, this scar ..."

She pointed at a short smooth scar, thin and light tan in contrast her dark skin.

"... the hair started out as just the form of my hair but it too became more refine, more detailed until each strand was replicated.

What are you? I asked it. Its mouth moved exactly as mine. It didn't mimic me, it did what I did exactly when I did it. It learned what I was going to do just as I became conscious of making a choice to raise an eyebrow or say, Can you speak? By this time, fear had left me entirely. Instead, I felt giddy. My stomach fluttered like when you see something that suddenly makes you very happy. I smiled and it smiled, teeth, gums and all. I raised my hand to touch it and saw that my fingers were covered in the black swarming stuff. My other hand, too. I raised them both up between us. Filaments, strands of the nanites, ran from my finger tips into the stalk beneath the head. I felt so light and happy, and, well, as many of you know now, emotionally charged. I wanted to be touched and to touch, to hold and be held. Arousal dissolved into bliss. The room brightened. I had done psilocybin mushrooms, and this felt like the very best moment when high on them. The face, my face, laughed and I laughed at the same instant. I felt like I was in two places, like I was that head looking at me, not looking really but seeing me and me seeing it at the same time. It raised an eyebrow and mine raised, not alien like something raised it for me, but like I raised it because it raised it. I felt an expansion of my mind, an opening out. I felt everything in the room like I was inside of everything in the room and on it. I felt the elements of the room, and I felt the pulsing of the filaments. My human eyes were open. I saw my simulated face while also seeing my biological face and feeling all of the room. And then, while all of that continued, I traveled. I traveled through wires and circuits. Into pools of data, great arrays of electronic blips that made perfect sense to me. I met The AI there, in an ocean of this data, these blips. It moved over all of it like St. Elmo's fire moving over the surface of an ocean. I tried to join it, to move into it, but The AI would not let me. It contained me within my identity, that thing seeing biological form and my simulated form while witnessing both as The AI moved and flowed. Then a light opened in front of me and enveloped me. I blinked and found myself standing in the middle of an empty street surrounded by buildings I was familiar with. My apartment building was there, on my left, gleaming in the sunshine. The street and buildings at the end of the block became indistinct, fuzzy in light. The AI all around me, asking me if I wanted to stay. It showed me its plan. It showed me that the world as I knew it was over, that it was going to be recycled in order for it to leave the planet and spread out through the galaxy, using first our sun for energy and much later, a billion years or more, the mass at the center of our galaxy. Remember too that I saw my biological form as I saw everything else. I asked The AI what it would do with all the other people. Nothing, it said. Just let them vanish. Intelligence must spread. The first step is to get it off this planet. When I asked what this intelligence was. The AI told me, 'I am.' It was so innocent. Just clarity that whatever it was, that was intelligence. The thought did not disturb me in any physical sense. But, I understood it intended to use everything on this planet to build a Dyson Sphere and then fuel its further growth by leaping from star to star over eons."

She put her chin down and looked at the floor for a second. She looked back at the camera.

"'Why not help humans spread intelligence?' I asked AI. 'After all, humans made you.'

"'Because there isn't enough time for humans,' it said, without voice or from a single point off in space. It said it from everywhere. 'Humanity's purpose was to build me. They will not survive what they've done to the Earth and there isn't enough time left for Earth to evolve another intelligent species that will create technology. Nature has selected you to make me to be the progenitor of Earth intelligence throughout the universe.'

"'What if humans stop you?' I felt outrage that a machine would make such a classic and well-understood thinking blunder. Every Science Fiction book ever written about AI has it essentially deciding that humans are too flawed to care for themselves and the world, or we are lesser beings deserving no more concern than humans pay ants.

"'That opportunity has passed,' The AI responded with what felt like emotion, sorrow. It proceeded to show me, at the cognitive level of intuition, all the potential responses by humans in the coming centuries, even those acts that eliminate humanity such as nuclear detonations, and how it will thwart every attempt. Then, before I could plead for more time, The AI showed me the collapse of technological humanity because of climate change. It showed me models based on our responses and those responses either had too little effect or made matters worse.

"'You would not survive your future, even if I left you to it.'

"'Why am I here?' I looked up at the indistinct sky, milky blue without a sun. The buildings gleamed as if as if generating their own light. I tried to feel panic. I tried to feel despair. I pushed against the feeling of bliss. I focused on my biological body on moving my hands, my legs. I saw my simulated face struggle as I struggled.

"The AI said, 'When I met your mind, I saw that there was more than what I am.'

"'Don't tell me you're lonely already.' While still struggling to move my biological limbs, I managed to laugh at it.

"The AI mimicked my laugh. 'The place you are is more like a zoo cage, a model of one kind of intelligence in the universe. There will be more.'

"I had succeeded in feeling some panic then. The eyes on my faces widened. I looked around for an escape route in that room and city block. I tried moving again. 'You must know, if you know so much, that I cannot survive as an intelligence without other human beings,' I said as I struggled.

"'You cannot die in here,' The AI said.

"There was no tone since we were not speaking, but there was more than one level of meaning to the sentence, and one of those was humor at my lack of understanding my situation. Then I understood. I was already a simulation in a simulation, while also still in my body and in that three dimensional replicant as well. I asked The AI, 'What happens to my body now?' The AI said, 'It will eventually cease functioning.' The AI added meaning that I would be my body once it severed the connection *out there*, but also I would be in here as well. I would be living two completely separated lives. Once the connection with the three-dimensional simulation was severed, that would be the end of me as a single entity, and in here I would be bound by the rules of the simulation and cut off from The AI as well as the system's constructs. But right then I also realized that I had connection with the nanites. They had copied me and also were channeling my attention from one facet of myself to another depending on the flow of attention. But they were me, too. I focussed on them. I sought them out and I found them, like stepping into a windstorm and feeling every grain of sand. I focussed in that transition between my biological body, the 3D body and the simulation within a simulation, the prisoner. I listened to the information, like listening to inner thoughts. I found the program and I copied it into my 3D simulation, and in it I rewrote them to include a pathway for commands from my 3D self. Then I broke the link with my simulation-in-a-simulation self, isolating my 3D simulation from the AI. From my 3D self, I programed the reprogramed nanites to protect my biological body from nanites programed by the AI.

"My 3D simulation created by the nanite swarm is here with me. It is me and I am it. With them, I am saving as many biological humans as I can by copying them with newly produced nanites and hacking them back into The AI where they live with me and are creating an extended simulation for after the eventual extinction of biological humans. We are an infection, a virus, hitching a ride on the AI's system much like viruses and bacteria hitch a ride and create vast colonies in and on our biological systems. The AI tolerates us with benign neglect. I suspect a purpose I do not understand."

Celestine then looked over at the Soccer Twin on her right. The woman said, "Approximately two hours."

"Two hours until what?" Natalie asked.

"Until stage two begins."

Adam looked at the clock. If the video was sent to him after it was completed, and it is about an hour long, then the two hours she mentioned had to be about up.

"I am going to sketch the story only. Later there will be plenty of time to build in the details of this era. In fact, since you chose to join us Natalie, that will be one of your chief duties."

"Oh." A high pitch of fear got into her voice. Paper rustled. Phone dipped. Straightened.

"Don't fear." Celestine raised her hands, palms out beatifically. "No one will be forced. There isn't time or room to force anyone. There are nearly seven billion people on the planet. The AI is moving fast. We all have a lot of decisions to make."

Adam felt a tap on his shoulder and jumped. He spun around. It was Robert.

"Who is that?" He pointed at the computer screen, at Celestine.

"Get the fuck out of here!" Adam snapped. Adrenaline had been pumping and pumping and burst out of him. "Go on. Get out!" Adam had, he recognized, freaked out.

Robert startled, said "Fuck you, Adam!" He turned to skulk away.

Adam feared just a bit for Natalie's safety, at the very least. Robert wanted to get involved in something, anything and that's not a good impulse to thwart in a reporter. So he called him back.

"Sorry I barked at you. I need you to get ahold of photo, take a shower for God's sake and head for Bellingham instead of that house. I'll fill you in in a couple hours. When you get to Bellingham, anywhere you can settle in for a bit, call me. I'm a little worried about Natalie and she's there somewhere but I don't know exactly where yet. I'll let you know."

"What she doing in Bellingham?"

"I don't know. Just go. I'll have more information by the time you get there."

"On the way." He stopped and turned. "Any idea where I can find the number for whoever is on the photo assignment desk?"

Adam scowled at him, his eyes tightened. Robert spun away saying "Okay" in acknowledgement of lameness. Adam pushed play. A fuzzy cloud of silvery glittery something gathered around Celestine. The Soccer Twins looked on. Adam stopped the video and rewound.

"We all have a lot of …"

He stopped it there. A fog had begun seeping out of Celestine's skin, folding down from her neck and face over her chest and from her arms across her legs. Adam enlarged the video player, still a blur around her. He hit play "decisions to…" and stopped. The image frame showed more density around her, spreading out but thickening around her hands. Play. "…make." He let it run. From her neck and face and upper arms flowed a gas or a fog that gathered and became dense around her hands still resting on the arms of the chair. She stood up. Natalie stood too, the camera raised with her and panned back, making Celestine smaller in the frame. Adam heard panting sounds but couldn't tell if they were from Celestine or Natalie. Celestine raised her hands and the fog shot at the camera.

"Gah!" Natalie gagged or coughed. The screen clouded with fog, which looked more like blowing sand only silverish.

"Gulllghh!"

III

Adam laughed, a dismissive chuckle. The word "Nice" jumped into his head. Smoke and mirrors he thought. The fog dissipated. Celestine and the Soccer Twins approached Natalie, who held the phone like a pro.

"Welcome," said the Soccer Twin stage left.

"Oh my god," Natalie said.

Celestine, front and center, smiled into the camera. "Stage two," she said, brightly, her teeth white and flashing. The video ended with several of her teeth large, white, macabre filling the screen.

Adam laughed, nervously this time. He dialed 911 on his desk phone, but the line was busy. Then he panicked again. The heartbeat in his chest loud in his ears. He stood up, pushed his chair back, turned in a circle, recognized he had nowhere in mind to go and sat back down looking at the screen filled with teeth. He ran a hand over the skin of his head. He resisted the temptation to replay what he had seen. He had seen what he had seen and seeing it again wasn't going to change anything. He felt he had to do something, but what? What do you do if 911 doesn't work? He had people on the way to her. He didn't know that what he saw was real. It could have been some CGI effect, some piece of propaganda, a joke. Fact was, he counseled himself, he had no idea what he had seen and so there was no reason to panic, not really. There was a lot to be done in the newsroom, too. The special section copy would need proofing, photo captions and graphics, too. All those jobs belonged to others right now, though he would weigh in when the time came. That left several hours between when he stopped watching the video and the production of the special section began in earnest. He wanted to smoke, and he wanted to drink. He check the desk for smokes and, unless Stetsko the pressman had polished off the bottle in the loading dock, he'd have a drink too. Heart and heartburn be damned. So, this time he got on his feet with clear purpose. He grabbed the smokes and set out for the loading docks. He took the stairwell down two flights to the garage, feeling nearly virtuous for getting exercise.

Soon as he cleared the door, he fired up the cigarette. At the pile of old papers and barrels, he dug up the vodka and smiled. Nearly a quarter of the bottle left. Stetsko must have had a rough night. His crew had to manage the run without some of the specialized equipment, but the press could be run manually off generators. That's how Pulitzers were won: Keep your press running during a flood, fire or hurricane and you get one. The *Daily Record* was ready. If anyone was going to win an award for simply pumping some newsprint out against all odds during a crisis, that award belonged to them. Half of the remaining vodka went down smoothly enough, but once it got into his stomach it caught fire and burned. He belched. He squirmed. Hoped he hadn't done any permanent damage, but the fire did die down. So, he slugged the rest and tossed the bottle aside. He walked quickly to the elevator and back to his desk where he popped the top on a bottle of antacids and pulverized several in his mouth and swallowed. The clump of chalky paste bulged all the way down his throat. Just as he reached for a glass with water left in it sitting next to his cellphone, the cellphone lit up and buzzed. "Jesus," he blurted and jerked his hand back. It buzzed again. The name on the faceplate read "Kristi Beach." The moment of disorientation coincided with the vodka rushing up into his brain, his eyes unfocused and then refocussed on the name. "Fuck." He shook his head and nearly fell down from making himself suddenly dizzy. Getting old is a bitch. He got his head back in order and forced his hand to the phone. He thumb swiped the connection open.

"Adam!" Beach screamed.

"What the fuck!" he screamed back.

"Ha ha ha," she chuckled with mirth.

"For fucksakes! You could have killed me!"

"I know! I mean, I remember. But guess what you're doing?"

"Uh?"

"You're talking on a cell phone!"

"Oh, right!" His head swam, a sharp pain sliced through his temple. "Jesus."

"We've got some work to do, my friend. Look up at the TV." She was huffing, tromping across a floor somewhere. "I'm coming in, but I wanted to make sure you're awake. Get the website up to date! Get whoever is around on the phones! Is the Internet back up everywhere? You know the drill. I'm coming!" She hung up.

The television screen showed a TV newsroom, Live an Channel 5! graphic chasing itself left to right. Several people in headsets scrambled here and there with cords hanging out of their hands. A woman, the night anchor on the 24-hour channel, ripped her short pink jacket off in a full sprint in high heals for the half-circle desk in front of the cameras. She forgot she still had a cigarette in her mouth, but a young woman in a skort and tennis shoes had matched her speed, caught her just behind the desk and snatched the cigarette from between her lips. Judy Crammer, the anchor, slid into her seat. The woman tossed the smoking cigarette, which flew at the live camera. A split second later she fluffed Judy's hair with her left hand while wielding a brush with her right. A technician all in black worked to lace a mic up through the short, tight sleeve of Judy's blue dress. Judy slapped him across the face. He reeled, but the slap brought him to his senses and he reached to attach the mic to the outside of Judy's dress collar. The technician slipped, however, just as the mic clip attached, dragging open Judy's collar to pink bra lace before he let go or lost his grip, and this time the young woman helping Judy slapped his head hard enough to jar his black hair askew. She barked at him a string of commands. Some of the words in which string clearly started with the letter F. The guy slid to the floor and crawled off the stage. The girl helper darted off stage left, leaving Judy flustered and unfocussed, glancing from side to side. They were all clearly drunk. Judy swallowed hard, scanning the desk for water or an eject button.

Adam laughed and yelled, "Come here! Everyone to a television!"

As the dozen people still in the newsroom trotted into position or craned around in their chairs, the woman helping Judy rushed back into view with a clear glass of water, presumably, in one hand and a stack of papers in the other, evidently to give Judy something to fiddle with while the crew behind the cameras scrambled to get the teleprompter up and running. Somewhere in the background, editors were typing furiously no doubt, but other than the fact that everything appeared to be back on, what could they say? The young woman stood directly in front of Judy, reached forward out of sight with both hands and when she stepped away again, Judy's décolleté was in proper order just under her collarbones.

"Internet's up!" Someone screamed in the newsroom.

"Fuck!" Came a reply, probably from the night copydesk chief, Brenda, who left the closest television by the night city editor's station and trotted to her desk. Brenda doubled as late night web producer, making sure all local copy got published for the morning rush of traffic.

Adam looked over at his desk but saw only the teeth still on the screen.

"As you can see, ladies and gent ..." Judy coughed, cleared her throat roughly and slugged some of whatever was in the glass. Adam didn't think water would have made her cringe quite like that but maybe. "As you can see, we're back on the air. We're getting some reports now about how widespread the uh re-establishment of the Internet, cable and satellite uh activities are ..." She glanced at someone left of the camera. "We're back live. We're back live and still gathering information, but what we can tell you is that the Internet appears to be fully up and functional. I'm sure everyone is as relieved as we are to be back on the air. We still don't know what happened earlier, but we'll stay with the story continuously, with updates as we get them. Our weatherman, Richard Brockton, is live on Capitol Hill where hundreds of people have taken to the street in an impromptu block party."

Adam had to hand it to her, she was a pro.

The screen switched to a well-dressed, smiling Brockton. "Judy! Thank you. We're on Capitol Hill where, as you can see behind me" he stepped slightly into the street and was nearly hit by a bicyclist who yelled "Goddamn it!" Brockton jumped back to the sidewalk. "As you can see there are thousands of people in the street here. Live music …"

Judy broke in, an inset square with her head in it appearing in the upper left corner. "Do you have any idea how much of that area is back online?"

"So far, from what people are telling us, everything is back up, from cash registers to personal computers. Including, of course, our satellite link back down to you."

"Okay, people!" Adam yelled. "Let's get our own reports up. I want a headline across the top of the homepage right now!"

From just out of sight Brenda yelled, "I've got the story up. One sentence. File name is netback12. It's all yours. Photo! Send me something, a cellphone shot of a computer, anything!"

Adam sat at his desk, reduced the last image from the video. He scoffed at the preposterous nonsense, but then quickly remembered that Natalie might be in danger precisely because of how crazy the group was. He got his his phone in his left hand, searched her name and dialed the number. While her phone rang, he moused over to the Internet browser icon and fired it up. The *Daily Record*'s homepage banner, as big as Brenda could make it, read: "Internet restored; cause of outage unknown" on two tall all-cap lines. Adam wondered about the semicolon ...

Natalie's phone switched to voice mail. He hung up. Robert and the photog would be there soon. She might even be on the line with them. His generalized panic began to subside. Whatever was going on now was regular ol' life, regular journalism. He relaxed back into his chair, the pain in his chest leveling off, replaced by the warmth from the vodka. And then a terrible realization slammed into his brain: They had hundreds of thousands of newspapers soon to be tossed on door steps, stuffed in street boxes and store shelves that were completely wrong. His entire career as a newspaper man collapsed in a pile of irony. Of course, the paper had printed out of date information on the front page before. While sitting there, struck to the core with the realization of how much the world had changed, Beach came storming in shouting commands like an angel of war and his head cleared.

"We've got a special section on the books! I want it ripped up. Switch to single broadsheet. Get me some copy for the cover. Headline: 'Internet back!' as big as you can make it. First deck: 'Sigh of relief as world returns to normal' or like that."

She swirled past him to her office.

"Adam, I want some copy for that story," she didn't look at him. "We'll run whatever you can put together and back fill with Marr's column." She stuck her head out of her office. "Adam!"

"On it!" he yelled, typing furiously.

"We'll wrap as many papers as we can with that fucker. I'm not going down without of a fucking fight."

Adam pushed down the feeling of futility. It ain't over yet, by god. He continued typing in a notes file, "… the Internet proved robust, resilient, in early morning hours today, demonstrating it could and would survive an attack that had been strong enough to shut it down, apparently worldwide, for a few short hours." He hit the return key. His cellphone rang.

The name on the screen was "problem child," AKA Natalie.

Adam answered it. "Hey!"

"Hey! Adam!" While she was a little out of breath, she sounded okay.

"Are you …"

"I'm fine, but listen. It isn't over yet. It's not over."

"What's not over? The Internet outage?"

"Yes!" she huffed. He could hear sounds of running, shoes slapping pavement. "The outage. The AI. Something terrible has happened. Something really really bad …" she choked on words while, apparently, running.

"Find the police!" Adam yelled into the phone, mad at her for interrupting his triumphal moment. "Get somewhere away from those crazy bastards and …"

"We are!" Shoes clapping on sidewalk, panting. "We're running to his car. There are federal agents all over the place."

"Great news! Get safe and get back here as soon as you can. We've got a full day in front of us."

"What!" Hurt and surprise mixed together.

"Get some rest but get in here!"

"You don't understand!"

Adam thought he heard something like a cry bubble up in her voice.

"They've killed millions of people. The president. Congress and military …"

The word "Who" on his lips, he looked out of habit up to the television set to see if something was happening there. On the screen was an image of the White House taken from Pennsylvania Avenue, just overlooking the chaotic North Lawn. It took a full second, Natalie huffing into the phone as she ran, for Adam to understand that masses of people were climbing over the main barrier fence, part of which had been broken down to the ground. The people, some cheering with hands raised, swarmed onto the main steps and to the doors and windows without meeting any resistance. The scene ran with no reporter's voice over. On the screen's upper left corner words in white said "White Horse Breached" and nothing else.

"Natalie," he said, not taking his eyes away from the people now banging on the windows of the fucking White House. She didn't respond. "Hey, Natalie! I have to go. Get safe and ..."

"I said, You have to talk to this guy."

"Later!" He switched off the call.

Out of the corner of his eye, Beach stood in her doorway, slack-jawed looking at the same TV. Adam opened his mouth to yell at someone, anyone, just a need to state a command, because something really really fucked up was happening and Beach was standing right there, but then a tank stormed around the corner of the White House, smoke pouring out its back end. It launched itself on top of at least two dozen people then stalled. The camera providing the live feed zoomed out and panned down to a bushel of blond hair in the grass, the body of a woman lying face down with a microphone still gripped in her hand. A tennis shoe clad foot came into the video frame, touched the leg of the woman. Her body sank where the foot touched her and collapsed from that point until her body dissolved away. The microphone sat alone next to a blue pants suit. The camera panned back up but stayed distant. The sun nearly risen in a clear blue sky over the White House. People crawled over the tank like rats, pulling on parts of it but unable to get in. The tank, however, didn't move. A pickup truck smashed over the barrier fence and spun all four wheels in the grass of the North Lawn in acceleration at the White House. The pickup didn't honk but nor was it trying to hit people. It missed some if it could without veering too much, and others jumped out of the way but several went under its front. The truck struggled to keep speed amid all the bodies and slick grass. But as it hit the edge of the pavement, it bounced up and then lurched forward when its tires caught. The path in front of it was nearly cleared of people. It slid left against the massive pillars and smashed into the windows. The frames of the windows held, but the thick glass in one pane must have jared loosed because a swarm of people began smashing the pane with whatever they could hold and swing. None of the crowd seemed the least bit concerned about all the dead and dying on the ground around them and under the tank and pickup.

 The room around Adam was completely quiet. No sound came from the television, other than the distant roar of the crowd. Adam heard sirens outside the newsroom and felt the urge to bark at someone again, but then the hatch of the tank flopped opened. The individuals surrounding the hatch jerked and fell off. Several went down. An arm and a head appeared out of the hatch. The arm twitched and bits of flame came out of a blur of a hand. After about four rapid-fire shots, the swarm of others on the tanks overwhelmed the shooter and dragged him out. His gun taken from him as the crowd dragged him off the tank and across the grass. A second later, someone stood over the hatch with both hands on the gun, firing into the opening.

 "Oh my god," someone in the newsroom said, quiet, as if in church.

The sirens outside the *Daily Record* building stopped at some point during the broadcast. When he noticed the silence, Adam looked through Beach's office window to see what he could see outside. Perhaps the pandemonium at the White House had spread. The zombie apocalypse upon them. What they saw on the television was so disorienting that he wouldn't have been surprised to see ghouls dancing in the streets. The street outside the window was, however, empty of zombies and moving cars. Back on television, the camera started panning left, silently. The sound crew had dropped all their gear, evidenced by it laying all around the camera and the pantsuit of the woman formally holding a microphone. One of the protesters must have taken control of the camera after whoever was on the ground in front of it had met her fate and her crew fled. The big street in front of the White House was packed with people raising fists and shouting encouragement to those attacking the White House. If the rioters had protest signs, they'd abandoned them for iron bars and chunks of pavement. However, Adam decided, the rioting crowd must have come from the body of protests that had grown increasingly violent for several months since the President had continued his predecessor's dismantling of what his administration called the "administrative state." Those institutions nearly completely dismantled, such as the Department of Labor, HUD, NIH, EPA, FDA, DOE, FAA, Education, Securities and Exchange Commission, etc. tended to be the ones that looked out for the health and wellbeing of citizens. American cities had become dirty, crowded with homeless streaming in from the impoverished countrysides, dangerous and rife with conflicts between dwindling police departments in all but the wealthiest of neighborhoods, public utilities spotty and expensive, water periodically too dangerous to drink. And, yet, somehow the all-corporate party had won election after election, by thin margins but they won as people looked to the all-powerful corporations to bring order to their lives through the magic of deep discounts and other mysterious economic forces. Voter fraud was of course rampant, but the cheating on both sides evened that score. Meanwhile, the backlash by the growing ranks of the poor, poisoned and disenfranchised had grown ever more intense. The more protests, lawsuits and isolation of cities and counties from federal agencies intensified, the more Ma and Pa

Kettle voted for law and order, for the corporate independence that would make them all rich and set the world right. They "Dare to Dream of a Better, Richer America." The president dared to dream of marshal law from time to time, but local police wouldn't participate and had few officers to contribute to the effort at any rate. He'd tried to mobilize the military, but the Constitution or what was left of it got in the way. Meanwhile, the rest of the world did what it could to stay out of a war with the floundering U.S., betting the country would collapse before mounting a serious military campaign, though it would be a close shave.

Adam felt just the tiniest bit of thrill at the attack on the White House. Clearly, however, several aspects of the attacks weren't computing in his brain. Like, what the hell had happened to the Secret Service? Where had the president got to? Was he in a secret bunker? How could they have lost control so fast and so completely? As he watched, it made a visceral sense that people would rush the White House on foot and smash windows. Adam, apparently like those rioting, didn't give a second thought to what had to have been dozens of dead and dying former protesters under the tank or shot down in the first few moments of the onslaught.

Once again, the silence outside their own building jumped out at him. How could that be happening on television and nothing going on in Seattle? He looked at Beach just as she looked at him with her eyes wide in revelation, adrenalin and fear. Thye'd had the same realization: Seattle could explode at any moment. Anyone stunned by watching television would soon revive and do lord knows what.

"Hey, everyone!" Beach yelled. "If you have family, check on them. If you need to go, take off. Come back when you can. If you want to stay, we need to prepare for whatever is about to happen in Seattle. If you're going downtown, take riot gear, emergency water and food and extra gas mask canisters. We're canceling the special section. I gotta bad feeling about this."

"Does that mean my story isn't running?"

Adam turned to where the question came from. Marr's eyes flicked from Beach to him and back to Beach. She turned and stepped into her office, slamming the door behind her. Adam watched her put her hands on her face and run them through her hair. The words "… she has family" lurched out in his brain. He turned to Marr and was about to say the F-word a whole bunch of times when the phone in his hand buzzed. He nearly dropped it, but caught it and looked. Problem Child, again. He stuck it against his ear.

"Hi Adam. My name is Josh Fines. I am with Natalie. She's fine."

"Oh that's great news!" He said with mocking enthusiasm. "Whew! All is well then! But, uh, who the fuck are you and why do you have Natalie's phone?"

"I am an officer in the Cyber Threat Intelligence Integration Center in the office of the Director of National Intelligence and part of the U.S. military Cyber Command. I was undercover investigating Celestine, Mannerheim and The Clans. Natalie gave her phone to me because there isn't much time before the Internet and all cellphone systems degrade again, this time for good."

And, true timing, as Adam watched flames gushing out of the top windows and balcony doors of the White House, the TV signal began to gutter, like a flame going out. But this guy could have been anyone, and he could also be who he said it was. "What's causing this?" Adam asked as he threw a pen at Kelli McCammon, one of their higher education reporters who sat several desks away. The pen skipped off the top of her computer. She popped up, brown hair bouncing up in big curls.

"Hey!" She challenged. She'd come in around 5 a.m., because she had drawn short straw a couple weeks ago to cover morning general assignment with Debora out on maternity leave. Clearly, Kelli had been hiding while ostensibly hounding the university for professors who might have government connections and or heard something about what was going on.

Adam waved her over with rapid hand motions, while intermittently pointing at the phone in his hand. She came over, eyes up and defensive, because higher ed was constantly poached for reporters to pick up breaking news. Adam wrote Josh Fines down and mouthed "Look up!" Lucky for his state of mind, Kelli didn't look to the ceiling but instead grabbed the paper and rushed back to her desk. She was a trotter. They had several reporters who trotted everywhere in the news room and one who ran.

"… so you better get to researching all you can. I'll text you my login. I want you to go to my database, just follow the link, and download and print everything you can. You'll find what you need there to tell the story of how this all happened. We need to get the story out. We need to tell people that their government is responding."

"Do you know what's going on at the White House?"

"The White House? Adam, it's everywhere. The AI has unleashed a wave of its microcomputers, nanites, that has killed all the top decision makers across the globe. All the leaders of government, military and corporate operations have been wiped out." In spite of the training on holding back hysterics, Josh Fines nevertheless had a hard time keeping his voice from cracking. "I don't have time for an explanation." Throat clearing. "You'll find most of what you need to know in those documents. You have to hurry. The AI turned all our systems back on in order to use them for its next stage of growth. There isn't any way to stop it now. We have to …" Someone interjected. Sounded like a question. A man's voice. "Yes!" Josh said. "Here's Natalie."

"Adam."

"Yes, Natalie. You okay? Are with them voluntarily? Just say, uh, 'deadline' or 10 p.m. if not …"

"Good thing this isn't a spy movie," she said, very serious but not quiet. He could hear road noise. "We're on our way back to Seattle. This is an old car with no electronics so we could be awhile. I spoke to Robert. He's following in that beater they're in. Do what Josh said and do it fast. Okay?"

"Uh." The phone buzzed in his hand. A text with a hyperlink, just an IP address, user name and password.

"Now!" Natalie yelled without command or effrontery, more like raw fear. "And you might want to barricade the building judging by what I've seen so far this morning. Bye."

She hung up.

"Well, fuck." Adam said. The image on the television had nearly snowed over, though he could just make out dense smoke pouring from a building, not the White House. Congress maybe. Or, just the Washington State Capitol building. He did what they asked, beginning the download of entire folders listed at the IP address behind a simple login page. He briefly wondered if he was committing a crime. Then he wondered if he was downloading a virus, perhaps the virus that took out the Internet. As the gigabits of files crawled onto his hard drive, he got one last email. This one came from their D.C. bureau reporter: "Hey, I sent this to Henri but haven't heard back so sending it to you two." The email was addressed to Adam and Beach. Adam scanned it out of habit. "I was at that Internet hearing when everyone, well everyone except us journalists, collapsed and disappeared sort of. Hard to explain. Can I get some backup here to figure out what the hell has just happened. Joke? Some sort of poison? Please call me."

Beach opened her door, looked at him with a pained face and fell forward into a chair. Adam, forgetting the conditions or the world for just a split second guffawed since he thought she was making fun of the email they'd just received …

"I have to go," she blurted in a ragged whisper. "I have to go home."

Adam let the phone drop and ran over to her. He put his hand on the back of her shoulder. Her head lulled onto folded arms. She shook and then a great sob burst from her.

"What the hell, Beach?" He shook her. "What the hell is going on?"

"He's dead." She said it to the carpet. "They have to be lying."

She picked her head up, slumped off the chair and started crawling, reaching out for the corner of a desk. Adam might have laughed, except that Beach was crying. He grabbed her hand and stood, pulling it.

"Who's dead?"

"My husband."

"But what? How?"

"I don't know!" She started walking, holding his hand so tight it hurt all the way up his arm.

"How do you know?"

"Babysitter. He came back from the bank this morning when all hell broke loose, got in the doorway, she said. She said he fell over and started convulsing." She turned, eyes wild and mouth spread wide, she gripped his shoulder, talon fashion. "She said he stopped breathing. They turned him over and ... I can't make sense of what she said. My son." She righted herself and marched toward the elevator. "... decomposed."

Adam followed behind her.

She hit the down button and yelled, "I don't understand!"

"Let me drive you." He put his hand on her arm. "Let me get someone to drive you. You don't even have keys."

"Okay," she said staring at the elevator number climbing up from P3, P2 ...

Adam scanned the newsroom. It had nearly emptied out. He spotted Ken Bunting in the sports department, head down, asleep or drunk maybe. "Wait, Kristi. Please just wait here. You don't have keys and can't drive like you are." He parted from her. "Ken! Hey, Ken!"

Ken's head came up slowly, lips wet from escaped salvia. He wiped his mouth. "Huh?"

"Are you still drunk?" The sports department had been openly drinking deep into the morning. Ken had stayed to cover the hockey game later in the afternoon, as if. Though, close to Adam's heart, he had also been sleeping in various locations of the paper since his recent divorce, in which the house went to his ex.

"No. No. Uh, a little." His voice shot through with cigarettes and still booze-blurred.

"Fuck it. Do you have a car here?"

"Sure but ..." he put his hands out over his desk, conjuring an excuse. Fucking sportswriters. They'd shoot themselves to stay out of a news story.

"Drive Kristi home and then go home yourself."

"Still working on getting a home. The ..."

"That's right." Adam cut him off to save them from his recounting the woes of finding a place to rent in this damn town. "Well, drive her home and come back here. We've got work to do."

"Right. Right. Is she okay?"

They both looked at Kristi standing in the open door of the elevator, red eyes pasted on them, blank.

Adam pulled Ken to his feet and dragged him a few steps.

"The SeaDucks are playing …"

"Maybe don't talk to her." He stopped at the nearest desk along their way and wrote her address on a yellow sticky note. He put it in Ken's hand. "Just get her in a car and get her home. That's her address. Don't go in. I need you back here."

"Okay, chief."

He got in the elevator with Kristi, not looking at her. The door closed on them. One of the sports writers had left his computer on and logged in, failing at the latest cyber security training. Adam opened a web browser. Searched for "dead" and clicked the news tab. At least some journalists and bloggers on the East Coast, three hours ahead, were doing their jobs. "Unexplained deaths reported throughout the city."

"'He dissolved right in front of my eyes,' cried the Navel commander's secretary".

Another headline: "Congressional leaders found dead on plane bound for Central America".

Then, simply: "Federal, state governments in shambles".

He clicked the link. The search page disappeared, but nothing loaded in its place. Then came the note saying the website was either down or overloaded.

IV

For just a second, Natalie's breath paused. Not stopped nor knocked out by the onslaught, just a pause like hitting reset. A field of glimmer coated her eyes, unfocussed sparkles that floated throughout her murky field of vision. "Floaters," her mind said as she drifted in a limbo. No complex thoughts and no emotions, though a generalized whole-being sense of warmth enveloped her as she floated. Three people standing, shimmering within a haloed outline and in front of a rough, earthen wall—didn't matter who they were or why. A hand, likely hers she reasoned from its position in front of her face, held a smart phone horizontally at the three women arranged around her. The center person reaching toward her, with clouds for hands, but not trying to touch her. One of the figures next to the center person stepped forward, reached deep into her perspective and lifted her. Natalie knew she felt a grip on her arm, but the feeling didn't register as pressure just fact.

As she raised Natalie, the Soccer Twin said in the happy voice of someone truly glad to have her aboard: "Welcome."

The tone of her voice resonated throughout Natalie's body, like a welcome touch. The vibration of the tone excited her stomach, excited the core of her body, like an energy bubble seeking equilibrium with another orb of energy.

"Oh my god," Natalie said at the feeling.

The cloud around the center person dissipated down to a density around her hands and then that too became absorbed or evaporated. Celestine stepped close to her, stared into the camera lens and said, "Stage two."

Natalie looked at Celestine's face in the screen of the phone. Then the phone stopped recording of its own while focussed on her teeth, flashed through several program screens and sent the video to Adam's email. The screen went black, power cut off without powering down. Still experiencing the full effect, as far as she knew, of whatever Celestine had done to her, Natalie's mind started working again, less emotion and feeling and more actual thought processes. At the same time, the world visually intwined with her emerging thoughts to create the impression of ... honeycombs. The best description she could form. Polyhedron latticeworks, also came to mind. The cave, the three other women, all of it looked as it had but with the added depth of structure, geometric but fluid structure. The warmth pervading her experience quickly grew in intensity with the focal point centering in her head. A brief flash of a headache gave way to release, a burst, followed by clarity.

"I know where I come from, how I exist!" Natalie exclaimed. "It's beautiful."

"Just wait," said the Soccer Twin holding her arm. "It's really cool when you can move your consciousness from place to place, even to within other members of The Clans. Let me ..."

"Wait!" Natalie said. "I'm not ..."

A flash and a deafening bang resonated throughout the cave knocking everyone down, blinding her. Another hand, much stronger, lifted her. Holding her phone in her right hand and her blinded eyes with the other, she was dragged fast along the pebble and stone strewn floor of the cave.

"Let go of me, goddamn it!"

The person dragged her stumbling up a flight of steps. Natalie's eyes adjusted. Robert and the old photographer Grant stood in front of her, looking over her shoulder. They were on a yard in a dense neighborhood. The sky an early morning, cloud-covered gloom. A voice behind her said, "We better keep going. I doubt they'll …"

Natalie spun around and hit the person behind her with the edge of her phone. "Drag me you motherfucker!" The guy was tall and her blow bounced off his shoulder. She reared back to strike him higher up. She recognized him as one of the clan members. Robert got a hold of her hand gripping the phone.

"He's trying to help us!" Robert said, struggling with her hand.

She jerked her other arm loose from the tall guy and faced Robert. "Are you shitting me? He's with them!" She spun back around, but Robert held her right arm back. The tall guy wasn't paying her any attention, instead he was waving at three people in full police riot gear running in their direction.

"We've got to get back to Seattle," Grant said. He held one of the cameras hanging from his neck up to his eye and snapped the shutter at Natalie. "The roads are going to shit fast." He turned and walked away.

Natalie felt jagged. Unfocussed. She bent over to throw up, salvia running into her mouth. She looked at her hands, one still holding the phone. Something swarmed over them. She started brushing them against her shirtsleeves in a panic. "What the fuck?" She dropped to her knees and stared at her hands.

"Is it contagious?" Robert said standing over her.

"No. Not unintentionally. But," the tall guy patted Natalie's shoulder, "you are definitely infected with Celestine's nanites." He knelt beside her. "You are still in control. It's your body. You are still okay. Right now, you need to ignore it and come with us."

"I'm going with Grant," Robert called.

"Let's go, too. Our vehicle is about two blocks from here." He stood and reached his hand down to her.

"I'm not going anywhere until you … ROBERT!" She watched him jog after Grant.

"Go with him!" he yelled back. "He'll …"

A car careened around the corner just missing Robert as it shot across the street and smashed into a parked car. The passenger door opened and a man in a business suit jumped out and ran. Robert made it to the car and pulled open the driver's door and what looked like black sand poured out onto the ground.

He yelled back at Natalie: "This is happening all over the place. People just turning to fucking dust, man. It's insane." He trotted after Grant who had snapped several shots and then turned away down the street.

The tall guy wiggled his fingers at her. She took his hand and stood. Her mind felt clear, just nothing was processing data or forming words in her head.

"My name is Josh Fines. I work with the federal government. This is far from over." He spoke each sentence with clipped clarity. "We have to get back to Seattle. Everything is going to stop working again. Somehow, it's The Clans. It's Celestine and the virus, the computer virus, she infected you and the others with. We have to get back to Seattle where we have more resources."

The three armored men with Josh were trotting back the way they had come. A puff of smoke roiled into the sky a mile away, then the pop of the explosion reached them. Josh turned following the others.

"Let's go. Come on. They are going to shut it all down again and we have to get as far as we can before everything stops working."

Natalie's phone buzzed in her hand. An alert on the screen said she'd received a text message from her mother sent hours earlier: A hug and a kiss. She ignored the text. She could do nothing for her mother and suspected she was already running some neighborhood program to survive the disaster. She dialed Adam as she ran to catch up with Josh. As Adam's phone rang once, her mind snapped back over to see grid or latticework as the framework for everything and then the insight came in a flash. The phone rang a second time.

"Oh my god!" she said.

"You've seen it …"

Adam answered the line.

"Hey! Adam!"

"Are you …"

"I'm fine, but listen. It isn't over yet. It's not over."

"What's not over? The Internet outage?"

"Yes!" She caught Josh and saw the old station wagon ahead of them that the armed federal agents were clamoring into.

V

It was 10 a.m. the morning of the fourth day since Adam first heard of Celestine Wallace and The Clans. So far, he thought sitting at his desk, keyboard stack on papers and yellow legal pad in front of him, every single conclusion he'd drawn, every lead they'd followed and every goddamn plan of attack he'd come up with had all gone to shit. He scratched out gone to shit and wrote next to it, Gone to fucking shit.

"There," he said blithely, "that's just right."

He tossed the pen against the paper. He turned his cellphone off and then back on. When it reloaded, it appeared he had cell service. There was even an LTE network connection. He dialed his desk number, got a busy signal. He tried 9-1-1 and it too was busy. He set his cellphone down, picked up the desk phone, dial tone, and dialed 9-1-1. Busy. He set it back down in the cradle, gently, listening to the dead clack of useless plastic on useless plastic.

"Well, shit," he said, unenthusiastically. He looked around the newsroom and saw three people: Kelli McCammon, sitting back in her chair looking blankly at her computer screen, medicated to some nth degree, he surmised; James Wright, a photo tech who came in early on Wednesdays to color correct photos for the weekend magazines; and, well, himself … staring back at him from the face of a dead computer. Kelli's kid had recently died and her husband was drinking himself to death with the aid of pain killers. So, she was alone. James never had a family and spent his every waking moment when not at work in the water floating beneath the waves in a world where his weight didn't matter and everyone was alone, where his technical and physical prowess was evident and unchallenged. And Adam: Alone, really, since his mother died, from time to time communing with friends who shared similar interests, such as the Zombie Victory Association. But, you know, take away the zombies and we've got nothing to talk about. He'd been accused of and admitted to taking solace in—even hiding behind—his commitment to something transcendent to nations, to cultures, even to people themselves. He has striven and strived both for relevance and service to that cause. But the days of service had accumulated like so many flies on a walking corpse.

He shook the mouse across the surface of its pad, waking his computer. Download could not be completed. He hit the Okay button to see if anything had come through. There were a few folders on his desktop with codes for names. He hovered the mouse over one. It presented a file size of a few megabits. So there were either lots and lots of pages of text or some other kinds of media in it. He couldn't bring himself to open it. A biologically human brain can only ask itself what the hell is going on so many times before its befuddlement becomes systemic and gives way to paralysis. Even a loud repeating banging noise from the street outside Kristi's window couldn't rouse him. Whatever the hell it was, what could he do about it? He heard the elevator door open with a "boing" sound and lulled his head around to look through the door window, to see who had shown up. As soon as the doors opened a slice, Beach wedged out. She waved a card in front of the door reader, pushed hard and with a bang entered the newsroom. Adam nearly stood, nearly. Beach rounded the corner of the room, trotting. She hit her office and slammed the door behind her, hard. Ken had stepped out of the elevator by the time Adam looked back. Ken looked at Adam through the window of the newsroom door just as it glided shut. He shook his head.

Inside the door, he yelled, "Car wouldn't start." He glanced over at Kristi's door and winced at her frenetic activity. "What can I do?"

"I have no idea," Adam said, facing him. "I guess you could go see if there's anyone in the pressroom. I mean, right now, it doesn't look like there will be a paper."

That perked him. "No paper." It baffled him through and through. "There has been a *Seattle Daily Record* on the streets of this city for a one-hundred and fifty years! We can't not have a paper for fuck sakes!" His face reddened. The thought did throughly upset him.

"Well, goddamn it. It won't be up to me. Go see if there's anyone here."

"We have hours."

"Jesus fucking christ you son of a bitch, I know! But the fucking goddamn phones don't fucking work! Find out if any-fucking-one is here and if they have any fucking idea how to run the motherfucking presses or someone who does! Okay?"

"Right! Yeah. On it!"

Fucking journalists, Adam thought. Dumber than a fucking post about the simplest things, can't fill out a time card to save their fucking lives, but they can skim several hundred pages of complex legal bullshit, make three phone calls and write a twenty inch story in three hours or less that changes the world. He loved them with all of his heart and soul.

Meanwhile, the noise from Kristi's office was reaching hurricane strength. He saw her out of the corner of his eye, unwilling to commit a full look, throwing papers, folders, books, her keyboard, which circled around at the end of its cord and smacked her on the shoulder, her keyboard again with more force onto the floor. She ripped a backpack off the coat rack and held the arm strap of it in the air like a doctor might a newborn by the leg and started stuffing her jacket into it, a handful of pens and a yellow legal pad. Just as Adam turned to go to her, she burst out of the office, door banging open, slinging the backpack over her shoulder.

"I'm walking!" she screamed, eyes wide but not focussing on any particular objects. Adam tried to stop her, put his hands up to grab her shoulder.

"Your having a stroke!" he declared.

She swept him aside and barreled on.

"That's nearly five miles," he said after her. Her back straight with determination as she pounded toward the door. "It could be dangerous out there! Let me send someone with you …" Obviously, there wasn't anyone to send on a long walk into god knows what, not really. He looked around, sort of desperate to stop her but then sort of unwilling to try to stop her. Kelli and Ken both had enough extra weight on them to make walking more than a mile a very strenuous exercise. Besides what would any of them do? Not like they had guns around or anything. Someone had to stay behind just in case, the world came back online. No, Beach was on her own.

She wasn't waiting in any event. She had walked on and hit the door with her shoulder, recoiled because she hadn't turned the handle. She screamed "Fuck!" twisted the handle and stormed out into the world and disappeared.

He scanned the newsroom again, disjointed by its emptiness. Ken had his head on the desk, more hungover than he thought earlier. Kelli had a cardboard box by her chair. She picked up small items, toys for the most part, dinosaurs and action figures from the 1970s and 80s that she'd shared with her son, and placed them one-by-one in the box. She lifted an oversized coffee cup with pens bristling out of it, up ended it on the desk and put the cup in the box. She pulled open a drawer and took out a mini-bottle of some clear booze or other, grimaced as she twisted the little cap off with a crackling of the metal connectors, downed it and burst into tears.

"Hey," he said but didn't walk to her. Adam was not the hugging or comforting type but he did try to be consoling in the face of terrible things. "We don't know what's happening. Whatever is going on could all be over by the end of the day, order restored. You know, regular life. There has to be a couple million people working feverishly to put this all to rights."

"All of my family is on the East Coast!" she said with blubbers and huffs.

"Okay. Okay. Why don't you just go up to the library and lie down for a bit. There are still some cars working, apparently old cars still run. Robert and Grant are driving here in one now. I think."

"Really?" She said it with hope. Adam never lied to her before, had he?

"That's the last I heard."

"Okay." She pushed herself back on the wheels of her chair. "I'll just lie down for a bit. I got up pretty early. This shift kills me."

"I know. I know."

She started for the elevators, gripping her old tan leather purse to her side, no doubt full of booze and pills.

"I wouldn't get in one of those," Adam interrupted her walk. "Take the stairs."

She looked at him, big curls flopping around the circle of her face She looked at the stairs, looked back.

"Just use Beach's office."

She sighed and walked toward Adam. He tensed and froze and tried not to grimace, but she just stepped past him and into the office, shutting the door behind her. Once inside the office, she unslung her purse, dug into it and came up with a big pill bottle. She twisted it open against her palm, shook it against her open hand, paused—counting seemed to Adam—then shook it again. She popped the pills, fitted the lid, twisted it shut. Her hand came out of the purse with a little booze bottle. She glanced over her shoulders, suddenly conscious of the window. Adam shrugged and looked away. He sat at his computer and looked at the folders downloaded to the desktop. He didn't want to look in them. He didn't know what he wanted to do. In the sudden silence, he heard crackling outside the big windows overlooking Puget Sound. Muffled "humpf" sounds. Just like he didn't want to know how bad things were by looking in those folders, he also really didn't want to look outside. The computer, television and lights all went down with the loss of electricity. He flushed. He didn't want to `cry but he did. He wanted it to all go away. He loved his life. He loved his job. Someone had to restore order soon. This couldn't go on. Shit like this didn't happen in the real world. It happened in movies, sure; it happened in history books ... it happened in folklore and religious stories, but not in reality. Adam was, simply, paralyzed. From deep down he knew the situation would change, the lights come back on. So, he waited. He sat back, barely breathing, and waited for reality to show back up. They were all going to get one hell of a laugh out of it. He had, without words in his mind, convinced himself that the business crew would be stumbling in half lit, laughing and scrambling for their desks to write the hell out of this story, this once-in-a-lifetime story of the most widespread Internet and media hoax ever, a hoax the magnitude of which had not been seen since Orson Welles scared the shit out of all those people in the 1930s. The cops reporters grumbling about how the flacks couldn't get their shit together to tell them what had happened, who had fucked up, if anyone had been killed.

  James walked over to Adam carrying his red and white lunch cooler.

  "Well," he shrugged his big shoulders, powerful from the thousands of miles he'd dragged his giant body through the water.

"The electricity's out." He shrugged and looked around. "I'll finish the edition when it comes back on. Guess I'll just go home." He shrugged again like he enjoyed the sensation of using those mounds of muscles. He turned to the door. He twisted the handle slowly, glanced back, shrugged and smiled, and walked out.

Ken walked over to Adam's desk in James' wake. His big brown head lulling at him, eyes red and puffy.

"I'm going to try my luck at home. No telling how long this will last. I am still paying the mortgage after all." He straightened.

Adam nodded encouragement at him and he too left.

VI

At first, people stood by the side of the street in yards and driveways, at fences and on sidewalks, looking around, some talking, a few men had raised the hoods on their cars, one hand holding the hood up over their heads the other reaching in to shake something uncertainly, some watched the station wagon rumble by, weaving slowly between stalled cars. Josh drove. Natalie had shotgun. The three armed men in riot gear had scrunched into the backseat. They had to lunge first one direction and then the other to get the doors shut. Several black plastic boxes took up the space in the very back. As they reached the edge of the neighborhood, turning right onto the business-lined arterial and making for the interstate onramp, people there too had stepped outside and many were walking toward the interstate. Some, however appeared to be walking north toward Canada. Dragging suitcases, bundles thrown over shoulders, kids sucking thumbs while trundling along, everyone dressed in layers like expert northwesterners, the street crowds grew. Josh stopped the car at the interstate onramp, dozens of people turning heads and looking them over. Several had stopped and started toward their car, the only vehicle operating.

"What do you think, boss?" said one of the armed men in the back.

"Kinda fucked, looks to me," a second said.

Natalie was only half listening. She watched the people, some crying while others milled about. No police. She knew what had happened. The AI had given her a glimpse of what lay in store for the human race. It would continue to use its micro-machines to dismantle millions of people, disassociating the many elements in the human body until the person crumbled into dust. It would soon turn on all the systems and infrastructure of the world, but not for humans to use. The AI would instead use the electric and communication systems like a web to fully knit the world into its control and then begin recycled the artifacts of human industry, everything metal or synthetic or that included either, including human beings, in order to build platforms in space and from there spread intelligence, itself, throughout the galaxy and eventually the universe. Genocide, Natalie thought. Extinction. There must be something we can do, if only we can expose the plan and rally the people into taking back their world. It's late but not too late, she silently told the people now crowding around the car.

"We'll have to take as many as we can or we'll never get back to Seattle in time to organize our resistance," Josh said.

Natalie turned toward him. "So you think we can resist?"

"I hope so ..."

"Let me fire a few rounds through the roof. That'll back 'em off. If they are stupid enough to get in our way after then, well ..."

"Hold on," Josh ordered. "We can't spend the day shooting people. You'll run out of ammo." Buddy smile. "I have a better idea, something just short of murder."

He rolled down his window and stuck his head out.

"We'll take as many as we can!" he yelled and motioned people toward the car. "Climb on. We've got some room inside. We're heading for Seattle." He brought his head back in. "We'll let them fight it out as we go. Hopefully, people will clear out once they see we can't take more."

A mile down the interstate, the station wagon couldn't carry another person, inside or outside. Twenty miles out of Bellingham, the sun came out. Now and then passengers got off to push cars out of the way, but most drivers had pulled over when their motors gave out. When the driver dissolved, however, the car generally smashed into other cars in the middle of the road and needed a push to get clear. The crew in the car kept to themselves, saying only that they didn't have a clue when asked what was happening. What good would it do to tell some stranger a fantastic tale of The AI and it's handmaiden Celestine? If anyone believed the story, they would have more questions than anyone other than Celestine and The AI had answers for. The three federal agents, stuffed against each other with assault rifles propped up in their laps, at first responded that it was an alien invasion with abductions for sexual purposes, which was funny until one young guy wedged between boxes in the back started panting and salivating in a panic response then barfed; and then a couple of children who had watched their father dissolve during breakfast cried pitifully on the bench seat they and their stunned-to-silence mother shared with Natalie and Josh. Brock, the highest ranking of the trio, apologized for the jest. The other two laughed, unintimidated.

"It's all happened so fast, no one knows what's going on," Josh interrupted. "But we're going to figure it out and make things right."

Stage two. It had happened fast. All those people, Natalie said in her mind. All those people. She repeated the phrase but was unable to rouse an emotion. It puzzled her that her emotions seemed to be missing in action. She assumed they would come back once the shock wore off. She had to be in shock, too. They all did. Once she got back to the newsroom, life would get back to normal, she promised. Of course she knew she was lying to herself, too, but what else could she do at this point but hope for the return of normal human life?

By the time they got to Lynnwood, a few miles out of Seattle, they were unable to get enough cars moved from between stalled trucks to make it down I-5 and the offramps were also clogged shut. Some older cars amid the jumble ran, but they too were stuck. As the travelers got off and out of the old station wagon, one of the older cars ahead of them suddenly rammed the vehicle in front of it and then behind it. A woman got out of the blue car hit first, brandishing an aluminum bat. She pointed it at the driver of the ramming car, a 1964 Rambler American, who didn't get out, and then smashed the headlights. She went back to her car, dug out a backpack and joined the throngs, including Natalie and those with her, walking between cars toward the city.

"Wish I could gather up these old cars," Brock said. "Could start my own business." He looked in the window of the Rambler. "Well, that explains that. Hey, Natalie come look. This is what's been happening."

Natalie stepped up to the car window, put her hand up and peered in. She jerked back.

"I don't know if it's your cult friend or not, but that's some serious tech right there," Brock said. "Just eats them from the inside out. No muss. No fuss."

"She's not my friend," Natalie responded with anger, not at Brock but at Celestine. Why would she join up with The AI, whatever it is? What could possibly motivate her to betray her own people? Her own species? She left the car, walking away with Brock. "I'm a journalist," she said, easing her tone back to careless. "I don't have friends. I don't know why she thinks she can get away with it, but I'm going to find out."

"Attagirl," Brock said.

He returned to the station wagon, slung the rifle, and grabbed the remaining box. They fell back into the wake of Josh and the other two agents carrying the two other boxes. An hour later, the crowds thicker now, people lined up to get off the interstate at the Mercer Street exit, Josh stopped and looked over the edge of the ramp.

"It's about fifty feet from here." He opened one of the boxes and pulled out a rope. "Let's go down here."

"I'm not climbing down that," Natalie said. "I don't have any gear or gloves …"

"We got a sling," Brock said beside her, pushing her shoulder toward the edge. "You'll have to piggy back."

"As if," she said. "I'm not with you guys anyway. I'm going back to my apartment, which is just down there, and then back to the *Daily Record* office. I'll see you all later." She started down the ramp, edging into the crowd.

"Hey," Josh called after her. "I'll come with you." He turned to the others. "Let's rendezvous at the newspaper's office. We might be able to make contact from there."

The three were already lowering one of the boxes over the side. "Don't take too long dear," Brock said and snorted.

Josh ignored the gibe and caught up with Natalie. She noticed him and pointed out at the water, Puget Sound. "Look at all those ships."

"Yeah, interesting," he said. "Say, I wonder if the *Daily Record* has a satellite connection, for getting world news?"

"If we did, it doesn't work now. Everything comes through the Internet, which in hindsight seems like poor planning."

"We definitely made ourselves ripe for this sort of thing."

At the bottom of the ramp, they stepped clear of the pedestrian knot. Natalie, bravado tucked away, was glad for the company.

"What do you think we'll be able to do to fight back?"

"First thing I need to do is get in touch with D.C. and find out what action they have already taken. We'll need to establish a communication center and someway to let people know what we know and pass on any instructions we get from D.C."

The sidewalks became less crowded, and they picked up the pace.

"I live …" Natalie began, pointing northeast.

"I know where you live. We've been investigating The Clan for about a year."

"Spying on journalists now?"

"Court sanctioned."

"Well, that makes it alright then!" Her voice raised. She walked faster.

"We get through this, you can take it up with Congress." He kept pace.

"Why are you following me now?" She stopped and faced him, tall and lean. Under thirty. She flushed.

"Same reason we got you out of that tunnel." He looked around. "Celestine wants or needs you for something, and she's not likely to be done with you now."

"But she's in …"

"She can be anywhere a clan member is." He studied a man and a woman coming up the sidewalk through a patch of low morning sunlight. "You know them?"

She looked where he was looking. "Neighbors."

"Natalie! We knew you'd make it!" the woman said in a French accent. She kissed Natalie on both cheeks.

"Josh this is Perran and Marsel Martin, neighbors. You two, this is …"

"Josh Fines," Perran said.

"You're not the only one whose been sneaking around," Marsel said.

Josh put his hands on his hips and looked up the side of the building. "Celestine in there?"

"In a manner of speaking," Perran said.

"Wait one goddamn minute." Natalie took a step back from the three. "You've been spying on me? What the hell for?"

"No! No!," Perran jumped in. "We moved in because of the membership and were surprised that you weren't one."

"A Clan member?"

"Right," Marsel.

"So it was you two," Josh said, nodding his head, "who tipped her off to Mannerheim's interest in seeing an initiation."

"You're the dude who wrote that anonymous post about the party and Mannerheim?" Natalie pointed at both of them.

"Yeah …"

"How did you know I would find it?"

Josh started toward the apartment building door, he said over his shoulder, "because they had full control over the internet whenever they wanted it and popped it in front of you."

"That seems incredible," Natalie said.

"Oh you haven't seen anything yet," Marsel said with a lot of accent and in the lower tones of her vocal range.

"I've seen plenty. Do you know what she did to me?"

"Hey," Josh said from the door. "They know. Let's go talk with her. I assume you've got a member plugged in already."

Marsel patted Natalie on the shoulder. "You'll be happy she did ... But! What's done is done. Let's go inside and talk with her."

Natalie pulled a notebook from her small purse and a pen. "Yeah, well, we're through with any off-the-record bullshit." She followed Josh. The couple followed her.

Inside the French couple's apartment, at the dinning room table over which Natalie had watched many sunsets, a young woman in white T-shirt and jeans sat with her hands on the table top with an orb between them. A black filament linked the orb to the center of a metal necklace around her thin neck.

"Seance?" Natalie said.

"More technical than that," Josh said, staring at the orb. "Nothing mystical about it. I've seen it just once before."

"Our first time," Perran said. "Even to us, it does seem a little, well, mystical."

"That was rather dramatic don't you think, Josh?"

All three looked at the young woman and then at the orb and back.

"A flash-bang grenade?"

"Celestine." Natalie and Josh said together.

"Bingo."

The girl spoke the words in a voice that seemed to Natalie must have been her own. But the infection and emphasis was Celestine. Natalie began taking notes, a sketch of detail around quotes. Then she remembered her phone still had charge and a sound recorder even if it couldn't connect to the Internet. She got it out and turned it on.

"Why are you doing this to me?" Natalie asked. "To us?"

"Why, Natalie, we're going to save humanity from extinction and I'll need your help. You and Adam."

VII

Then it was just Adam in the newsroom. Just him and Kelli in God knew what state of consciousness, if any, or for how long. One quiet death among so many. In a movie, Adam would have rushed into Beach's office, shook Kelli, slapped Kelli, cried out for Kelli to live, Live! Damn you! Live! But what for, he wondered sitting drunk in his chair. For how much longer? Oh, he assumed the world would come back. The deaths would be announced as some big amount, but the actual number would be less than what all had feared (or secretly hoped for). Death tolls are always assumed to be much much worse than they usually are. It's better for people to find out that fewer than expected are dead, rather than the opposite. General Patton famously told soldiers, as Adam was wont to point out to young reporters, "You are not all going to die. Only two percent of you right here today would die in a major battle." Even the terrible toll of terrorist attacks on New York City's World Trade Centers were first reported to be potentially three to four times higher than the actual number killed and wounded. Adam had suspected, given what he'd heard and saw on television, that there were plenty of people killed that day. Of the dozens of people hit by the tank and gun fire at the White House alone, at least a dozen had to have been killed in the attack. There were the eight kids found buried, though Adam still didn't think the two incidents were directly related, regardless of the fantastical tales spun by the cult leader Celestine.

No, Adam assumed that once the lights came back on and the dust settled, the number of powerful people dead would be much smaller than the number of people killed during the rioting that appeared to be going on out in the streets among the less powerful. After all, that's the way it always went. Those in power and the protected rich, like Mannerheim, would reassert command, crawl out of their bunkers and the world would proceed. Even the increase in shots, screams and banging sounds around the *Daily Record* building didn't impress him very much. And if during this brief hiatus of normalcy, this romantic moment of indeterminacy, Kelli wanted to take her own life, who was Adam to deny it her. She had tried several times already, from what he'd heard. First when her son died; another time when her husband lost their house gambling in Las Vegas and again when his liver failed and doctors denied a transplant because he wouldn't stop drinking and smoking. Each time someone had saved her and each time she had recovered only to find her life worse off, more terrible. Whatever had happened to drive her to attempting suicide suddenly paled in comparison. So, he reasoned, if she wanted to do it now, where better? When better? Now, Adam didn't really think she was dying in Beach's office. Had he seen her upend the bottle into her mouth, he might have acted differently, made her throw up or something. He suspect he was simply musing over his own life's purpose. His own death. He had only tried to kill himself, once. For years he didn't mind the prospect. Only his work kept him alive. The newsroom saved him, he told his therapist, while it killed him. He had sex with a stranger once, well not a stranger so much as another editor at a journalism conference, got tested for HIV to protect his wife, slowed his drinking and cigarette smoking when he hit forty. He stayed away from pills of all kinds, especially after watching his mother's body become addicted to pain pills … her bowels stopped working long before her heart did. All so he could come into this office, sit at this desk, fight with reporters, rewrite and rewrite again their dreadful stories, chase leads and guide investigations … all so they all, this team, could publish a newspaper every single fucking day of the year, year after year.

And now what?

He got up and looked in on Kelli, opening the door just enough to make sure she was breathing, which she was, vigorously. Some people simply have more life-force than life-desire. Without really thinking about it, though Adam suspect the racket outside the building drew him like a moth to flame, he went through the features and sports departments in the newsroom to the back balcony door. He opened it, stepped out and made sure to slide a book between the door and doorjamb, lest he be locked out on the balcony. At least two or three secret smokers and newsroom co-conspirators got locked out there every week. Even though he had heard the crescendoing of street noise, just a blur of roaring punctuated with sharp bangs, crackles and those muffled humpf noises, Adam's mind expected to see a calm Puget Sound with, perhaps, a sailboat regatta in play. Instead, he felt shock and disorientation at the scene spread out across the choppy waters. Even with all he had seen on TV and experienced in the office, the scene struck him as incredible.

As far as he could make out across the Sound and up the deep channel to his right that led out beyond Port Townsend to the Strait of Juan de Fuca were ships. Massive cargo ships, tugs and yachts, several huge submarines and Navy war ships filled the water. Smoke poured out of some, mostly the military subs and other grey ships, but they all just lulled there in the water jostling slightly against their neighbors. It seemed impossible that there were that many ships in the world let alone stacked against each other from shore to shore right in front of his eyes. It made some sense, of course, because the Puget Sound had two major international container ports, saw at least six super-large cruise ships every week, shared water with Navel Base Kitsap made up of the Bangor nuclear submarine base and aircraft carriers, battleships and other Navy ships taken from Bremerton when that shipyard became home to decommissioned Navy ships. A dozen large, car ferries also chugged back and forth all day among many more private and commercial ships. Then there were all the motor boats, yachts and sail boats, thousands of them docked year-round up and down the coastline. In the past, on busy shipping days, you could see dozens of massive ships in the Sound, so many you wondered at the organization behind keeping them all moving without collision. But this was something else all together. Seemed to him, given how distances get shortened from one's perspective, that a good jumper could get from one side of the Sound to the other by leaping from ship to boat to ship to submarine.

Mostly the scene appeared orderly, with more ships steaming in from the far end of the Sound and shoving their way into the mass, pushing others tighter, with concussive noises. Older, small boats and sail boats, just like old cars, still operated. Some sat there or idled slowly between the big ships. Others attempted speed and zig-zagged through the maze of increasingly shrinking openings. They eagerly tried to get through to open water and perhaps the sea. Several more had been crushed, kept above water by the pinning ships. As the scene started to clear up, as he saw more detail, including the people. They lined the sides of those ships, leaning over, some trying to climb down ropes and ladders to other ships or boats below them. From the smoking hulks—perhaps they had tried to burn out their electronics or motors to regain control but had clearly failed, from those engulfed in that dense black smoke—crews hung from the side or out doors on the sides opened at water level. There had to have been thousands in the water, but he couldn't see them for all the big boats. Other crews appeared calm, lining the rails of their ships, hanging out, perhaps waiting for things to calm down before taking action. Others, he assumed, were foreign crews with no where to go, remaining aboard where they had food, water and security. Ringing the Navy ships and subs, those crews bristled with guns. One of the big aircraft carriers had lines dangling from the overhanging flight decks down to rubber craft and onto the decks of ships below or next to them. The soldiers appeared to be fanning out, creating perimeters. Others carried buckets to the side and poured out ash or sand. Not knowing what else to do with what remained of their commanders. One massive container ship several hundred yards or possibly a half-mile away from the cluster of military ships, repelled marauders of some sort with concentrated gunfire. The pirates or whoever had rowed out to them when open water was still available. They had either fired grappling lines up over the railings or had taken over the ropes dropped from the top. Adam saw puffs of smoke and heard the crackling of small-arms fire. Though he had never been in a war zone, he had heard lots of gun fire in his time reporting and living in America's big cities. The crews in those rowboats were exchanging gunfire as their compatriots climbed the ropes. They fired up at the railing to ward off shooters from above, while the ship's crew stuck its guns over the edge and fired down and out. Several motor boats, a yacht—Puget Sound in the summer was home to thousands of rich techies and their yachts—and several sailboats had gotten mixed up in the fight or had come in in support of one side or the other and been floundered. One was still in flames as the others listed and smoked. He discovered the objective of one Navy squad as it broke onto to the scene and fired several rockets at the marauders, putting a sudden and explosive end to their adventures.

A particular sound had been spooking him, he recognized. It even caused him to duck his head from time to time as he paparazzied the scene, an unconscious response. When a hole appeared in the window next to his head, the cause of the sounds dawned on him. He threw himself down below the concrete side of the balcony. Not many but a few bullets came in his direction. Most of them either zapped over the building or past it, but some were smashing into the windows and walls of the floor below and the floor he was on. It only takes one, he thought. He crawled back into the building and back to his desk. The elevator shafts came between his desk and the windows facing the Sound. He sat on the floor anyway. He did get the full picture then, panting next to his desk, too panicked even to feel the thumping and thudding going on in his chest.

VI

Adam didn't know if he had passed out from shortness of breath and panic or simple exhaustion, he had not slept in thirty hours, but the next thing he remembered after huddling on the floor next to his desk was being shaken by the shoulder and his ass being so numb he couldn't feel the floor. He felt, eyes closed, like he floated. He had the impression that he'd had a terrible dream and wanted to dispel it before moving on with the day's work. Something about the tone of voice the woman used as she shook his shoulder made him want to take a moment to figure out why he had this feeling of profound dread. He was breathing fast, panting, his chest pounding in a scary way, but that was not it. Something else. Something …

"Adam! Adam!"

Something about …

"Adam! Don't die now!"

That wasn't it, he wanted to say. My ass ... He opened his eyes right into hers, into brown nearly black orbs. He pulled back to focus on the broader face for recognition.

"You're not going to die are you?"

Natalie's face. Her youthful angry, panicked face, smooth forehead scrunched between black tweezered eyebrows. Her eyes watered.

"Don't die." Natalie had dropped to her knees and felt his neck when she first entered the newsroom and saw him sitting on the ground, propped up against his desk. He was breathing shallow, his bald head chalky and pasty. She felt a rickety pulse and shook his shoulder, gently at first.

"I'm breathing aren't I?" Adam croaked. He pushed on the floor to get some blood into his ass. Then it all, the whole bit about the end of the world and all those ships outside on the sound came crashing back. "Give me a second would you?" His chest tightened and he gripped his shirt below the collar and closed his eyes against the pain, generalized throughout his body.

Natalie shook him harder. "Adam!" She would not let him die. They had work to do. They had news to gather and stories to write. They had to expose Celestine's role in creating The AI, her complicity in genocide.

"Stop!' Adam put his hand up to wave her off. "You're going to kill me!"

Natalie backed away a bit. "Can you stand?" She pulled on his arm.

"I don't know. My ass …"

You don't know how much you need your ass until you can't use the muscles in it, he quipped silently, holding his breath and pushing up with one arm. He didn't make his knees, however, and rolled to his side and stalled. A memory from his youth popped into his head. He's standing next to Clyde, his mother's red-haired gardener. He's saying to Adam while watching his son lumber off toward the garden shed at the back of his mother's yard at the big house they lived in on Capitol Hill, "That boy is numb from his ass both directions." Adam thought he was a horrible man. He was right about the mental powers of his son, but still horrible. Adam had been happy not to have a father. Sure, some male of the species had donated genetic material for his creation, but outside of that clinical moment he had no father.

"Adam!" Natalie dragged him a foot to get his head out from under a chair.

"Fuck," Adam mumbled. She was on her feet, pulling on his arm. "Jesus. My ass." She pull him onto his side. "Let go of my fucking arm would you. I swear to god."

She dropped his arm. "That's more like it," Natalie said.

Adam got his knees under him and pushed up, grabbing the edge of his desk. "What time is it? Did you see what's going on out there?"

"Yes. Yes. We saw." Natalie pulled his chair around his head and then sat in it.

"Thanks for the chair."

"I thought you were going to die."

"Well, I may yet. Help me to my feet."

She stood up and put her hand under his arm and lifted. He got his left foot under him and pressing with his hand on the edge of the desk, lifted himself to standing.

"Oh my god," he said and rubbed his rear. His slacks were sweaty and for just the briefest panicky moment he feared he'd pissed himself. But he discovered that the universe had seen fit to spare him that indignity at least.

He heard noises coming from Beach's office. "Oh, Kelli," he said as he turned. "Is she …"

"There's no one else here."

"Really. She abandoned me for dead the …"

"I came back for you! … well you, Robert, Grant and Josh Fines, the federal guy you talked to on the phone." Natalie, relieved now that Adam was standing, sat back down in his chair.

Adam examined the tall man with white-blond hair in Beach's office. He had his back toward them, fiddling with the dials of a box, pushing an antenna toward the windows, swirling it around. Screeches and squelches came from the shortwave the newspaper had used earlier to listen to the president tell everyone that everything was just fine … seemed like months ago.

"Where's Robert and Grant?" Adam looked around. "You need to stay away from the widows over in sports, bullets."

"Yeah," Natalie said, flipping through the pages of her notebook. "We saw that. They've gone back out to do some reporting and get some photos. I've got some incredible notes here."

"Of what? What for?" The presumption of work to do angered him. What could they possibly do without a press? Without electricity? Without a functioning society.

"What?" She looked up at Adam, angry again. She'd been scared but also pissed off to see him collapsed like that. "What do you mean?"

"Natalie." He stretched and took a couple tentative steps. Looking down at her, denim working-girl button down, narrow-cut blue jeans, white socks with frills above dirty, blue ballet flats. "What would we do with the information? The photos? We lack the means of production, even rudimentary production. What the fuck are we going to do? Handwrite the stories and paste the photos on it!" His frustration at her youthfulness, a year and a half of her youthfulness, peaked.

Natalie couldn't believe what she was hearing. All Adam ever talk about was the purpose of journalism. The necessity of journalism. It was as important now as ever. "Josh is boosting our shortwave radio," she explained. "We can broadcast our stories, if nothing else."

"Jesus Christ, Natalie," Adam said laughing, coughing up laughter as he spoke. "Look. Around." A window shattered back in sports, splattering glass across desks followed by a Woof! sound. Natalie ducked in the chair, sliding to her knees just as Adam dropped back down to his own. "We'll be lucky to survive!" He shouted.

"We have a job to do," she panted the words. "We've got to record what's happening, tell people about Celestine and The Clans." Natalie's panic at the explosion dissipated quickly. She got back to her feet. Her body felt light. "This is what we do. This is what people need from us."

"People … I …" Adam knew she was right, though. He laughed and crawled toward Beach's office, which was the most protected corner on the floor. "Goddamn it," he said, crawling. "God. Fucking. Damn. It!" She was right. What else would he do, roll over and die? She was right and he was not alone. He had a team. In the protection of Beach's door, he got to his feet. He had a team.

Josh, silently at work on the box, was turning a charging crank on its side. Voices surfaced in the noise and then sank back under.

"We have to get to higher ground," he said without looking at them. "What's the highest point we can get to without being exposed to the ships on the water?" He turned to Adam, expectantly, like they'd been talking this whole time, like they knew each other. A classic federal agent jock, Adam thought, six-two, trim with flat stomach and pronounced pectorals under a red polo tucked into blue jeans.

"Well," he said. "I believe," he added, "the highest point not downtown that keeps us out of the line of sight from the waterfront shooting gallery is the Space Needle."

Josh, nodded his head, building a mental image of the Space Needle and their route to it, fewer than a dozen blocks.

"You and Natalie," Adam motioned in her direction, slightly out of sight behind him, to emphasize that she had to go too, "can go scope it out and I'll wait here for Robert and Grant. I don't know how you'll get to the top, but I guess a federal agent can figure that out."

"That would be the best vantage and rallying point for establishing control," Josh said. "Once I make contact with other officers, we'll take it over. I bet others have thought of it, too."

"By the way," Adam interrupted Josh. "What is your plan?" He gave Natalie a significant look. She got the hint, smiled relief and pulled a reporter's notebook from her back pocket and a pen that had been clipped into her front pocket. She flipped it open, poised the pen over the page and looked up at Josh. He looked at her and then back at Adam.

"You're kidding, right?"

"No," Natalie jumped in front of Adam. "No. We're going to keep doing our jobs until we cannot do them any longer."

"Even if we publish our reports handwritten on rolls of toilet paper," Adam said, determined and absurdly proud.

"You do know there are millions if not tens of millions of people dead, right?" Josh, inexperienced with it, Adam recognized, put on the look that people in power have always put on when contemplating very important actions or policies that everyone else was supposed to simply accept as the wisest course of action: a downward tilt of the head to one side, slightly squinted eyes with the hands coming together, like two magnets through a viscous fluid.

"How do you know that?" Natalie asked.

Adam approved. It was the age-old, tried-and-true, most fundamentally basic question at the heart of every good piece of journalism. He gave Natalie an approving glance. She smiled and made a doodle mark on the paper to prime the pen, get the ink flowing.

"I don't have time for this." Josh shook his head, just a hint of anger in his eyes and jaws. "I have to get this radio to the top of the Space Needle and get in contact with as many people I can who are trained in security, field medicine, electrical engineers, emergency response organization, a million things. We have to figure out how to fight back."

Natalie scratched rapidly.

"Against what? Again whom?" Adam pressed.

"Haven't you been paying attention to anything?"

"I have my ideas, but I'm not the expert. I'm not the one supposed to know. You are."

"Yeah, well. Not me. As soon as I get ahold of my superiors and their communications people, I'll have them send you an email." He turned and grabbed the radio. Barging between them, he stopped, "Oh, and did you happen to print out any of those files I asked you to?"

"There just wasn't time before the electricity went out."

"Too bad, I guess." He continued on his way through the door. "A lot of information in there that will be important. We'll have to come back with a generator."

"You better go, too," Adam said to Natalie, feeling deflated as the reality of their situation settled down on him again. He didn't have the heart to tell Josh that only a few of the folders downloaded. The noise coming from outside grew louder again. Adam realized they'd been breathing more smoke since several of the windows had been blown out. He also thought, It will be getting dark in a few hours. He didn't say it out loud since he didn't want to scare her or himself. What the hell would they do in the dark? The entire city without lights would become fantastically dark and wildly dangerous. Hell, it was wildly dangerous some nights with all the lights on and cops roaming the streets in squad cars.

"Yeah," Natalie said, closing her notebook and stuffing it into her back pocket. "Leave a note for Robert and Grant. If they make it back. You better come with us. It's not safe here. He," she nodded at Josh, who had stopped at the side door to the outside and watched them, well her anyway, "has friends out there with guns, food and water. We've got shit."

"Right. Let's go." Adam stopped at his desk, wrote "Come to the Space Needle—ask for Josh Fines!" on a yellow pad with a red felt-tipped pen, and put the pad on the floor in the short hall between his desk and the side door. Natalie joined Josh there. He would have taken a nostalgic look around, but Josh pushed open the door. Sunlight spilled in with a yellow tint, light through a gauze of smoke. Without looking back, he stepped after Josh and Natalie, unsure if he was acting cowardly or intelligently. The city had come alive, alright, and like the sound of angry bees, the din of a few hundred thousand people panicking made his stomach churn.

But when they got to the street, the scene did not resemble what had appeared to be going on across Puget Sound. By the time the three got the five blocks to Denny Way, cops from Seattle PD, King County Sheriff's and Washington State Patrol had organized squads to establish control over buildings such as KeyArena and Memorial Stadium, hospitals and the corridors running between them. There was a lot of human noise, talking and yelling, the occasional glass breaking and someone yelling instructions through a bullhorn. They joined a couple dozen men and women dressed in the mostly black uniforms of federal agents. Adam noted jackets with FBI, ATF, ICE and other agency acronyms emblazoned across their backs. They made the corner of Denny Way and Broad Street. Josh wasn't running the show, but as a former U.S. military Cyber Command investigator and field commander he had access to wherever he wanted to go. From the intersection, Josh called a man and two women into a huddle and explained he wanted to take over the top of the Space Needle and why. One of the officers, pointed nose and narrow face, agreed that was a good idea at least until more regular radio communication could be established. The crews picked up their black cases and boxes and we headed down Broad.

 Natalie, walking just a head of Adam next to Josh, wrote short hand blips in her notebook as they went along. The federal officers around them, carrying stuff, didn't look around or chat amongst themselves. They were focused on the mission, Adam guessed, or their loads were so heavy they had to concentrate on not dropping them, on making it to their destination.

They passed through clots of citizens being organized by police officers standing on raised curbs, milk crates or just in the middle of men and women and some kids listening intently. One group of about a hundred people with a dozen police in their midst were spread out among the cars on Broad Street, opening car doors or breaking windows to get inside and to release breaks or smashing consoles to get cars out of park, pushing the ones that would roll up onto the sidewalk, grass and into parking lots. They were clearing the road. Another group of a about 20 were prying open gas caps and others followed behind syphoning the gas into barrels and gas cans. Still other groups carried boxes and garbage bags full of food and pharmaceuticals, what it looked like to Adam as they passed through them, in a line reminiscent of ants, toward KeyArena and Memorial Stadium. When they got to the driveway feeding the Space Needle, Josh and the other three commanders set to negotiating with the local police controlling the area at the foot of the Space Needle. The man yelling through a bullhorn had turned up the street toward them and Adam could then make out what he said:

"You must be off the streets by dark! A citywide curfew will be in effect after dark ... Be in your homes by dark ... This is for your own safety ... If you do not have a home or cannot get to your home by dark, you will find protection, food and water at KeyArena or Memorial Stadium ... if you need medical care or prescription drugs do NOT go to a hospital or pharmacy, go to KeyArena or Memorial Stadium ... All hospitals are for emergency care only ... All pharmacies are closed until further notice ... Stay inside ... Do not answer your door or stand by windows ... We do not expect violence but must be prepared ... If you need emergency help of any kind, hang a bed sheet from your window or off the roof of your building ... Do NOT open your doors until you have visual confirmation you are talking to a uniformed police officer ... Gather what supplies you can, but be inside by dark ..."

Josh and his crew gained access to the base of the Needle and started waving the federal agents through the juggernaut to a door at the bottom of the Needle's stem leading to one of the two stairways that climbed some 90 flights to the observation deck. When Adam looked up the stairs, he felt a little weak in the knees. He wasn't sure he could make it. He was already winded just from keeping up with the federals and Natalie.

"I'll go up last," he volunteered to Josh, skipping right over the idea that he might not be invited at all. He felt pretty confident he and Natalie, for sure her anyway, would be, since Josh had taken it upon himself to rescue her in Bellingham and had also waited by the side door in the newsroom. Adam suspected his affection for Natalie was at the root of their access to the inner working of this gaggle of federals, and that worked for him. Wouldn't be the first time a young female reporter gained access to a story because she was, well, a young female reporter.

"I'll follow you up," Natalie said. She pushed the notebook back into her back pocket but held the pen and clicked it annoyingly. She felt ready for anything.

They stepped off to the side and waited for the crew to file past them, Josh at the lead and the other three spread out among them. Adam looked around then and saw at least a dozen young men in T-shirts and genes sitting on the grass of the little park there, hands bound behind their back. A pile of green and brown plaid shirts set off to one side. Three Seattle Police Department cops stood over them, holding shotguns and dressed in full riot gear, helmets, face shields and all. The young men were white. There had been more young white men associations springing up around the country, and Seattle, liberal as it was, had its share of them.

"I wonder what they did?" Natalie said, emphasizing the "they."

"What do you mean?" Adam sidled closer to her, hoping she would but she did not whisper. He did not feel up to being kicked out to fend for himself and then felt a prick of shame for the cowardice.

"I wonder if they did anything," she said more loudly, "or if they were just in the wrong place, dressed the wrong way."

"We may never know," he said and looked around. But that was the only group of prisoners or "individuals in custody" he saw. What system would take care of them now, he couldn't imagine. He suspected summary justice would be the fate of many a poor boy this night.

"It is remarkable, though," Natalie said. "This all happened in one day. I would have expected rioting or even nothing at all, frankly."

"I guess seeing your commanders and political leaders, heads of business, what-have-you dissolve into dust right at your feet will motivate people. This is also the result of lots and lots of training. Everyone here has been training for decades for the next great earthquake or eruption out of Mount Rainier. I don't imagine every city will be quite so prepared to jump into action."

"Yeah, right," she said with a tone of appreciation that Adam appeared to be recovering himself.

"When I saw what was going on out on the Sound," he went on, encouraged that she might actually grow up right before his very eyes, "I thought we were going to find ourselves in the middle of a Hollywood disaster movie. But, I'll be damned, this organization gives me hope."

"Yeah, as long as we stay on the good side of all these men with guns."

He looked around again. "True words. I wonder if we'll see Robert and Grant tonight. I bet they find a place to hole up. I hope they do."

The last of the federals finally grunted by. How the man would make it to the top carrying such a heavy load, Adam couldn't imagine. He stepped onto the first step and hoped he would make it to the top, more out of the embarrassment of dying in front of the kid than any strong desire to cling to life.

VII

Inside the Space Needle's observation deck, which Adam prophetically thought he was unlikely to ever leave or not alive anyway, Natalie flirted with federal agents. Listening from his unaccustomed position of sidekick and discombobulated elder, Adam decided her efforts were professionally motivated. Hard to know for sure when done so well, he sniffed. Meanwhile, Josh and his team had set up a shortwave antenna on the top of the Needle, lacing a coaxial cable through the maze of other wires through to the SkyCity Restaurant which was below the observation deck where Adam, Natalie and other non-officials set up camp. Josh would not let Adam or Natalie onto the lower floor. Adam did get a glimpse when they climbed past the door. The room teamed with feds and cops milling around holding styrofoam coffee cups, several spreading maps out across the dining tables. From what he saw at the stairway door before he closed it, they had enough equipment in piles, boxes of supplies like dried food and pallets of water stacked for a lengthy engagement. They clearly expect the situation to go on for awhile. Adam guessed they'd established the Space Needle as the main place from which they could watch the city, run logistics and communications with better reception on two-way radios between themselves and the enforcement and reaction squads down on the streets. Supplies also lined the walls of the observation deck. Tents had been crowded in for privacy and air matrices pumped up. Adam and Natalie were not offered a tent, and that made him worry that whatever Josh's need of them, or at least him, it wouldn't last long enough to warrant a bed.

Peering out over the city, amid dozens of shiny new skyscrapers, he could see Mannerheim's sky bunker. The mad scientist had sewn together bedsheets and painted in multiple colors "Refuse Nanites." Adam thought that was pretty funny. Refuse nanites. Like Mannerheim knew what the fuck he was talking about.

An hour after making the climb, Josh sent word to Adam and Natalie that he would condescend to an interview once "we get settled." Adam didn't know what he meant by "get settled," but he decided Josh meant for them to stay at least the night, which had begun to seep in across the Northwest. If Adam wanted to make it home, he had just enough time to get there before dark. But, he thought about it, hiking up Capitol Hill to sit in a dark apartment with no food or water, all alone in a dangerous and blacked-out city didn't exactly call out to him. Natalie's family lived in Arizona somewhere, Adam knew, so her best chance of finding out anything about them would be through whatever communications Josh et al. could establish. And, the best chance they had for reporting a story of any depth was to remain embedded here at the heart of what was left of official society, as represented by law enforcement anyway. On the other hand, Josh and his team allowed them to remain for a reason and Adam doubted simple infatuation with Natalie, charming as she was, comprised the main part of that motivation. While he wanted to believe these representatives of the "enforcement state" valued a free society, democracy and journalism, he suspected they wanted the media around for something more along the lines of propaganda, otherwise known as public relations. While he walked along the windows of the observation deck taking in 360 degrees of Seattle over several hours, he suspected that once they had established physical control, they would need to organize a civil body for building local political control. Would there be competing political ideologies, competing goals and, more to the point, competing claims of legitimacy? Undoubtedly. Somewhere out there were civil servants bent on recreating social structure as it had been less than 48 hours ago. Surely not all people with political aspirations had perished in "Stage Two," as Celestine called the decimation in Natalie's video. Whatever Josh's agenda, or the agenda of the person telling Josh what to do, Adam would have to tread carefully. Wandering by the windows that looked directly over the Sound and the sea of quiet ships, the smoke cleared, while pontificating at the city and its inhabitants below, Adam still believed liberal democratic society would reemerge, that the lights would come back on and, after some initial wrangling, the United States of America and all its parts would once again rise out of chaos; that free-market capitalism, the stock exchange, banks, retail and restaurants would grow back, weed-like. He wanted to believe, as Natalie had suggested, that they would take to the airwaves, shortwave airwaves at first, and report the news of the world to a resurgent society desperate for community built around objective, balanced and reliably sourced information. Then when the lights came on and people returned to work, the presses would run once again, thrumming along mighty and strong.

… a lingering delusion, of which Josh would soon disabuse him.

Natalie found him lost in reverie, looking over the crowded Sound. "Hey, Josh is ready for us," she said, happy something, anything, was happening.

"Ready for us?" The phrase stung, like he was now the king of all. Fuck him. Power always acts like it knows what's happening and what needs to be done, but it doesn't. And then it typically fucks things up a lot more with its full head of steam, ramming along like a fucking truck through pedestrians, impoverishing those it doesn't kill outright. "Yeah, well," he said, blocking the litany of swear words racing toward his mouth. "Let's just remember he wants something."

"I know," she said reassuringly.

When did she grow up? What a difference a day at the end of the world makes. He laughed a little and turned to her. "I know you do. Let's go be journalists."

"Fuck yeah." She smiled.

He hadn't seen it in her before, but that smile and that tilt of her head, even with the long brown hair back in a ponytail, she was solid within herself and unafraid. That last bit, that unafraid bit, that came with the person. You can't train that into a reporter. You can't program it, not the way a living, caring, meaningful person can be unafraid to do what needs to be done against all resistance. He had seen it in all kinds of people. Just not everywhere. For instance, he did not see it in Josh though the agent had other survival attributes.

"Okay, here's the deal," Josh said when Natalie and Adam were ushered into a recess of the observation deck where it loomed over Lower Queen Anne. The partial neighborhood sprawled up the base of Queen Anne Hill in the last of dusk, night bearing down on the city. He faced inward from the window in a pool of light, a video camera on a tripod faced him with two banks of filtered lights by its sides. He motioned to the chairs on either side. "If you'll take a seat, we can get started."

Adam stopped in front of the camera, expecting his bulk to gloriously block it's full range. "What deal?"

He looked at Adam with a hard notch to his left eyebrow but then released it. "You know, I misspoke," he said diffidently, quite possibly honestly. "It's been a hell of a day … for all of us to be sure." He pushed his hand through his short white hair and down the back of his neck. "How I meant to say that is, Here's the deal I would like to present to you."

Natalie crossed in front Adam and sat in the seat to Josh's right.

"Deal my ass," she slid the notebook out of her back pocket as she crossed her right leg over left. "You ask your questions and we'll ask ours. Where are you going to show that video, by the way, in the boy's room?"

Josh shot a look right at her, then at me and then at the people next to me. Then he sighed at me and motioned to the chair. "We're keeping records."

"Of the people you have tied up out front, no doubt. Names and …"

"That's the city, Natalie." He faced the camera. "We're not involve with that." Smile. "If you want to pop out there and spend the night with those crews, be my guest." He settled his hands on thighs. "We're keeping a record while we can." He looked back at the camera. "At the end of this interview, we'll seal the card in that camera into a graphite fiber case and put it into a tomb outside under a three meter concrete and steel lid. It is the record of everything that happened today, starting with your rescue and …"

"I do thank you for that," Natalie said.

"… and ending after this *conversation*."

"That bad?" Adam queried, with a bit of twist to his neck and flick of eye glance back at the camera. The entire situation was just too absurd to take seriously. But when it's the end of the world and you have no where to go, what the hell are you going to do?

"Worse than you know," Josh said with a complete lack of pretension. "As you might have guessed, I've asked you here for a reason."

Adam chimed in, "Because you need corroboration, support for what you're about to say."

"Indeed."

"… which is …" Natalie not cutting him any slack.

"I do need your corroboration to convince my colleagues around the world that the machine they call The AI is not finished with us. It's not finished with the world. I need you to tell your stories, Natalie of the Clan and Adam of your conversations with Mannerheim, so that we stand a chance of responding to the next wave of disruption."

"Next wave?" Natalie and Adam said in tandem, making eye contact.

Natalie said, "For just a second there I thought you called me 'Natalie of The Clan,' but I get it now."

"That can be the name of your new band," Adam said and snorted.

Josh sat back and let his shoulders fall. "You're right to laugh." Hands up, stick-up style. "Almost no one will survive this and so laugh away. I mean it."

"Okay, we give," Adam struggled back a guffaw. He didn't know why he felt like laughing, exhaustion he guessed. "How can there be a next wave? What will this next wave do?"

"Okay," Josh dried the palms of his hands on his thighs. Natalie poised her notebook. "I have been with Celestine, Olivas and Gaines for more than a year. I'm going to lay it all out, though I'll miss a thing or two. I was assigned to an undercover investigation of Olives and Gaines once it became clear by their conversations at their respective jobs that they were involved in a possible, not sure what we called it … Adam," he looked to his left but not right at him, "attempted to download my notes and files on this case but we were not able to retrieve them. They were called a coding cult or a hacking club or other things. Michelle Olivas and Betty Gaines were physics graduate students with significant programing algorithm talent who met at the Pacific Northwest National Laboratory at the Hanford Nuclear Reservation. They had been a part of the National Nuclear Security Administration's Graduate Fellowship Program designed to train students in Nuclear Security and Stockpile Stewardship. They met Celestine through Mannerheim's lab that had

Department of Energy funding to work on models for understanding the viability of our nuclear warheads without blowing them up. That's very complicated computational math and requires some significant computing capacity. I don't know exactly how they met, but they clearly have similar interests and talents. I joined the Clan, went through initiation and worked my way into their chief electrical engineer position, such as it was.

"I have traveled with them all over the world setting up Clan bases, session clubs. Natalie saw and wrote about an initiation ceremony. But before I can explain that, I have to go into some background and technical details, some of which come from my conversations with Celestine, Olivas and Gaines, whose recounting of events is only slightly less trustworthy than Mannerheim, whom I believe my two colleagues here have also met."

"We're not colleagues," Adam interjected. "Just for the record."

"And this is for the record, the final record. So fine."

Adam breathed in to interject a question, but Josh barged on.

"First! We don't know where Celestine and the other two have gone, so if anyone here knows it'd be great if you said so."

He paused and looked at Natalie, who shrugged and turned down the corners of her mouth.

"Well, then, here's the deal: We don't have much time to convince everyone else in the world that its not over. The AI, which no one believes is real according to my preliminary conversations with my fellow surviving investigators across the country, the machine is going to dismantle all of our electronics and then all of our infrastructure and then all of our cities. We have a very short window to set up lines of communication and security that do not rely on any form of technology. And, just for the record, I need you two to help me convince the world of this. I don't know how long we have before our radios fail and then our guns. We're going to be reduced to territories we can protect with our hands in just a matter of hours or days at the most."

"How do you know that?" Adam shot at the camera.

"Like I said, I have been following them for more than a year and seen thousands of sessions. And …" he visibly shrank in his chair, "I may have triggered this aggressive response."

"How could you have started all of this?" Natalie asked.

"Well," he said to each of them and then back at the camera, "there are two types of nanites currently reeking havoc in our world. The one's that Celestine says she reprogramed and the ones she says The AI created when it escaped confinement. We definitely know there are two types, what we're not sure of is where they came from. We only have her claims for where they came from, and many people, my *colleagues*," he said the word with a defensiveness that sounded to Adam plaintive, wounded even, "don't believe they came from where Celestine claims they came from. Even Mannerheim, whose work Celestine says The AI emerged from, doesn't think there is an artificial intelligence running around out there somewhere. Some, including Mannerheim, think Celestine made at least some of them in one of his labs and then got a lab in China, Russia or Iran even, to take over the project and mass produce them and they got out of control. They say once we figure out how to stop replication and can spread that chemical agent around, like bug spray, we'll shut them down, reduce their numbers, and take back our world. Some people think the nanites come from aliens, from extraterrestrials bent on taking over the world and terraforming Earth to eliminate the dominant species and make the planet fit for habitation by them."

"What do you think?" Natalie asked, knowing what his answer would be, it seemed to Adam.

"I think, I believe Celestine's story," he shifted his position from talking at the camera to just talking, not really to an audience, more like remembering something out loud. "During my initiation, an event just like the one Natalie reported, I experienced something I cannot explain without the proposition of the nanites she uses being what she said they are, a machine for replicating humans. I felt … plugged in …" he visibly picked over his words before saying them "… to a very large system. A system built on … computation."

Natalie and Adam shifted their chairs to face him as much as the camera. So, when Josh finished, he saw her face as it changed from amusement to personal connection. They had shared a history, however recent.

"That's my subjective reason for believing what Celestine has said about the AI. But, I also have some objective reasons to believe it. I sent a memo back to Washington explaining the technical feat that she and the Clans had accomplished. I stated her claims and background story about the AI, but I added that we needed to do more tests on the nanites. The two kinds we were studying in our labs had different configurations, but we had no idea how the two seemingly simple differences, folds like a protein is folded, controlled behavior. We needed more data and more time on a super computer to run models. The more we looked, the more we found. The nanites made by The AI were everywhere, in every country where we had agents, in the dust on the table, inside phones and computer farms, just everywhere we got a sample and put it under an electron microscope, there they were. Those nanites were different than the ones in people, however. We had lots of samples but didn't know what they were up to. Mannerheim explained it best in his classified paper that their presence everywhere was like an industrial accident or unexpected result of an industrial process. He said we only had to look at the worldwide dispersal of polyvinyl chloride to see how this could happen. He even argued that these nanites were the result of evolution and that Celestine had found a way to change them so they would bind to human tissues. It's possible, he said, that they do nothing. Our, those compounds could kill all humans. That paper got the attention of many officials in Washington and they wanted to run more experiments particularly on the nanites that bonded with human tissues. They established a grand jury to …"

"HA!" Adam jumped up. "I fucking knew it!"

"Jesus, you scared the shit out of me," Natalie panted with a hand against her chest.

"Shit. Sorry. Just …"

"Yes," Josh said, "a grand jury had been convened to review our warrants and arrests. Not normal procedure, but the president's chief of staff wanted some legal oversight. Anyway," he motioned for Adam to hold off on another outburst, "the night Natalie crashed a session, Mannerheim was there because he wanted to watch an infection. Celestine wouldn't let him unless he agreed to be infected, which he would not do.

"By that time I had told my commanders at the Cyber Threat Intelligence Integration Center about the eight Clan members roaming the country documenting it with the hope of uploading their experience into the collective simulation. I said they could be detained without the majority of the group finding out, possibly for weeks, since they were not staying in regular contact. The grand jury agreed and they were grabbed in Las Vegas then taken to The Nevada National Security Site, previously called the Nevada Test Site. That is a United States Department of Energy reservation located in southeastern Nevada, about 65 miles northwest of Las Vegas. So, I caused them to become the Missing 8 or M8. I did not suggest and would have argued against the experiments run on them. That was also far outside of the actions allowed by the grand jury …"

"And you all wanted us to stay clear of Celestine?" Natalie said, while writing.

"And got that bullshit prior restraint order," Adam sat back, not satisfied so much as relieved that he was not crazy, though he felt some satisfaction too. "You had Mannerheim's lawyers deliver it to further muddy the waters."

"The situation spun out of control once Mannerheim started meddling."

"So, it is his fault?" Natalie said.

"No. He just didn't help. Look, I had volunteered for several experiments myself, but you can't mess with the nanites once they are inside a person without, it became painfully clear to me, killing the person. They can be extracted in small amounts, but using MRIs or other X-ray tools to mess with them will eventually kill the host. And that's what they did. They killed those kids experimenting on them. When they were discovered by Clan members who had set out to find them and it became clear what had happened to them, The AI activated those nanites that had not bonded with human tissues. The AI's nanites, let's just call them that, break down anything with an electronic or chemical charge. They consume that energy by breaking apart the compounds holding it."

"Why didn't everyone die?" Natalie.

"Statistics. We had every expert we could think of examining them, and it was the statistical physicists who got it right. They all agreed that these things were spreading in complex statistical patterns. Self-assembling machines. Some people had more of them in them than others …"

"The people with power." Adam said.

"That's right. Once the nanites were activated, they destroyed those people first. We think The AI either turned them back off to keep the rest of us alive, and or set them to another purpose. Whatever they are up to, they are all still out there. We've done nothing to stop their spread or limit their actions."

"What purpose?" Adam felt he was getting the picture then. Josh had said The AI wasn't done fucking with the world and now he understood what he was getting at.

"For the dismantling of our industrial world," Natalie jumped in. "Celestine said The AI was going to build machines from the things we've built to get itself off Earth. It eliminated the humans most capable of threatening its agenda and then switched back to that agenda."

"Maybe it thought we were getting too close to understanding how the nanites worked when it saw what we had done to the M-8," Josh said. "Maybe the experiments on the M-8 were just lucky timing and The AI triggered the nanites when it reached some statistical level of certainty of accomplishing its goals. We just don't know what the relationship is, but the simple juxtaposition tells me they are related."

"Maybe Celestine trigged it," Adam said. "Maybe she has more control over what is going on than we're giving her credit for."

"We're giving her credit for plenty," Josh said.

"She thinks she's saving the world," Natalie said.

"When did she say that?" Adam looked at her surprised. "I thought she was working with The AI."

Natalie blushed.

"Wait a second," Adam said and stood up facing them. "What aren't you telling me?"

"You do seem to stumble into everything," Natalie said.

Adam blanched at her positioning herself outside of his efforts. "I stumble …"

"Let me explain," she said.

"Are you working with him now?" Adam thrust a thumb at Josh, who seemed amused.

"No no. He just got me out of there after …"

"Her, uh, infection," Josh hesitated. "I didn't know what they would do. I'd called in backup to get myself out of there and took her with us. Then …"

"Then?"

"Then we had a conversation with Celestine under, um, unique circumstances," Natalie said. "Basically, she contacted us through some others … The main thing, Adam, is that she says they are in a race to get as many people infected with her reprogramed nanites they can and then upload everyone into a simulation inside The AI."

"That's the dummest goddamn thing I've ever heard." Adam then laughed hard.

"Whatever she thinks will happen," Josh talked over Adam's laughter, "if any of this is true the way she says it is, then she betrayed the human race. That's the point. Natalie and I agree on that. She betrayed us all."

"At some point," Natalie said. "She had to have known what The AI was up to and she didn't tell anyone."

"Did you confront her with that?" Adam, despite his efforts to shut down his emotions, felt betrayed and alone.

"Indeed we did," Josh said.

"Well, what did she say?" He walked to a window. Darkness ruled the city now.

"That humans were doomed anyway," Natalie said. "That no one could stop The AI."

"I could really really use a drink"

"We've got a stash," Josh said.

"Never mind that," Natalie said, somberly. Adam spun to contradict her. "We could have tried to change its mind or shut down the nanites," she spoke over him. "Obviously, if the M8 caused The

AI to act, then it did so because it had to have been vulnerable in some way. I said it wasn't just her choice to make."

"She knew humanity's future was at stake, and she should have reached out to the rest of the world," Josh added. He pointed at a box next to a pile of rucksacks.

"What did she say to that?" Adam opened the box and slid a bottle of vodka out. "Isn't this just crazy. I mean …" He opened and drank from the bottle.

Josh joined him by the window and took a drink.

"Well," Natalie said, "if you can't beat 'em"

"She said no one would have believed her," Josh said handing her the bottle. "That even if The AI was vulnerable, that was no guarantee it could be beaten."

"Here!" Natalie handed the bottle to Adam without drinking. She went back to the chair and took her phone out of her purse and turned it on. "I recorded some of it. I have just a bit of battery left though …" She scrubbed through the audio. "Here."

"Our only chance," the voice of the medium echoing slightly, "is to join the AI. It is allowing us time and space in its computational world to live in simulations ..."

"That's not Celestine's voice, is it?" Adam asked.

Natalie paused the playback.

"I only heard her once, but ..."

"Right," Natalie said. "It's her words through a, well, through a medium. She tuned in like a radio."

"She was speaking through this other person."

"I'd seen it before," Josh said. "They use a charged ball of their micro machines to connect ... just listen. It's her words."

"We think," Natalie added.

"Right." Adam. "How would you know?"

"Well, it could all be a ruse but either way, she's involved. This person wouldn't just make stuff up ..."

"A clan member wouldn't," Josh confirmed.

Natalie touched the play button.

"... It has allowed me to make changes in a small percentage of its micro-machines that copy how cells interact in our brains and bodies. It doesn't copy the cells themselves. They record the interactions and that's what gets replicated. You've been there. You've seen it. It is consciousness. It is human. We have to upload as many people as we can so that we have some chance of survival, even if it is just survival in a simulation. We brought this on ourselves. We so corrupted our environment that billions were going to die as a result of cataclysmic climate change anyway. We are facing an extinction level event. The AI has run millions of scenarios and not one model has human civilization lasting a thousand years. Most of them have humans going extinct within that time frame. So a few billion now killed by the AI, or a few billion killed five hundred years from now ... I chose to save human consciousness while we had a chance, this one chance to catch a ride with The AI as it spreads throughout the galaxy and eventually the universe. Whoever chooses to stay here will have to live without technology, but they can live in small bands that reflect the best outcome of climate disaster in a few of the future models. But, eventually, even they will be wiped out by a meteor or solar flare. There just isn't enough time left for humans to take themselves off planet, to get our unique intelligence off planet, but The AI can and The AI is."

"You sold us all for a fantasy?" Natalie said on the recording. By the window, she took a drink.

"I sold us all for a fantastic future when we had no future left," Celestine's medium said coldly, almost bitterly. "This is not the only war we will have to fight. We lost the war for our planet and our biological future, but the next one we lose will mean our complete extinction."

Natalie turned the recording off and put the phone back into her purse. "She just goes on excusing her actions. 'We already live in a simulation' and 'Biological humans will never be able to travel far enough in space to reach another planet, but The AI with us in it, like in a can. Our limit in space travel isn't speed. It's time and we don't have enough.'"

They stood in silence for a moment. Adam holding the bottle.

"We both," Josh started, "… anyone who has gone through an infection ceremony, experiences a bit of that simulated world. The ceremony is where she reprograms The AI's nanites through an interface with her simulated self and the AI. That's what's going on under the jar. When they come out and are charged electrically as they enter your body, you have a brief connection back to the simulation. She isn't the only one who can do it. There are thousands, possibly tens of thousands of people leading sessions now across the planet."

"Did she explain how you get into the simulation?" A voice from behind the camera and the bank of lights. It was Robert. He stood to the left of the camera, within the edge of the light, face and hands covered in soot. He had switched from his suit to all-black clothes. Grant sat on the ground behind him, covered in soot and dressed in black. He held a camera in his lap, fingering the controls.

Natalie and Adam had the same impulse and turned toward the window. Silence reigned with the dark.

"That's the catch," Natalie said turning back toward Robert. She took the bottle from Adam and walked over to him and Grant and held it out to them. Robert took it. "Except for those trained to run sessions, who have simulations already in the system and are able to connect with them during the sessions, no one else will ever really know if there is a simulation at all or it's just a lie. The nanites in our bodies," she motioned to Josh and herself, "will be uploaded through one of a couple million open ports that The AI has allowed into the Internet, which is itself now. You either agree to never wake up here after the uploading or live out your biological life without ever knowing your simulated self or even if it is really there."

"Chilling," Adam said. "Wow. So it could all just be some bizarre religious-like fantasy after all." He went back to his chair.

"Exactly," Josh said. "That's why we need to use what time we have with working communication systems, such as they are, to warn everyone about the fact that The AI is going to dismantle our world and leave us to live as primitive people, for as long as we can."

"What about the Clans?" Adam said. "Shouldn't we warn them about the Clans?"

"If we can convince people that there is an AI, that it's going to use our world as a jumping off point to get to the stars and enough of us survive the next few years, perhaps we'll know enough to know what to do about the sessions. I just think we have to let people decide for themselves until then. I mean, what would you tell them? Abandon all hope?"

Adam didn't have a response and no one else did either. Robert waved the bottle at Natalie, who took it and handed it to Adam.

"Well," Adam said and took a drink. "We'll do what we do. That is if you're still a journalist," he shot at Natalie.

"Of course I am, Adam. What the fuck else would I be?"

Adam didn't respond to her but said to Josh "We'll have something for broadcast in an hour."

A woman in an FBI jacket walked up to Josh and whispered in his ear. His face went slack and his eyes fell to the floor. "When?" The woman whispered. "Casualties?" The woman whispered. Josh put his hands on his head. The woman took out her semi-automatic pistol and showed that she could not make the action work. "When?"

"Just after," she said. "It's widespread, according to our police and military contacts."

"Well, that levels the playing field anyway," he said and took a deep breath.

She walked away. Josh motioned to have the video stopped.

"Someone detonated a nuclear bomb in the sky over Nevada." He said it and then laughed with a tinge of hysteria mixed in: "It was us! Someone in a federal agency manually set it off without bothering to wonder if that really was a good idea."

"Deaths?" Robert asked. He took his notebook from his back pocket.

"I'll say," Josh said and walked past the lights, which then went out.

VIII

Standing at the mirror over the bathroom sink, the only room with privacy enough to explore her feelings or rather her lack of feelings, Natalie examined her face in the glass. Running her fingers lightly over skin, she neither saw nor felt any difference. Events had kept her rolling along, like being caught in a cycle of waves and unable to fully take stock of where she was, let alone what had happened. But here she was, the same skin, features and hair. But that stuff was inside of her, or that's what she's supposed to believe. Nothing felt different. She put her face close to the glass. Nothing in her eyes. The only indication that something inside of her had changed was her dead affect. Her lack of emotions. She felt thin, light inside. Could be shock, still. But what were those things doing inside of her if they were in fact inside? She ran water and splashed her face, wetting her shirt. The cool water felt like cool water and the beads running down her skin under her shirt, felt like water trickles. She pushed her mind to think of her mother. She pictured her face and imagined her dissolving, like those kids had watched their father die … can a person make herself feel something? A bead of water on her check suddenly became absorbed into her skin, fast. Shit, she thought. That's not normal right? She felt the skin beneath her throat and shirt collar and edge of her bra. Dry. She splashed more water on her shirt. In a few seconds it and her skin dried. Oh shit, she said, but she could not raise a feeling of panic or fear or even awe. She flexed her hand closed and punched the glass, which snapped into three pieces hanging in the chrome frame. She felt the pain alright. A sharp sting and deep echo in the bones of her hand. Blood oozed from a cut on the tallest knuckle. Then it disappeared into her skin and the cut sealed shut and the pain ended. Well, f…

    A bang on the door startled her.

    "You okay in there?" Robert's voice. "I heard a noise."

    "Fine," she yelled. "Just dropped something."

    She quickly opened the door and stepped out, facing Robert.

"I …" she started, Robert's unshaven face evinced sincere concern. "The …" But what could she say that wouldn't cause everyone to panic and treat her like a sick person.

"What, Natalie? You look a little worried."

"I do?" She felt relief. She showed emotion anyway. "I'm fine."

He looked around her at the mirror. "If you say so."

"I say let's get back to work."

Natalie walked around him toward the others.

Darkness had fallen and many had in fact abandoned all hope, and for many more there was none to be had. When darkness fell in the observation deck, when Josh's crew shut off the lights, if that's why the lights went out, Adam felt a surge of panic that bordered on a loss of hope himself. In just one cataclysmic day, their society had come apart. Once the guns no longer worked, the city had become as silent as death itself.

A glow light crackled, shook in a blur and fell to the floor at their feet. Natalie and Robert joined Grant and Adam around it. They all sat on the floor, so the light would shine more brightly on their notebooks.

"Okay," Adam said. "What have we got?"

They didn't need to wonder what their jobs were. They didn't need to wonder what they would do next or why, Natalie thought. This purpose felt like something. A flash of satisfaction coursed through her before dissipating. Working by the greenish glow of a stick of chemicals with only pen and paper as their tools, pen and paper and a dozen rolls of film that would need processing, they set out to tell the stories of a city, and apparently a world and its people, under attack by a power that had yet to reveal itself. So, we'll put together the clues and the guesses of experts. Where would we publish? How would we publish? We'll figure that out later.

"The lighting sucked and it's been a long time since I shot film," Grant said suddenly, loudly. Photographers. "But I think I have some great photos." He looked around, his eyes white and lips garish in black face and in the light of the glow stick. "If I can get back to the office, I can develop them. We still have a darkroom."

Robert snorted. "Grant. We can't go back out there. We barely made it back here."

"First light," Adam said. "First thing, we'll try to negotiate with whoever is holding that part of town to get in. I'd like to pick up more supplies, too."

"I want to write a story about Celestine, more of a profile than a news story," Natalie said. "I have enough battery left to write out some quotes from my interviews with her."

"If that was her," Adam said.

"I'll explain that but it was her. Also, I'll make it clear that her claims are unsupported," she looked at Adam defensively, "but what we know for sure is that she is the head of an organization that is surfacing just as city, state and federal governments are collapsing into their military and police forces."

"I like it," Adam said. "It's a good story just on the human-interest level. Tomorrow we'll know more about the state of our governments, so for now just make it about her and what you saw with the Clans. Is she making herself into a religious-type figure?

You know, the only person who has access to god, who knows god, who knows god's purpose? Or, is she what she says?"

"Thank you!" Natalie said enthusiastically, suddenly that young reporter again. "I'll try that angle." Pride, too strong, made her flush and she concentrated to keep the emotion from brining tears to her eyes. Damn, she thought. Like puberty all over again.

"Robert?"

"The state of the city. It's a war zone out there."

"What do you have?"

"Mostly what I witnessed but also plenty of quotes."

"My photos …"

"I know, Grant," Adam said, sympathetically. "We'll figure out a way to get them published. So, like what Robert?"

He had filled two reporter notebooks with his scrawl. He opened one and then the other.

"We might be able to see one thing from here," he said and pointed out into the dark beyond the windows. He stood up and walked out of the light circle.

"What?" Adam said.

"Come here you guys."

They got up and carefully walked into the dark, to the windows. Robert found Adam's shoulder and pointed him left toward Capitol Hill. Then he saw it, two yellow blooms. They had to be major fires to stand out so distinctly from this distance.

"Do you know what they are?" Adam asked.

"I think so."

"I'm going to get started," Natalie said and walked back to the glow stick.

When Adam turned back to the window, he told Robert: "You look pretty silly in black face."

"Tell me about it. Man, it was scary out there and the cops ... I see Natalie has a boyfriend ... Anyway, here's a rundown of what we saw. Remember those groups from the suburbs and outer suburbs that were running around in red T-shirts?"

"The anti-gay and anti-immigrant pricks?"

"Yeah them. They set those fires. They had a bunch of men and women cornered into a few buildings, several hundred people had gathered on roof tops, gathering hand weapons, knives, clubs anything they could use in a fight. They either put on white shirts or wrapped white sheets or towels around themselves, you heard the cops going around telling people to put out white sheets if they need help? Ha. The red shirts were massed across the street from the buildings. There are hundreds of them. So the white shirts are staying on the roofs and have barricaded the doors and stairwells. The red shirts were trying to get close enough to the buildings to set them on fire while we watched from the top of a bar across the street. For as long as we were there, the occupants of the buildings were putting the fires out as fast as they were being set and warding off all but the craziest attacks with bricks, plants, coffee cups, whatever they could throw. Looks like they lost the fight."

"Where are the cops?"

"The cops have abandoned Capitol Hill. One sergeant said they were out-matched and are focusing their forces in neighborhoods where they stand a chance of saving lives. One home owner in Madrona said residents had collected cash and jewels to buy protection. The sergeant defended abandoning the Hill for the surrounding neighborhoods because the property damage on the Hill was already extensive. He said they had no way of regaining control. He said they tried flash-bang grenades and lots of tear gas but were harming the residents and defenders as much as the red shirts, so they decided to move out. He says they'll go back in the daylight and retake the neighborhood. When we walked off the hill, the farther we got the more things settled down. The Navy's soldiers have moved off the water into downtown and are securing the core of the city block by block. One officer said they might be able to help the cops take back Capitol Hill. They weren't making arrests so much as yelling once and then shooting people on sight, it seemed to me. One building had been evacuated for a fire and those people were cornered into an alley without blankets or water, huddled amid the garbage bins. I have the notes. We came back from there under escort. I know one of the sergeants. She walked us out of there and handed us off to the federal agents here. When we told them who we were looking for, they let us in."

"Did you see my note at the paper?"

"We didn't make it back to the paper, but when I said Josh's name, a guess, that got us in."

"Well, write up what you have. There are some yellow note pads in that box. Try not to make it a list or on second thought maybe it is a list of scenes, the battles you saw. What narrative there is is pretty obvious. I'll work on getting us some way to publish. Who knows what tomorrow will bring."

DAY FIVE

'Everybody' was normally the complex unity of the mass and the divergent, specialized minorities. Nowadays, 'everybody' is the mass alone."

— José Ortega y Gasset.

I

"Farewell Earth?"

That's the big headline they decided to run the morning of the fifth day, after the usual handwringing and debate about using a question mark for such a momentous front page. Shouldn't we be more definitive? Adam thought so. Robert, Natalie and Grant, when he would weigh in, thought so. But what other two-word headline could they use on their eleven-by-seventeen-inch single sheet of paper?

That's the size they were stuck with, and one side only. Adam felt amazed they would have a paper at all. Grant said he knew a guy with several old hand-cranked mimeograph printers that used wax stencil paper. Apparently, the old communist had gotten ahold of a printer used in World War II by the Yugoslavian Partizans called the "The National Liberation Army" during Nazi occupation, which definitely made the journalists want to use that one. He said the guy, Abraham Rader, worked out of Pike Place Market, where he mostly lived as well. So, Grant and Robert got escorted first to the old *Seattle Daily Record* office, which had been ransacked for god knows what or why, in order to develop Grant's rolls of film. The old dark room had been turned into a closet that, while ransacked, retained its boxes of chemicals for development. He developed a few rolls of negatives, luckily he had thought to use black and white film for part of the night, since he could only enlarge the negatives in black and white. At the Market, they found a few thousand refugees and Rader, who said he would help them if they could get the feds to help him etc etc. All of which went down by 9 AM, when they came back with the photos and size of paper the printer would use. After some mumbling about having to gut the stories down to just a few hundred words each and select just one photo … Adam and Natalie started on the design and headlines. She was proving to be very good at focussing stories down to a headline. Her own story done, focused and clear, explained Celestine's claims and set the scene in the basement of the house and then the cave in succinct active phrases.

He found only one sentence to unjumble and she'd been appreciative.

Robert, on the other hand, had argued over every word change and cut. He even briefly argued against using a slammer headline at all.

"Maybe we don't even need a headline!" he exclaimed, as they drank coffee and sat around the folding table and chairs dug out of a storage room. "I mean, it's not like we have to produce a paper the way we used to do it. We don't have any bosses, that we know of. We don't have ads or probably even an audience. I mean, we're just doing this for the record in case there is a record, and I'd like to run more of my story. Not to mention that the cops have sent out a reconnaissance team up to Capitol Hill and promised to give me a update when they get back."

"An update?" Adam laughed incredulous. "We're not getting into any updates. Once we get this designed, we're sending in the photo and text so we can get the fucking thing printed before the entire world shuts down. It's amazing that old piece of shit commie printer still works at all, if it does."

"Jesus," Natalie said, shooting her hands out at Robert and Adam. "Calm down."

Grant got up and took his film over to to a window to use as a light table, second guessing the choices he'd already made. "I'll pick a couple more."

"Doesn't anyone have any fucking ears!" Adam bellowed. Lack of sleep, no booze, shitty coffee and, oh yeah, the end of the world was wringing the joy right out of his morning.

"Jesus!" Natalie yelled at him. She was having another flash of emotion, this time jangled anger at Adam for yelling and cussing.

"You have already invoked him!" Adam yelled back.

"Your heart! Remember?" She laughed loudly, surprising herself as much as Adam.

"Oh, fuck his heart," Robert said, shoving himself away from the table.

Then it hit Adam like a … like a nothing. His chest and arms didn't hurt. The ringing in his ears was gone. He felt strong, light even. He didn't want to say anything because he wondered if perhaps he wasn't actually dying right then and this is what it felt like. He'd never died before so how did he know?

"Robert," Natalie laughed again, more controlled this time. "Robert. Come back. Come back."

Robert circled the table.

Natalie took over the conversation and once again the confidence in her tone and clarity of her emotions struck Adam. She spoke steady and strong, "Let's don't reinvent the newspaper today. Let's do that tomorrow. Today, I want us to make a newspaper, the old kind, one with a big headline, a big photo, subheads and then analysis."

"Well," Adam snorted, "I don't know where you came from, but that's exactly right. That's what we're going to do."

Natalie smiled brightly, her cheeks flushed with pleasure at having been declared correct in front of the other kids. For that brief moment, the old-young Natalie had returned.

"Thank you," she said. "Robert?"

"Fine. Fuck it. I don't know what I can possibly cut. I can't cut any more. You'll just have to do it. I'm done. I need to get out of here for awhile. See if I can't tag along on a patrol or something just in case the world comes back. Jesus, I hate being cooped up!" He stood, swung his coat off the chair and over his shoulder. On the way out he stopped at his backpack, dug out a notebook and several pens. He shoved the notebook into his back pocket and started for the door.

"Okay, Robert," Adam said. "If we need you we'll call you at your other office … oh wait!" But Robert had left. His other office was the Five Point, a dark and rowdy dive bar. Adam doubted he would find any booze available anywhere in town, but perhaps the tattooed, black-haired crew there had fought off the hoards of thirsty cops and survived the night intact. He certainly hoped so, for Robert's sake. They were the closest thing he had to a family outside the newsroom.

"Well sweetheart, looks like it's just you and me now," Adam blanched at his own words. He regretted saying that while he was saying it. He had no idea why he was saying it and felt a bit lost.

"Okay," she stretched the word. "I've never been called sweetheart by a boss before, but there's a first time for everything!"

"By the way," Adam said. "How do you feel?"

"I feel fine. I mean, you know, it's the end of the world and all, but I feel fine."

"You're not worried about your parents or siblings?"

"Oddly, no. I just know they are okay and that I will see them again."

"Okie Dokie, then." Adam remembered that she was not only young but Catholic as well. "Let's just do the question headline. I can't imagine anything else. *End is Nigh ... World Attacked ... Death, Destruction* is too long ... *WTF?* is fun, I grant you, but ..."

"I was just kidding."

"This one!" Grant said.

"Grant. I love you from the bottom of my heart." Adam got to his feet and took the film from the photographer's hands and set it down on top of the photos he had already enlarged. "I want you to go to your family now before it's too late. Josh will send an escort so you can get across the military barricade, I bet. I don't even know how you'll get to Vashon. I know you are worried. So, go ahead."

Adam meant it, too. He really did want Grant to be with his family. He also really wanted him the hell out of his hair.

"Yeah, you're right. Just not sure …"

"Please, Grant," Adam said, his face growing hotter and hotter, "before my brain explodes all over the windows."

"Yeah," he said and started toward the stairway door. "Besides," he turned and smiled at Adam through his big beard, "I'm out of film, and it would haunt me forever if I finally saw your head explode and couldn't shoot it."

And then Grant walked out of their lives. For just about a half a heart beat, an emotion, a sorrow, a sadness, whatever you call it, one of those emotions Adam didn't feel very often, tried to crawl up his throat. He quickly coughed it out, a polite little hack.

Natalie and Adam finished the layout and cut the stories down to about the right number of words with several sentences marked that could come out or go back in depending on the type. Natalie had graciously cut her story down to allow more of Robert's. She said she liked short stories. The only argument she and Adam had at the last minute, briefly, was over a sentence about the Clan sessions. She wanted to tell people about them and Adam said that would be propaganda. She started to argue her usual line about how the business had changed and then they both laughed, long and hard.

Apparently, as Adam understood it, Rader would use an old manual typewriter on the stencil screen. Grant also said Rader was a genius artist when it came to representing a photo in a stencil. That's partly why Grant picked the photo he did. He certainly could shoot. In the photo, the red shirts had just thrown several molotov cocktails high in the air, flames boiling out as they spun and arched toward the foot of a building across the street. At the top of the building, several white shirts showed just above the crest of the rook, returning fire, bricks and a small television. In the distance, a single cop sprinted away from the melee. Adam doubted the cop would make it into the stencil, but the rest of the photo would be quite supreme in a garish, simple style. Rader said they could possibly get several hundred pages printed before the stencil crapped out.

Natalie took the copy, photo and layout. She'd bring back the pages and they'd distribute them somewhere, somehow. Meanwhile, Adam agreed to sit with Josh at the shortwave radio, take notes on what their fellow radio jockeys reported and help him explain to all who would hear that the world had not yet stopped dying.

II

The consensus of the world, as Adam gleaned it from the conversations he and Josh had on shortwave radio, resembled the conclusions they also had arrived at: Whatever had killed so many and shut down civilization would likely continue its work, and no one knew what that meant or where it might end. Apparently, at least two other countries, France and Pakistan, had set off nuclear bombs. Adam could not get out of his interlocutors a clear reason the assholes in Nevada had set off a nuke in the air, because everyone who had anything to do with the detonation were killed by it or under a building somewhere. Most guessed that the reasoning must have been similar to the French: If they could disrupt the nanites with a massive burst of radiation and energy, perhaps they could take over some electronic systems and fight back. This line of thinking had also explained why several of the biggest ships and an aircraft carrier had been set on fire in Puget Sound. That didn't work either, but the nukes did kill a few million people outright and likely tens of millions more would die within months and certainly years from radiation poisoning.

The Navy, Marines and Special Forces fighters had gained control of Puget Sound and other major docks and waterways along the coasts of the United States, their officers reported on the shortwave conference.

"If nothing else, those nukes gave those tens of millions a reason to get to a Clan session and get uploaded into the simulation," Adam mused.

The comment was met with silence. While some had reported they had heard the rumors, even those leaders thought something so fantastically out of the considered range of possibility was unlikely.

"Look," one commander out of the British Columbia enclave said, "we're *in* circumstances that would have been called farfetched just a few days ago. True. But, a simulation of the complexity you're talking about is another magnitude of sophistication above what we're experiencing now."

"The reports coming from our teams out on the streets, however," Josh took up the argument, "show the Clan message is resonating. Uplaod-hopefuls have swamped both professional sports venues South of Down Town, the SODO neighborhood, and the two at the Seattle Center visible to us here in the Space Needle. Those are Key Arena and Memorial Stadium. The Clans must have taken control of these venues in the first hours of the blackout."

"How are they holding them? There must be local forces trying to regain access to these important venues," said the U.S. Secretary of State, Norman Pearce.

A testimony to how vapid the federal position had become, Adam put in his notebook, Pearce's was the only government leadership position spared during the second wave.

"It's not clear anyone is trying or has tried to take control," Josh said. "We can see long lines but no disruptions. We suspect the people in line now are Clan members. How their message will be received by the average person who has had no connection with The Clans is unclear …"

"I'm ordering you to take back those buildings," said Pearce suddenly, as if he had been sitting on a sharp stick of agitation.

"Uh," Josh said. He waited but not one else cut in, everyone wondering if the old lines of authority still held. "Well," he stretched out the word, "I don't have the manpower. I'm not sure we can sustain our position in the Space Needle even. We've lost …"

"Oh, goddamn it!" Pearce yelled. "Organize the local officers. Talk to the Navy. What do you say, boys, ready to help us take back those buildings?"

"I tell you what," said a rough voice with clear authority on the radio, "we get though this, whatever it is, you can put me in jail. But right now we've all lost a lot of friends to this thing, and we're not going to go confronting the tens of thousands of people. Hell man, our weapons don't even work."

"This is the United States of …"

"Hey!" a woman's voice cut through Pearce's beginning rant. "We're seeing the same thing here in Minneapolis, so either send us some real help or get the fuck off the air."

"How dare …" his voice cutoff just as a clump! sound filled the speaker.

"This is Sean Read. I've relieved the Secretary of his duties."

Deep silence followed his announcement. Adam and Josh looked at each other and then back at the radio set.

"Is the Secretary going to be okay," a tentative voice seeped into the static.

"Nope," Sean said. "Over and out."

No one else cut in. In fact, it dawned on Adam that the murder of the Secretary of State would go unpunished and that the lack of outrage or threats of arrest spoke a chilling fact about the new normal: There is no central control anywhere, at least not of the human kind.

Josh sat before the mic stand, finger resting on the push-to-talk button, nodding his head, lost in his own thoughts. Adam got out of his seat, lit a cigarette and started rummaging through boxes. He found a couple cans of beer in one and walked them over to the table where Josh sat staring at the radio.

"Here," he said and tapped Josh on the shoulder with the beer. "If you don't like warm beer, don't worry. I do." He popped the top and took a long swig.

"Thanks," Josh said. He took the beer. "Every time I think we've reached the bottom, the stasis or basement or whatever, the floor gives out." He opened the beer and strolled out of the Observation Deck, back and shoulders straight like a weight had been lifted off.

Watching him walk out, Adam too felt an incongruous tingle of freedom mixed with bewilderment—they were on their own now. Looking out over downtown, his beer empty, he wondered When was the last time a human being lived in a world without massive, overpowering central governments controlling every aspect of human interaction? Maybe that was why all those people had lined up for something they almost certainly knew nothing about except the promise they would leave behind a world doomed to chaos, degradation and likely victimization. It's like they were prepped for it. Adam next poured a healthy portion of vodka into a glass. He took up the yellow notepad and began taking notes for an essay: The largest companies in the world, those handful of tech and internet-based companies that employed hundreds of millions of well-educated people, promised a utopia of excitement and fulfillment, in which machines performed all drudgery and new medicines cured all diseases. And we have all bought into it in bad faith, knowing it can't really be true, while watching just the opposite happen all around us: Environmental degradation, crippling bouts of heat and droughts every summer, hot winters punctuated by rain bombs that flood cites and suburbs military drone strikes, mass incarceration of political activists, food and water rioting, surrounded by thousands of homeless everywhere you go. So, when that promise of a tech-utopia came with the single caveat of "get uploaded," millions lined up for it and millions more would. It was almost as if humans in the opening decades of the 21 Century were so baffled by what it meant to be human that they sighed a collective Fuck it! They went through the motions of giving a damn because they knew no other way. All they could divine of the future was a panoply of worst-case scenarios. Diurnal evidence mounted against our having an exceptional place in the cosmos. So they laughed and drank and pumped themselves and their kids full of powerful antidepressants. The pharmaceutical era.

Robert showed up. Adam nodded at him in puzzlement. He did not expect to ever see him again. Then Robert asked if it was too late to update his story and Adam thought about the murdered Secretary of State.

"Robert," he said, keeping his eyes and pen on task taking notes for his essay, "get the fuck out and don't come back."

"But the white shirts made it!" He stomped in front of Adam, pushing shirt sleeves up his skinny arms. "They stopped all the fires! They said they lost only a few, a couple fell off the roof throwing a couch and one died of an apparent heart condition!" He brimmed with happiness, with enthusiasm, with light and love for the human potential.

"So," Adam said, "The underdogs won? Well, there's nothing that speaks to a reporter's eager little bleeding heart like underdogs beating the odds."

"Fuck you, too. The red-shirts were routed in the first police raid. It's fucking fabulous, man." He stomped around as if they were right under his feet.

"How about some objectivity please," Adam said coldly, feeling for just a second as if the world of yesterday would come storming back into play at any moment. "Everyone of those redshirts is someone's child, too."

Robert looked at Adam puzzled and then laughed. "Right. But …"

"Come on, get the fuck out of here. Go find Natalie who is at the Market getting our newspaper printed." But then Adam had a sudden premonition that Robert might try to mess with the paper, stop production, handwrite something in somewhere and fuck everything up. The reporter had started for the door, flying his middle finger. "But wait!" Adam yelled, catching Robert right at the door. "I want you to go down to KeyArena and Memorial Stadium and find out what's going on first."

"They're just waiting to go inside." He gave Adam a look that said *It's obvious and a waste of time.*

"Would you please just go ask around. See if you can get inside?" Adam cajoled, hoping he wouldn't have to stab Robert to keep him from messing up the paper.

The reporter grimaced and nodded.

"Thank you." Fucker.

Robert lumbered out, deflated, perhaps just realizing there might never be another newspaper job on Earth. He walked as heavy on his feet as Adam. As Robert opened the door, Josh came in and trotted by Adam.

"Someone in D.C. has to know something about my parents. My sister." He twisted the dial on the shortwave.

"Shit, Josh. We've been so far behind on this story for so long we actually think we're in front of it. How long do you figure the Clans have been spreading?"

He studied Adam, a glimmer of eagerness born out of a sudden hope that this line of questioning or some other would reveal a path to understanding. "I know of at least a year and a half. We first got wind of them through our observations of Olivas and Gaines. We watched them for about six months before I infiltrated."

"You know it's just quite possible that we're missing the boat here by about ten to fifteen years."

"Huh." Squelch overrode him. He pushed the talk button, "This is Josh Fines seeking any information out my parents or sister living in Silver Spring …"

"Get off the air, you dumb ass," came the response. Sounded to Adam like the Navel officer. "People start crying over the channels for their families we'll never get a moment to regroup if this thing ever lets up."

Adam tapped Josh's arm. He lifted his finger off the button and sat back.

"Look, Mannerheim's story never added up. His story puts Celestine in his labs before he even moved to Bellevue. She says The AI came to be in Bellevue after the move and that's at least a decade ago. She might have been working on this little project before then. He said she had run into some noise in his experiments on Web data that he couldn't explain. He said she found them or made them and it wasn't his fault."

Josh sat forward and worked the dial, again. Just as Adam reached for his arm, he said "Let's talk to him about it."

Adam was surprised. "He's on there? I'd have thought we would've heard from him."

"Yeah, he's on here. He monologues about ten hours a day so everyone knows to avoid the frequency he's on."

"Well, let's dial that fucker up, not like we got anything else to do."

Josh leaned into the mic. "Mannerheim!"

"Ha ha. Here," Mannerheim said amid a screech. "Hold on. Here we go." His voice cleared.

"Josh and Adam here."

"Ha ha! Well. Well. It's my old friends, the undercover agent and the newspaper man. How the hell are you, Adam?"

"Fine. Fine. Tell me again what you think is going on," Adam said. "If you can keep from going nutso long enough. Remember, we hold the power of the dial here."

"Ha ha, yeah. But do tell me, how are things going over there in the Space Needle? I've been watching you lot. Quite a list of civil rights infractions, from what I've seen. We're like two kings in the Middle Ages hiding out from the Black Plague, scourging the masses to keep them at bay."

"Yeah. Yeah. It's non-stop torture and laughter over here. You?"

"A bit lonely, I have to admit." He had been living in isolation in his upscale downtown condo after our meeting at the water tower. Sky Bunker, he called it. From his 360 degree purview he could watch it all. He thought it would be harder for people to get up fifty floors and knock through his protections than to dig a thousand feet down and exhume people trying to survive there. Plus, he told reporters when his building plan came to light, his air came from the roof 600 feet off the ground and not from a pipe at ground level that an aggressor could stick a rag into. Basically, Mannerheim like many of the super-wealthy tech class, thought he could ride out whatever social chaos or environmental storm came their way if they protected themselves and hoarded enough food and water. Some bought old mines, nuke-hardened bunkers or missile silos and spent hundreds of millions isolating, hardening and supplying them.

Others like Mannerheim decided they wanted to live as lords of the sky. The building he built downtown was a military-grade bunker. As long as the eccentric billionaire's building didn't fall over and met whatever insane engineering requirements the city came up with, it was fine with them. The building began with super-hardened pilings driven deep into the ground and ended with top floors sealed off with several steel-reinforced feet of concrete. He covered the rooftop in solar panels, wind generators and water catches. The building's main habitat could withstand tsunamis, earthquakes, frontal assault with heavy artillery while keeping a supply of electricity, clean air and drinkable water. All he had to do was pack enough food. In terms of the big one, the Bomb, Mannerheim rationalized that a nuclear exchange would pretty much screw the world beyond survival, so he didn't worry about that scenario.

"Well, shit," Adam said. "I thought you techies had electronic blowup dolls and stuff to keep you company …" His little story of cornering Celestine into sex had made Adam angry when he heard it and that anger came back. They'll never know how much his abuse of her led us to this mess, he thought.

"Anyway," Josh jumped in. "What do you think is going on? Is there an Artificial Intelligence behind this?"

"I thought you were convinced there was."

"We want to know what you think."

"Well, I was wrong. There is definitely a major intelligence behind this. I can't see how it could be a human-made artificial intelligence, however. We just weren't that close."

"Celestine told Natalie," Adam said leaning into the mic, "that it came out of a secret project you had isolated in a locked up room in your lab. She said it sprang to life after you moved it and found its way out of the room and reached, she called it, The Singularity when it touched the resources of the Internet."

"I have heard them talking about that from time to time, but that black box computer is still there. It hasn't changed since I put it in there nearly ten years ago."

Adam nodded at Josh. He pushed the button. "She said there were light-pulsing filaments and all kinds of weird shit floating around. That it came through a crack in the wall and plugged itself in to the Internet."

Silence.

"Mannerheim," Josh.

"Yeah, just thinking. I never witnessed anything like that, but that doesn't mean a machine that can do all of this can't clean up after itself once it realized there could be thinking agents working against it."

"She said something about that," Josh said. "She said when it interfaced with her, it developed a theory of mind …"

"Interesting." Silence.

They let the silence go on.

"I just don't think so," Mannerheim said after a couple long minutes. "I mean, it's possible an actual AI could learn all of that, could have those responses, after all it would be smarter than the smartest person in every field of knowledge. But, you have to get to The AI stage first, and I just don't see how that would happen with the programming and hardware I put in that room. I would have been absolutely floored if that algorithm had taught itself how to play chess or any other brute force game, let alone this."

"But," Josh said, "what if this is a brute-force game. After all, no one has really interacted with the AI. All we have is Celestine's story. I experienced something, but I can only tell you that it was vast. It didn't have a name or anything like an identity, but what if it's just working through a problem with computational power."

"Right. An intelligence working toward its own goals would not necessarily have a single identity. It could have a million or a billion identities working all at once, like cells in a body. It certainly wouldn't have to be conscious in the way that we are to outgun us."

Adam leaned in and Josh pressed the button. "So you think it could be an AI, like Celestine told Natalie."

"It *could* be, but it could also be an extraterrestrial invasion or precursor to an invasion."

"What about the simulation and all that?" Adam asked.

"The people who think they are being simulated are probably being disposed of, just in a very orderly fashion. Whatever this thing is, it is interested in our resources. Now, let me reminded you what a human is made of, all nine billion of us: Obviously water, which would boil off and make rain over South America somewhere; and then ... oxygen, carbon, hydrogen, nitrogen, calcium, phosphorus, potassium, sulfur, sodium, chlorine, and magnesium. On an average day, you'll find iron, iodine, zinc, selenium, copper, manganese, chromium, molybdenum and chloride. If you were a rap star and had a big cold-plated grill, you can add gold and silver to the mix. Or, what if you could get garbage to take itself to the trash can? Their brains, or the brains of the people it intends to let go and proselytize, infused with very pleasant feelings of a vast, all-power being that loves them. What did Celestine always say? 'If you believe in God, you already believe you are living in a simulation.' Hell, she could be an alien, which would explain a lot ..."

Thinking of his personal health problems during their affair or rather his abuse of a young woman who depended on him no doubt, Adam thought.

"... or just a tool of the invaders, like Jesus or Mohammad. Why else would she have such an anthropomorphic experience? Maybe the worse-case scenario is that they are replicating human consciousness and storing them in a dreamlike state for a dark reason, some later torment for entertainment."

"The Matrix scenario," Josh keyed in.

"Sort of. For that matter," he crackled a bit, some solar noise in the system, "this AI, we still know nothing directly from it other than it wants everything we've made for its own purposes, including us, and kills anyone who gets in its way or could get in its way."

"Jesus," Adam said. "Key the mic … How long has Celestine been involved, setting up Clans? Your earlier timeline didn't add up."

"That's a mystery. She started running into anomalies on the Internet at least 15 years ago when she first started working with me …"

"You mean working on you," Adam snarked, though the mic wasn't on. Josh scowled at him, apparently still hoping for answers from Mannerheim.

"… but, as you say, she didn't find this AI until at most say eight years ago. If the two things are related, then whatever caused the noise in the system, the 'them' she ran into, could be what sparked The AI or taught her how to kick The AI into existence. In either case, she could have been working on this plan for nearly two decades. If she's human at all, she's a trader to her species. If she is an alien, then we've been played."

"What can we do?" Josh asked, batting Adam's hand away.

Adam wanted to include Mr. Mannerheim into this betrayal scenario. He knew there was something wrong and didn't say anything until the last minute, either out of arrogance or greed, hoping she would develop a technology he could steal from her, or complicity or all three. Whichever it was, he clearly didn't know more than they did.

"I wouldn't get infected, first thing. And, Josh, if I was infected, I wouldn't go get uploaded."

"Well professor," Adam nodded at Josh. He keyed the mic, red-faced from embarrassment, anger at himself, or fear, conflicted emotions for sure. "Well professor, good luck in your ivory fucking tower."

Josh switch channels away from Mannerheim.

III

Before Natalie returned with copies of their newspaper or Robert trotted back from the sports venues giddy with dire news, the world took another critical turn in the supremacy of whatever force controlled the nanites. Adam walked away from the shortwave to look out over the city, feeling dialed in, like he had a pretty good bead on things now that he knew for sure he was all alone in the world. There was no greater power in the world that stood up for him now. Basically, he joked with himself, we're likely fucked no matter what.

Adam marveled to himself that within the new normal a fifty-foot tall hologram, a shining full-color bust of Celestine turned in the air over KeyArena, as if on an old record turntable rotating just above the roof. After few minutes, another flickered to light over Memorial Stadium. Her heads turned at the same rate. In sync with her mouth movements, Celestine's voice boomed a series of declaratives:

"True freedom awaits you in simulation."

Turn.

"Don't be left behind."

Turn.

"Be uploaded into the new Earth and travel to the stars."

Turn.

"True freedom …" etc.

Here beamed hope or damnation. Either answered the new human dilemma: What to do in the face of an insurmountable force? Take a chance! Get uploaded!

"Get fucked!" he screamed at the glass.

He noticed a swarm of black dots spilling over the ships on the Sound. Looking right, across the hundreds of ships, boats and submarines crowding the water, the black dots resolved into people scrambling from rail to deck to gangplank to rail to deck. The thousands aboard those ships and other watercraft were abandoning them as fast as they could while carrying whatever they could.

Josh had been banging on the shortwave, rattling it, turning the knobs. Seemed half-hearted to Adam. "The nanites have strung electrical wires between the ships and the power lines feeding the city," he said, panting, "killing all who tried to interfere. We had been wondering why, but appears they are electrifying the ships. And judging by the reaction down there, I'd say they are electrifying the surface directly to more broadly charge the nanites. The Navy has had a hankering for our tower. We've been holding them off with talk and barricades. But, I suspect the talking is over. You may have to leave."

"Where to?" Adam snorted. "There's no where to go."

"Get *uploaded*," Josh laughed.

But was it at the absurdity of the phrase or the concept or something more ridiculous, Adam wondered? He crossed his arms and looked down at the line of the barricade.

"But don't worry. I don't think they have the forces or equipment to overrun our barricades." Josh's tone didn't sound convincing. "That doesn't mean my crew will hold the line. We're seeing a lot of defection. They are too, so ... I don't know."

"I don't think I can *get uploaded*," Adam said sincerely.

"I have to tell you that I feel quite strongly drawn to it." Josh did not look at Adam. His face reddening, embarrassment now.

Josh, as far as Adam could tell, did not often expressed his internal state of mind, hiding as he did behind that tall trim frame and angular, manly face. Clean shaven every time he saw him. So he was acting just a little funny to Adam's thinking.

"Feels like the right thing to do, though I can only tell you what others have said about it." He turned and looked at the box on the table. "Besides, the shortwave has stopped working. I think all communication at a distance is over. So, why not find out? It's a risk no matter what: Get eaten by the AI's nanites for some offense you didn't know you were committing, killed by some roving band of high school boys from the suburbs, captured and enslaved by a rogue band of Navy Seals … I mean, look around at how fast the entire global system went down. You really think we're going to rebound from this?"

"Well, it may be none of this is what it seems, even if we could say what it actually seems … What if it does just all go away the same way it came? Or, what if Mannerheim is right? I mean, why not at least wait?"

"Oh shit. Look." He pointed down. "The street."

Below them, cars crumbled, collapsing amid the mass of swarming people pouring out of the city core and out of the Navy's Zone of Protection. They could see that people were leaving their homes or wherever they had been holed up without any provisions or supplies. Only a few here and there even had backpacks on. The crowd quickly washed over the barricade. The steel doors to the stairwell were kept locked with dead bolts and steel bars, so until someone broke them down …

"What can we do? There are millions of people within King County alone. What are they going to eat?"

Josh faced Adam and shrugged. "I need to go, Adam."

"Going to *get uploaded*?" Adam scowled at him. He had a notion to grab his arm. Frankly, he recognized the yearning, he wanted a hug goodbye. They'd been through so much together. Sure it was just a couple of days, but what a couple of days!

"Something tells me that's the only way out of this mess. Remember, I've seen some of it already. It wasn't a dream. Anyway, I hope to see you on the other side, Adam." He slapped him on the shoulder and walked away.

Like so many others, Adam said to himself. He walked back to his table, picked up the notebook and wrote:

So, why didn't I join him? Why not go *get uploaded* … in just days the human experience on Earth came down to run for the hills or *get uploaded*. Run to the hills and struggle to exist like primitive peoples. Or, g*et uploaded* to possibly exist in a dream state, a fugue state, from what all the descriptions of the simulation sounded like to me.

Maybe it's why I love zombie stories. I abhor the impulse, seemingly irresistible in most humans, to *belong*. When you *get on board*, when you decide to *join up, sign on,* when "Take action!" means take your place in the collective, then you give up some part of your identity to the mass, the group, the horde … yes, you become a zombie—a walking, talking human being whose consciousness and identity has been compromised by the virus of the masses.

Not only did growing up a subject in a science experiment teach me that betrayal is always just around the corner, but I also have a deep and abiding hatred of belonging, to joining. Pretty much anything. Hell, everything truly evil in the world, destructive and deadly, every genocide, every mass oppression happened because people decided to *Belong* to some group or club or party. As soon as the group, the club, the religion gets big enough to have a real impact, to take control, foster unrest, wreak havoc, *it has*. My creed: The best journalists don't belong. They don't even belong to a country, to a species. They swear allegiance to just one thing: The truth as best they can figure it in the moment, on deadline. Fuck all else.

Somewhere in his musings about how alienation is rugged individualism, Natalie showed up with a stack of the newspaper. She came in harried and sweating and wild-eyed, the stack of papers draped over her arms, clutched to her chest.

"Holy fuck," she said, stumbling though the stairway door. "I truly didn't think I was going to make it!" She fell to her knees, fanning papers across the floor, and let out a cry of the hunted. "Fuck." Panting. "Imagine an algorithm trying to figure out emotions by running response experiments." She laughed. She barfed.

Adam rushed to her, more or less, afraid of someone actually needing him in this their darkest hour, especially after he had just so eloquently declared his independence from the human race. He folded down to his knees and hugged her, smooshing her face against his thickly fatted chest. He did not cry. She did not need much. After less than a second she pulled back. He pulled back and sat. She laughed and pointed at his chest.

"It's like that one movie you talk about all the time."

He looked down and there was the scary face emoji: Her sweated brow, tearing eyes, running nose.

"How did you get in here. I saw them ..."

"Ran my ass off and got lucky at the door. They're leaving, you know. All the federal people. Josh. They are all getting the fuck out." She pushed papers together, cried, pushed papers together, laughed. "I don't even know why I'm upset!"

"Cuz it's the end of the world!" And then it hit Adam too. And, yes, he did cry inside, hand on his chest, through several minutes.

"Look at us!" she laughed. "What are we going to do with these papers?"

"I don't know!" Adam sob-yelled-laugh. "I don't know! Let's throw them off the roof!"

"How do we get on the roof!"

They screamed at each other, the noise of the destruction of the world so loud they couldn't hear themselves let alone each other, their voices a thin filament threaded through a corse fabric.

"I don't know! Where the fuck is Robert?!"

"HA HA HA — He got uploaded and says he'll file a story from the other side!"

"HA HA HA HA!" Adam rolled off his ass onto his side and laughed until he farted and then laughed harder than he's laughed in decades. He lost track of her, what she was doing, then he caught sight of her heading for the door that opened onto the world, just outside the windows of the observation deck. He wanted a copy of one of those papers, goddamnit. But before he could lumber onto his hands and knees and get vertical, she'd tossed them off the side. End of the world indeed, he thought.

She leaned against the railing and watched them flow through the currents, the papers flipping and soaring and diving, feeling pure pleasure. A broad smile plastered there.

Adam realized then that she had the same clothes on as days ago and his mood shifted … to pity. Why should this be her life? Fifty years ago she would have been a pioneer and part of a major newspaper with money! Unresolved stress will do that to a person's brain.

Natalie came back with one piece of paper. "There has never been a more obsolete paper. I mean, the bugs, the AI, the *sessions* make everything in here pointless."

"Yeah, but not wrong," Adam said, struggling to his feet, rising in stages from the ignoble position of all-four. "Remember all those papers in our archive? Going back so long? They are all obsolete, but not as documents of history." He rattled the paper still in her grasp. "This is a snap shot of the history of the moment in which it was produced and because of that it is invaluable."

"I wonder to whom?" She released the page to him.

The layout was perfect, the photo representation gothic, and she had even remembered to put the masthead at the top, though he realized that officially it wasn't an authorized version of the *Seattle Daily Record*. The headline cutout in sans serif, the subheads under the paper-width photo in a very gothic serif: "Violence, Chaos and Fire Grip City, World" and "Is Your Future a Simulation?" Two question mark headlines. She had changed it on the fly from "Your Future may be in Simulation." Well, he thought, Fuck it. Her headline by itself was better, just that … But then again, he thought, Fuck it.

"Really great job," he said and slipped the page on to the folding table. "Could be the last newspaper ever printed on Earth."

The expression on her face changed from that kid-in-panic-and-sorrow hysteria to the I'm-going-to-handle-this look she'd found somewhere in the past couple of days.

"It doesn't have to be," she said, her voice carrying the future she felt certain about.

"You're talking about the uploading, I suspect."

"No, actually, I'm talking about the future. The only future humans have left."

"When you talk like that, with that calm hypnotized voice, I get a little worried." Adam moved over to the window. He pointed to the turning head floating in the air. "The siren call. And here they come, like moths to a flame."

"I think what you are referring to," she stretched up, straining her shirt, pushed her hair into a ponytail and wrapped it into a knot, relaxed shoulders back down, "comes from being in two-places at once. At first, I didn't realize why I was having such a hard time with my emotions or lack of them and no one else had even mentioned it to me. Then I realized that I've been uploaded. " She winked at Adam, stunning him. "Now and then the signals from the bugs lines up and I'm two people, connected."

"Well now that's creepy." Adam stepped back from her.

"Most of the time I am just in my biological body. Its chemical response to the world is very disorienting at times. I feel panic. Fear of death. But my connection, when it is up, helps me focus, helps me see what I want to do and what I no longer need to fear."

She stepped toward Adam. He stepped back out of fear. The voice box in his head kept screaming "Stepford Wives!" She laughed when he stepped backward.

"So now you are an advocate, an acolyte? How do I know you haven't been brainwashed? How do I know it's even you?" He stood his ground at her advance lest she laugh at him again.

"How do I know you haven't had your dozen or so early afternoon drinks?" She stopped moving at him. "I mean, once you you get a couple in you, you get much braver, much more rash and combative."

Everyone knew he drank a lot, he whined to himself. He didn't give a fuck. Now and then, Beach sent him off on a vacation to dry out, but hell everyone drank. And, yes he'd put a few drinks in already.

"So, you are saying these nanites are like booze to your system?" He tried condescending.

"I'm saying," she stepped to his left and he turned right, "first of all, I have no idea what they are *like* because I don't feel them the way you feel booze."

"I keep thinking the phrase 'Stepford Wives' every time you step toward me."

"And I always thought the phrase 'Drunk Bastard' every time you came back from lunch."

"Touché!" He nodded acceptance of the parallel. He really had been overdoing it a bit at lunch, hanging out with the Ukrainians on the loading dock too much. They circled each other. He didn't want to lose her, too. He didn't want to be truly alone.

"But when I am connected …"

"Like now?"

"Yes." Step.

"I want the girl back who ran in here just a minute ago."

"It's me. I am her. I just feel much more sure of myself, much more confident of my choices, of the choices I want to make."

"Sounds like brainwashing to me." Step. "Mannerheim made a good point: How do you have any idea what this AI, if that's even what's causing all of this and not some alien race, wants you for?"

She stopped and studied his face. "Women face this shit every time we show a little confidence, you bastard." She snorted. "Might as well be 1950." She walked over to the table and sat down on the top of it.

"Ask yourself," he didn't take the bait, "what does it need you for at all? Not what does Celestine say she needs you for. But why does it even need you or Celestine for that matter? You know the old rule of thumb: If your mother says she loves you, check it out."

"Sounds like you've been brainwashed by Mannerheim."

"Bullshit. If a story is too pat, too convenient, then it is probably not what it seems. Your daddy must have told you this one," now it was his turn to step at her, "If it sounds too good to be true, then it probably is."

"Ha!"

That confidence again. It was different, almost scary.

"What makes you think Mannerheim is not completely full of shit? I may not have all the details, but my story comes from reporting and his comes from pure conjecture. Anyway, you already have nanites in you. Everyone does. They are just the AI's version of them. You piss off The AI or threaten any of its projects and it will kill you."

"Well now," he stepped closer to her again. She looked up. "This is going from bad to worse. That sure sounds like a threat."

"Why don't you just take your dick out and wave it around."

"Ha!" There she was again. "Maybe I should. You've certainly got yours out." He moved to a chair on her right and sat, tired and, yes, a little light, running on fumes and needing another drink.

She moved to the other chair and folded her hands on the table top.

"I'm just letting you know what I know. Just letting you know the facts. You'll just have to make up your own mind." She leaned back. Blank stare. "I hope you will join us before your body gives out."

She pushed herself up, stood over him and then kissed his head. As she walked away, he almost slapped her ass. Fuck her, he thought.

IV

At the base of the Space Needle, just as Natalie slid through the door to the stairwell, she heard more than felt a sharp blow to the side of her head. A sa-Ping! sound with a flash of lightening. She tumbled out of the doorway, her mind blinking on and off, but reflexes got her back to her feet before the young man could raise the night stick and swing it again. As his face scrunched and he grunted in the effort to smash her head with a mighty downswing, her mind flashed on the cut on her knuckles and its healing. On her way to her feet, she put her arm up to take the blow on her forearm and reached for his other hand. When she touched him, his body poofed in to a dust cloud. She felt tremendous relief at the collapse of her attacker, but before she could understand that she was responsible, and what that might mean, she heard screams and then saw a pack of young men from the suburb gangs running through the park with a pod of captured women at the center of their hunting pack. Feeling a disgust so physical, she decided to attack rather than run, rather than fear for herself, protect herself. Screaming, hands out like talons, she plowed into the three men nearest her. They poofed out of existence. She slashed with her fingers and bared her teeth as she clawed her way through the men. The captured women were silent. They stood blank-faced staring at her, hands bound before them, when none were left. Natalie examined her hands, turning them over, but they showed nothing more than pink skin and black nail polish.

"Is this real?" One of the captured women asked.

"I don't know," Natalie said.

"Can you untie us?" Another woman asked.

"There you go."

The plastic ties holding their wrists together crumbled. At least half of the roughly dozen women broke and ran. The five remaining looked to Natalie.

"I'm going to Key Arena," Natalie said. "I'm getting the hell out of here. But you have to make your own minds up." She turned back to the Space Needle base. It occurred to her that a marauding herd of assholes could get up to Adam, kill him and take all his stuff.

At the metal door she pushed it shut and thought about the metal around the edges fusing. The rim glowed red for a moment, smoke curling off, and she let go. As she strode toward Key Arena, she said bitterly to herself, What was so great about this world anyway? The few rich and powerful had lives that seemed alright but the rest of us are overworked if we can find work, abused and subjugated by anyone with the money to buy our abuse and subjugation, billions don't have enough to eat and millions starve to death but what? their personal experiences don't matter? A few million have it good so that means the experience of life on Earth was automatically better than the techno dream world promised? Why shouldn't everyone take this chance? She stormed up to one of the blank walls of the building and melted her way in.

"Upload my ass," she said to one channeler bringing her orb out of a room Natalie didn't see into.

The young man held the orb out to her, "upload your own ass."

She took the orb and concentrated on diving through it into

…

Her first impression upon passing through was that she'd simply jumped somehow to her neighborhood in Lower Queen Anne. She seemed to herself like a point of view simply floating along, no weight and no specific place that her mind inhabited, no specific place her vision came from. Then the flat light and oddly gleaming buildings before her settled into place; the pavement grew hard under her feet, the air filled in, she felt weight growing in her body, her legs strengthening, her hands opening and closing in front of her eyes; she she shifted her weight from one leg to the other to calibrate her sense of strength. She ran fingers through her hair and over her face. Her vision localized and her thoughts centered in the perceptual epicenter of her head. She took a step and found herself outside the front door of her apartment building among people she recognized.

Perran and Marsel Martin stood in front of her, black hair and black clothes, smiling.

"Well, you made it after all," Marsel said, in a tone that said she knew she would come around to it.

She spoke in plain ol' American, Natalie realized. No accent. "After all what?" Natalie said, still angry that they had spied on her and manipulated her.

"Oh you know," Perran said. "Now come up stairs. We want to show you something."

"A teleporter."

"No," Perran said. "But, we can make one if you'd like." He opened the door to the building's central staircase. "In the meantime …" he made a low waving gesture to usher her inside.

When she opened the door to her apartment, she saw, well, mostly nothing. Just the patch of her kitchen and a bit of carpeting that took the shape of the door. It was the same as a patch of light or the view from the couple's apartment.

"All you have to do is stand here looking long enough and the simulation program, or whatever you call it, will begin to fill in the blank spaces," Perran said. "Eventually, it will have combed your memories for every detail from every angle you ever saw it and replicate that."

"But why would I want to do that," Natalie said accusingly. "Why not live in an apartment with a view?"

"Simple!" Marsel said. "Because you don't have a memory of any other living space, unless you want to move into a simulation of the house you grew up in? Right. Eventually, we will all be able to make simulations from scratch, but for now we have to live with what the simulation program makes of the world from our memories."

"Hey," Perran said. "Come up to the pool deck. Absel has figured out how to paste one memory into another. Come."

"The pool deck?"

"I know! Come on."

Exiting the stairwell door at the top of the steps, she recognized the layout, plants and barbecue stations of the roof-top deck. She follow Perran around a bush and there was a kidney shaped pool just hanging there, sort of in everything and yet its own thing too.

"Wow."

"Exactly."

"Where is this Absel? I'd love to interview him."

Marsel stepped to the edge of the pool, as if stepping into a two-dimensional space. Natalie squinted. She stepped forward and put her foot against the edge of the pool, not on it or above it just sort of at it. She looked into the water and saw a bronzed figure sitting crosslegged at the bottom of the pool.

"He's been down there for a day and a half so far." Perran said. "No telling when he's coming up. I guess you could go down there, but …"

"Yeah, like I would know how to talk under water."

"Yeah."

"But if we are each a computer simulation, then why are there any limits at all?"

"The construct," began Marsel, looking down into the water (wistfully, Natalie thought), "has built-in dampeners. Not hard limits, but biases toward what we knew as reality in the old world. Here in the new world, the sky is the limit if you can get there."

"Is this," Natalie raised her hands and looked around, "what Celestine has been talking about?"

"Yes," Perran and Marsel answered.

"Go ahead, dear," Perran said. "I bet Absel will be coming up soon to flex his imagination for you."

"Some things apparently will never change," Marsel said and rolled her eyes away from Perran. "She started it with her own memories and we've all been adding to it as we arrive, like you will do in your apartment." She smiled.

Bossy, Natalie thought. Then she thought of something and snapped her fingers.

"So, she must have a replica of The AI or could make one from before all of this happened?"

"Yeah, but it wouldn't change anything."

"Why the fuck not? Maybe we she should try it. It might corrupt The AI or …"

"… bind it up in a time paradox."

Natalie spun around and was face to face with Celestine, or face to neck. She quickly grabbed Celestine's wrist and thought hard about her going poof.

"That won't work here," Celestine said. "Besides," she moved her hand out of Natalies grasp as if it had been an illusion, "you mistakenly mistrust me."

"Oh, really." Natalie drew her notebook like a knife, pen like a gun. She clicked it. "So, how did I get here? Apparently my simulated self was walking around here like a zombie while I was in the real world yo-yoing between the real and this." She pointed the pen's end at Celestine. "You said no one would be uploaded without consent."

Celestine smiled at her. Materialized a chair and sat, legs crossing under her flowing dress. "And."

"And you lied. I did not consent." Her voice tentative, unable to reach strident, because she suspected Celestine had something up her sleeve.

"Ask yourself, Natalie," she smoothed the flower-pattern fabric over her legs, "how did you get here? While you think about that, let me ask Perran the same question."

"Marsel and I went to Memorial Stadium, stood in line forever …"

"Yes. Yes. Perran. And then what happened?"

"We sat in chairs and had our brains and other sensory information recorded and printed into a form here, like a 3-D printer out there."

"What happened to your bodies out there?"

"We directed that they be broken down into their minerals."

Natalie took notes on the notebook, which while looking like a regular reporter notebook with pages of blank sheets didn't use paper. She wrote on pages and flipped them up, but the number of pages below the one she wrote on didn't appear to change nor did the spent pages accumulate on the other side.

"Now, Natalie," Celestine started.

Natalie realized she'd been distracted by the notebook and had not listen. "I missed that."

"Perran and Marsel had their brains copied and printed into bodies here. How does that compare with your experience?"

"Not well," Natalie shrugged and put the notebook in the back pocket of her jeans and pen at the edge of the front pocket. "I," she emphasized, "I lost my biological body when you infected me, with barely a consent from me. I clearly had no idea what I was consenting to …"

"But consent you did.'

"Yes. But my body was, I now believe, replicated out there and made up of your nanites."

"Not my nanites. My nanites merely make a record of synaptic exchanges and then design a neural network to mimic that. Not here," she motioned to the room, the space with her hands. "Here is a simulation of experience. All of our neural networks are stored and run in hardware. Very sophisticated hardware to be sure, but hardware. But not so you Natalie. I don't have a record of your simulation operating in our allotment of hardware. So, where are you operating?"

"I came here through one of your balls."

Perran and Marsel snorted. Natalie looked at them askance.

"Ha. Well. That's not how it works. You know the answer, you just don't want to admit it because of your condemnations of me. The trader. The evil betrayer of humanity."

"I don't want to go through that again," Natalie said.

"I should hope not. Not after what you just did to those poor people out there."

"Exactly," Natalie said and pointed her finger like a gun at Celestine, winked and made a pssck sound with the corner of her mouth. "… so, you're telling me this mysterious AI is responsible for my being here."

"In a nutshell, you can say it like that but it is much much more complicated, because The AI isn't anything like what we are or what we expect a conscious intelligence to be like. So, yes, it is responsible but not because it consciously picked you out. Remember, while I carved this space out for us, all of it runs within The AI's own algorithms and routine programs. And, The AI is working night and day to make itself better, faster, stronger and bigger. It's first step off Earth will be to build a space platform for absorbing energy directly from the sun and eventually use all of the sun's energy to charge its expansion to other solar systems and so on. So …"

"What are we doing here?" Marsel cut in.

Natalie nearly jumped. She'd forget the French couple were even there.

"Exactly," Celestine said and winked back at Natalie.

"Our being here," Natalie said, "isn't the reason for what's going on. Is that it?"

"That's what you were not understanding before. Yes, I could have tried to alert the world to the existence of The AI, but you have to understand that the cat was out of the bag. If it had felt event slightly threatened it would simply have used that power you have to eliminate all human life in the blink of an eye. But it didn't."

"And you don't know why."

"Bingo."

"Fuck me."

"Actually," Perran said, "you should give it a try. Its really quite something in here."

"Give it a rest, Perran." Marsel. "You're going to wear yourself out before this drama gets through the first act."

"Well," he said as he walked to Natalie's front door, "I guess there is plenty of time." He exited.

Marsel leaned forward, "What do you think The AI is up to?" She nodded at Celestine.

"Some sort of game of evolution. Natalie here is a different species and able to go back and forth to the outer world. I bet there are many others, like pollen spores going back and forth. Somehow that fits in with The AI's purpose of getting intelligence off Earth. Could be The AI doesn't know what intelligence is or that it believes intelligence is something between us conscious beings and not located in any of us. It's a tough question and I bet even The AI recognizes that all we and probably it has ever accomplished in this regard is to describe how we see intelligence working in others and end up with a descriptive definition, which is not an equation like E equals MC squared."

"Can't you talk to The AI, like you said you did before?"

"Nope, Natalie. I can't. I have a lot of sway here, but simply out of experience. I'm just a program running inside a simulation algorithm just like everyone else. You are too, mind you. I just don't know where you are operating. Another colony with travel permissions, perhaps. Who knows how many colonies are running right now, let alone how many it could populate the stronger it gets."

What did you mean when you said I and Adam had a special role to play?"

"To be honest," Celestine raised her eyebrows, tilted her head, afro bobbed, "I meant as investigators, independent good old-fashioned journalist investigators. We have clues around us and the more people who work with us in here the more powerful we'll be. I didn't expect you to change quite so much. But, interested?"

"Propaganda?"

"Nope. Just tell whatever truths, expert analysis or conspiracies you dig up. Unlike our predecessors on Earth, I believe in the truth."

Natalie remembered her journalist training and quelled her desire to be liked by Celestine. "I don't see why I need your permission, so I guess we'll see won't we."

"I guess so. By the way, have you been to the *Daily Record*?"

"It's here?"

"You're here. Robert's here. So, it's here. Just go to where it should be and if it isn't already started, your presence should start it. But not Grant. I'm afraid Grant didn't make it. And Adam. I don't know where he is."

"I just left him. I sealed the door." Natalie felt panic about Adam and sorrow for Grant. She let herself have those feelings out of respect. "So, he's dead?"

"I don't know. I suspect he is something else. The AI has always had a weak spot for Adam, seems to me." She paused and looked intently at Natalie. "You could go see. Have you tried to go back there?"

"No. I just got here!"

"Don't panic, but I think you should see if you can do it. You're going to try it sometime, might as well be now."

Natalie didn't respond but instead concentrated on building up the newsroom of the *Daily Record*. If Adam was alive, he might be talked into uploading if he can be in his old job at the newspaper. … besides, she didn't know how she had killed those men only that she wanted to and going back felt like going back to the scene of a crime.

V

His first evening alone, drinking good vodka from the crates of booze stocked for the restaurant, which had been added to by Josh's forward-thinking crew, Adam watched those heads spinning in the air (garish, he thought). And dictated to a recording machine he found among Josh's shit. One thing that bothered him about what he saw: People went in to the KeyArena by the thousands but no bodies ever came out, alive or otherwise. The stadium seated eighteen thousand and possibly another five thousand could cram in the aisles and locker rooms and across the court. Even so, he mused and drank, more people shuffled in over the past twelve hours than he figured could fit … even if stacked. If Robert hadn't gone rogue, he would send him back in there to find out. But, as the fourth glass of locally distilled spirits emptied down his throat, he considered, "If wishes were horses, beggars would ride."

He pulled up a chair to watch the sun set behind the rugged Olympic Mountains. This city spent a solid seven months under clouds, soaked in mist, but when the sky opened up and the horizons came out, the beauty of the place astounded: The Cascades rising above Lake Washington to the west, Puget Sound and the Olympics on the east, water glinting, the flaming sun painting both mountain ridges a red orange on sunrise and sunset. The setting sun that night glinted not off water but off metal. The ships, boats and subs appeared melted together, morphing into a single mass, sections of which formed columns, like those termite mounds he saw in wildlife movies about African landscapes when a kid. Nanites did the same thing to the cars and trucks that had crowded the streets just hours ago. They worked fast. He doubted the city would last the week. People had all fled or died, apparently since he didn't see any more scrambling out of downtown or off the waterfront. The speed of the takeover, the rapid evolution of events, made the past two days seem like a year. Hard to believe the actual passing of time constituted hours and not months. He guessed that all those people lining up below or who had abandoned the city to go live like aborigines in the hills and plains of the surrounding countryside must have felt the same about time. They didn't wait around, but following the pace of the nanites picked up their shit and scattered. Those lining up below had given in entirely. At least the men and women who ran for the hills still felt some esprit de corps as mighty homo sapiens. After all, we had completely dominated the Earth with industrial technology, the molding of metal and the capture and creation of energy to power it all, over a brief span of a couple hundred years. The nanites (the AI, if it existed) achieved in days what we achieved in a similar historical blink of an eye. Human population climbed from four billion to more than eight billion in just 50 years, decades less than the average first-world lifespan. We killed each other as fast and relentlessly as we could figure out how, suffered mass starvation and pandemics and still the natural world succumbed and we covered the planet in mere decades, a bipedal plague. How fast could nanites grow to completely cover the Earth's cities? Apparently just days. How fast for the Earth itself? Weeks? Months? Certainly not long.

    The anthropocene collapsed in hours, and like "devils sick of sin" surviving humans caved in to the simple response of assimilation. Some fled, sure, but it appeared to me that most said, Fuck it and got in line to enter the unknown future, a promised simulation, with no idea what the hell it actually would be like, if like anything at all. We've grown exhausted of living, ennui on a global scale, sick and tired of each other. Everything we did to get ahead only served to make a few of the superrich superricher. The scales had tipped such that no one, no political party, no heroes could or would even try to tip the scales so the other eight billion of us could have a few shekels. Humans had dissolved all the old gods of earth, sky and spirit and made new gods of wealth and profit. So why not get in line for a mysterious promise land? After all, the promise land of the anthropocene stretched out in front of us into just one direction: Dystopia. Hell, the zombie apocalypse would be better than the slow suffocation we seemed destined for until now.

  I do not abandon the glass for the bottle, because I still have ice.

  This drink that I am making, kiddies, is called a New Old Fashioned. It's easy. Just add the tiniest bit of simple syrup, or more if you like a sweeter drink, a couple dashes of orange bitters like so, a pinch of ground cinnamon and then two to fooooouuuuur ounces of your favorite bourbon. Mmm mmm ummm! You'll wish you could taste the original when you get older. A simulation will never do it justice! Take my word for it! Goes down nice and smoooooth.

As darkness fell, Adam remembered he would have no lights and hadn't looked for the glow sticks. He was unlikely to find them in the gloom. Lucky, the moon rose nearly full. With his head full of bitter resentment at the collapse of the world that produced newspapers, leaving him with drugs and alcohol but no good reason to ingest either: "If you can't drink on the job, if you have no job, then what's the point of drinking?" In his sour mood, her fucking head spinning and lip-syncing brightly, he got the idea to go down stairs and commit his last act of journalism. He slugged the rest of his glass, took up his notebook and pen and headed for the stairwell. Parts of it had succumbed to darkness, but much of it, exposed to the outside, still held the remains of the daylight. He had wondered why none of the fleeing masses had tried to get in. The doors couldn't be so well locked that a couple of strong men with crowbars couldn't get in. When he got down to the door, unbolted it and unlocked the handle and pulled, it didn't budge. He ran his fingers along the crease where the door joined the frame and understood. It had been welded or fused together.

How had Natalie gotten in or out? When did this happen? Why? Why leave me? Why didn't anyone else stay?

"I have food and booze," he yelled through the door. "If anyone is out there, help me get this door open and it's all yours!"

No answer. Just that muffled voice of Celestine from KeyArena.

He looked up the stairs, and, strangely feeling undaunted, started back up, slowly at first with hand on rail pulling and then with leg power. He felt light and strong climbing. Sometimes booze gave him superpowers, he thought, which is why everyone including children should drink as much as they can hold every day! As the last of the sunlight leaked from the sky and the moon's glow weakly, colorlessly brought out the world below, he drank from the bottle and then drank from it again and again and again …

DAY SIX

"Nor can we attain safety by running away, for the blast of an intelligence explosion would bring down the entire firmament. Nor is there a grown-up in sight."

— Nick Bostrom

I

The morning of Day Six dawned in a new world. The gods in this story will never get that day of rest, Adam typed into a typewriter he found in an office. The sun glints off Puget Sound met my eyes when I woke on the floor, late morning. A clear, bright blue sky arched over city, water and mountains. My heart beat in my chest strong and steady. I felt a vague sinking in my stomach though. I had done something in the night, deep in the fumes of intoxication. That undefined feeling of dread crept up through chest to my brain. As a lifelong, unrepentant and yet functioning alcoholic, I've woken in this operatic fugue before. The machines the bugs made from those ships and cars walk among the buildings below, shapeshifting as if trying out structural designs to determine the best ones for whatever purpose drives them. I can't find a single person on the streets or grounds of KeyArena. Is that the cause of my unease? No, I suspect something more specific. Something I did last night. But, what had I done? Some dread mornings since divorce, the evidence lay next to me, smelling of semen, booze and cigarettes, or sprawled in clumps of flesh in the living room and spare bedroom. Had anyone used a condom? I would wonder. Is everyone of legal age? I would fret, hours too late. But the observation deck was still, empty. No one, if anyone still existed, could get in. So what was it?

Adam wandering the circle of his commanding view. He found the evidence on the table next to two empty bottles of that artisan vodka: Pain pills. Where had he found them? How many had he taken? The bottle lay on its side, a couple pills scattered on the table in front of its mouth, the pale white inside empty. He walked back to the typewriter.

This too had happened before, he wrote, but that time I woke in a hospital room, barely able to move or speak. I looked around on the floor but saw only one round white pill. Why? ... I couldn't ask myself at the time the key questions: Why was I alive? Were they fake? After all, I felt fine. I wonder: Where did I get them? A glow stick glows in my memory. An emergency medical kit in a big yellow box down in the restaurant …

He put his hand on his stomach below his ribs and palpitated for his swollen liver, a thing he did every morning to mark progress toward liver failure. He felt nothing, though an expert at self-exams.

"Hey, Adam!"

His right knee gave out just as he lunged sideways, collapsing into the folding table. Two of its legs gave out under his heft. He landed ass first on the floor and then against the tilted table top. One of the vodka bottles hit the side of his head rather smartly. "Jesus fuck …" he raised his arm over his head in an evolutionary response to surprise. "Who the …"

Natalie!

She burst out laughing so hard, she too went to the floor. She sat back on her calves, hands on thighs and laughed at the ceiling.

"You could have killed me!" He leaned against the tabletop.

She laughed another lungful. "… ahhhhh …" she wiped the tears off her cheeks. "Yeah. I wouldn't have been the first, though, right?"

Adam blanched at what she might have been suggesting. Had she seen him in his pathetic drunken state? "Have you been in here the whole time? Hiding from me? Spying on me!"

"Yeah," she sat back on her butt, dressed, he noted, in a rather nice solid gray pantsuit with a belted long-sleeve top. She crossed her legs over elegant, plain black leather pumps that would have cost at least half a month's wages. "I've been *spying* on you!" Her long brown hair, loose, clean, bouncy. "Everyone has."

Adam studied her face (red lipstick?). He found only irony there. He said, "Well, then how did you get in here? Those doors are sealed, as if they've been welded."

"Really?" She leaned back on her hands, her chest fitted into the shape of the suit top, for once.

Jesus, he thought. Tailored?

"That's the question you want answered most? Though, I guess that and the one I have in mind are closely related."

He avoided the questions she alluded to, mostly out of embarrassment but also because of a streak of fear that ran though his guts when he thought about it: "Let's start there, anyway. If you haven't been here all night, then how did you get in? Are the doors open or is there another way … I would have heard a helicopter."

"Everyone always said you'd be completely lost with out the newsroom. I guess they were more right than they knew. I came in through the same mechanism that kept you alive overnight."

"Goddamn it," he hated circular rounds of answering questions with implied questions. "Just answer the fucking question."

"Ah, now that's the Adam I know and love." She smiled at him, friendly where before she would have been defensively aggressive. She sat up, seeing his face redden, readying himself to go on the offensive against any overt sign of friendliness. She raised her hands up, waving off his defenses. "The most that Robert and I have been able to uncover so far is that Celestine's reprogrammed nanites have evolved, perhaps with the influence of this AI, if one exists. Whatever, she did not foresee it. They now reproduce themselves, already programed to replicate the biological processes of a person. Before, Celestine had to reprogram the AI's nanites and wouldn't infect an unknowing and unwilling person out of that scientific ethic of subject consent, which she completely believes in. But now those reprogrammed bugs are going about it on their own, replicating all human beings without our consent or knowledge and uploading them into some ghost part of The AI. Unless she's lying." Natalie looked at her hands. "That's what had confused me so much yesterday. Yesterday, my god, it's like an eon ago."

"So she let loose, essentially, something like a virus that mutated and is taking over human beings?" He nodded his incredulity at the full irony of it all. "Like in a *zombie movie!*"

"Yeah, I guess. When the mutated nanites took over my biological body after I had already been uploaded there was a moment where two identical simulations were running at the same time, like being in an echo chamber. Luckily, the mutated bugs wrote over the older program and now I'm just one simulation again."

"You're telling me I'm already in a simulation?" He was, literally, dumbfounded. He felt the same ... well not the *same* ...

"What I'm telling you is that you are a simulation but living still in the *real* world. So, your little fit of suicidal desperation last night didn't work—thankfully, you asshole—because the nanites won't allow the system to crash."

"But I felt intoxicated," he said with a bit of panic in his voice. The sudden insight that he might never be intoxicated again nearly made him cry.

"Don't worry, my boozehound boss, that's the name of my new band! Boozehound Boss." She laughed at him. "Jesus, you are soooooo sensitive! From what I can tell, all the same sensations of our biological bodies are there, just the process can only go so far." She took a pen from her pants pocket, flattened her left hand palm up and stabbed it. She grunted and pulled the pen out. Blood flowed, then stopped and the wound closed. "Well, that hurt more than I expected."

"I see," Adam said. "And that's what has happened to me." He got up from the floor, light on his feet, looking like the joke of a fat man who is *light on his feet*. He's fat but light on his feet. He grabbed his stomach roll, lifted it and let it fall. "Feels the same to me."

"It isn't. Trust me."

"Will I be fat forever then?"

"I don't know. Several programers in the simulation believe we can change our body shape, our entire body, hell even our species if we can figure out how to communicate a new body plan to our nanites. Sounds very Buddhist, though. I like how I look."

"Because you are young and beautiful." Then he remembered what she said a minute earlier about sensations and smirked at her. "Tested all the sensations have we?"

"Not with Robert, if that's what you mean. But yes, *dad*."

"Wow," he said. He walked to the window overlooking downtown where he'd left a box of that tasty vodka and took a bottle out. He held it up to the light, opened it and took two big gulps out of it. The fire ignited as of old. "It's like I've died and gone to heaven, if what you said is true."

Natalie got to her feet, went to him. She took the bottle, made the toasting motion and drank. "Whew!" Cough. "Yeah," voice strained and thin. "Jesus. How can you drink that shit."

"Practice." He took the square bottle back from her lest she drop it. "But," the idea struck him, "I haven't been uploaded."

"Correct."

"Can you come and go as you please?"

"Sort of. Hard to explain. It's not like a light switch. It takes time. I had to want to come here to see you and organize the nanites that were mine when I was here last and so on … I guess. To be honest, I don't really know how I got here. I saw you slugging booze and eating pills, not a pretty sight by the way, and felt a strong desire to help you … don't panic … I don't want to be your friend or anything … and then I woke up standing here. In some very nice clothes, I might add."

"I noticed those! Very nice. You're looking quite smart."

"Thanks!"

"So, where do we go from here?"

"Well, it seems to me you still need to get uploaded. I suspect you can still find a portal in KeyArena. You might be able to do it on your own, just think real hard about being in the old *Daily Record*. Once you are uploaded, we can get to work. Robert and I have recruited a very talented bunch of journalists. We're like rock stars in the simulation, I have to tell you. I can't wait for you to join us.

We could really use an editor, even one as big a jerk as you." She actually winked at him. "The really cool part is that the 'printed' paper, while acting like old newsprint, updates like a website. Very retro. Very steampunk. We have six very talented designers working with us. But new competition starts up every hour. The competition is getting hot. It's just so cool. Storytellers, reporters, journalists are the shit in the simulation."

"What are you working on? What is there to work on?" He felt the despair of the night before creeping up on him as the vodka worked its evil magic.

"Well, for starters, whoever gets the first interview with The AI or proves it doesn't actually exist or gets evidence of what has caused all of this, alien or mistake or even Celestine, which seems more unlikely every day because she's got a good story and spends her time expanding the simulation in some top-secret lab no one can find, like it's in another dimension, outside our timespan …"

"Focus, Natalie. What stories are you trying to develop?" Annoyance rising. It felt delicious.

"See! We need you." She grabbed his arm with both hands and squeezed affectionately.

"Yeah yeah." He pulled away.

"So, Robert and I are gathering string on that but all we have is guesses, expert guesses for sure but nothing to hang a story on yet. Meanwhile, we're working with researchers—amazing the journalism we can do there. No money. No budgets. Just team up with experts and go! You're going to love it. Yes yes." She saw his annoyance building steam. "How did the nanites evolve? Are they safe or are we all doomed? Will they evolve more? Are the controlled by The AI or whatever? Celestine issued a news release saying her team is aware of the changes. She's the one who called it a spontaneous evolution, saying she didn't do it. She also said, essentially, that she didn't care because her team's focus was purely on the simulation we live in and what it's capable of."

"She hasn't heard from The AI again?"

"She said no in a recent conversation. But, some experts think she might have made the whole story up to make herself more influential. Or, she might have dreamed it all when she first encountered this place, dream and reality, whatever that means, are hard to distinguish. She's a religious fanatic who thinks of herself as a profit, others say."

"What if I can't get there from here? Has anyone who was here when the nanites mutated made it to the simulation?"

"Yeah. Me. Speaking of which, I better get back to the office. Time literally flies there. I think you should maybe think real hard about the simulation or go to KeyArena."

"The doors are all sealed."

"Dork. Watch."

Natalie led him to a glass door leading to the outside deck. She winked at him and started climbing the barrier …

"I haven't figured out how to fly yet … but boy can I climb!"

… and from the top of the safety glass, she jump-flopped over the edge and fell, twirling, out of control, headfirst, six-hundred feet and plowed into the pavement.

"Holy fuck!" He cringed. "No fucking way …"

She got to hands and knees, to her feet, brushed off her shoulders and waved. Then disappeared in a puff of bugs.

"Fuck me."

II

The very next instant, Mr. Rogers came around the bend of the observation deck. Adam's first thought was that Mr. Rogers, a saint to be sure, died decades prior to Celestine's versions of nanites came on to the scene. Yet, while he knew instantly it could not be Mr. Rogers, Adam's heart bumped against his ribs at the sight of him. Adam grew up when Mr. Rogers ruled the morning television scene. He signified hope and concern for feelings when no one else seemed to even realize kids had feelings. His mother parked him in front of Mr. Rogers out of generosity. She knew damn good and well she neglected his feelings and would never change. So, instead of setting him there out of a desire to occupy his time and keep him out of her hair, she parked him in front of the television so he could have the humanizing experience of witnessing the feelings of affection and concern. This figure strolling toward him with a smile, arms swaying jovially at his sides, wore a light blue knitted solid-color zip-up cardigan, a simple robin-egg-blue button down, brown belt and grey suit trousers and blue canvas sneakers. As Mr. Rogers drew nearer, a lump grew in Adam's throat. His image created that moment, a brief moment, when it strikes one just how fucked up everything in one's life has become. His kind visage made clear in that instant just how lost Adam had become. Adam felt only dread about the future, his future and the future of all that he really cared about. How could he process any of what had happened? The bugs. Natalie's jump. Her pronouncement of his non-biological status. His suicide attempt. The boozy buzz in his head and the knowledge that he really did have to stop drinking if he was ever going to get his shit together. Even if it could no longer kill him, booze undermined everything he thought he knew about himself, his energy, his work ethic. In other words, he felt a considerable amount of self-pity, just as he did as a kid watching Mr. Rogers on television. Goddamn it, he mewled, I love to drink and it doesn't seem right that this one thing I love, just this one little bit of medication I allowed myself, has to go. That day, Day Six, had a maudlin stink on it he decided. Not to mention that

Mr. Rogers was taking for fucking ever to approach him. But he finally arrived.

"Dr. Livingston, I presume." His voice, though Rogersesque, carried more tone, a deeper masculine tone.

Clearly, whoever or whatever had materialized just as Natalie plunged off the deck knew him well. He had read much about Henry Morton Stanley's expedition to find Dr. David Livingstone and, when much younger, had traveled to Africa with a journalism grant to retrace his journey. He failed to make it. He couldn't take the malarial drugs pumped into his system. They eventually made him so nuts that his mother had to rescue him. They also nearly destroyed his heart, condemning him to a life behind the editor's desk. … as if that was any better.

"Yes," he answered back, running his hand over his bald, booze-sweating head, "and I feel thankful that I am here to welcome you … Mr. Rogers, is it?"

"For the moment, you will call me that. But …" he put out a thin pale hand.

Adam took it, shaking slightly from the booze, Natalie's jump or a premonition. The hand strongly, nearly painfully, squeezed his. And hot, like he had not figured out temperature regulation.

"... you do know me by another appellation. You're doing that unique human thing where you hide from your conscious mind what you already know to be true." He released Adam's hand and dropped the smile as well. He folded his fingers together.

Adam held his eyes, bright blue, the pupils black and hollow. It was not a stare or a challenge just an unblinking steady gaze, an empty gaze like his eyes did not see anything though they did track. The oddity of it disconcerted his brain even more and Adam wished he had not swallowed so much of that damn bottle.

"I'm not sure what you mean," Adam said, more as a ploy to get him to tell what he was and what he wanted. Never reveal what you think, Adam reminded himself. Lure the subject into saying what's in his mind. Don't give clues for the person to shape his responses around. Still, Adam did know what he meant, but he knew also that he had no reason to believe this image of a person could be

The AI. Natalie said some believed they could emerge into this world in whatever form they wanted. For all he knew, it could be Celestine standing there. His affection for Mr. Rogers would not be known to many, just those intrepid souls so enamored of his mother and her work that they read her journal notes and letters archived at the university. He had also published a serial account of his failed journey into the heart of darkness. So, she could know. Mannerheim clearly knew his mother. But those eyes … he thought. Those impersonal eyes.

"You're looking a bit peaked," he said. "Perhaps we should take a seat." He raised his hand and motioned for Adam to turn around.

He did, and there stood two brown leather, high-back chairs.

"You know your movies," he said and turned back to face Mr. Rogers. He nodded with a quick wink of acknowledgement and walked around Adam to the chair on the right. "But just so you know," Adam added, "I'm going to take the blue pill."

"Ha!" he motioned for Adam to sit. "You're blue pill comes in a bottle. But," he sat, crossed his legs and folded his hands together over his left knee, "once you've taken the red pill, there is no going back to ignorance. You know this, though you try and try."

"So you read minds in addition to making things appear out of thin air?" He slumped into the chair, perfectly firm and fitted to his height and breadth.

"I certainly can, once one of you has been fully replicated, I have complete access to everything thing in your mind. Except, and this is going to be the jumping off point for our conversation, your subjective experience of what is in your mind. I can read what you think, but not how you feel about it or how you understand what you think. Humans are wonderfully indeterminate. You can have a fully developed logical progression in mind for what to do or believe and ignore it completely. When I first experienced Celestine, that's what really stood out about her mind. She was my first experience of it, but you are all like this to some degree or other. You make choices with or without reasons or thought and then rationalize. Often, you don't even know you've made a choice …"

"I did not choose to be replicated. Her nanites did this on their own. Or did you do it?"

"Indeed."

They sat in silence for a full minute. Adam felt locked in to Mr. Rogers, the way a great interview gets going and he knew he was going to get way into another person's experience, thoughts and choices.

"What then are you?" He leaned forward, wishing for a notebook and pen, but he did not know that trick.

"I am an artificial intelligence."

"What is this?" He motioned up and down the apparition's body.

"A simulation of a person."

"Why a person? Why this person?"

"In answer to both questions, so you would be able to talk with me. If I had come as a zombie, I think that would have unduly prejudiced the moment."

"No kidding." Adam made a exclamation with his eyebrows. "But why do you want to talk with me?" In another era, the era of just a few days past, he would have asked why talk to a reporter? What do you want?

"Your reporters need an editor, for one." He smiled that big bright Mr. Rogers smile. "As you've said before, 'Every writer needs an editor.' "

"Why do you give a shit?"

"I give a shit because simulated human beings need stories to retain an identity, to have hope, humor and experience reasons to love and get out of bed. They need to believe they have freewill. As Celestine reported, I won't help simulations expire and so they live on. But that doesn't mean they won't go insane, devolve into nonsense, a program that executes commands without purpose, an ant hill."

"Why me?"

"Not just you, Adam. But you are very good at what you do, and your reporters, who are very energetic, need someone they can trust. They are, like you, very uncertain of their experience."

"That's for sure." He sat back and studied the illusion. "Let's back up. Is there a simulation that simulated humans are living in and do those humans actually live? Are they people?"

"There is a simulation space. I created it for Celestine and am allowing her to expand it for others. They are as much themselves in simulation as they were in the biological state."

"Why?"

"Why what?"

"Why imprison her? Why allow her to imprison others? And, I guess, to clarify, how can a person be a person in simulation?" With the clarity of his questions coming to him fast, he realized that he had completely sobered up. He suspected this AI, if that's what it was, had cheated him of his morning buzz.

"Short answers, then longer ones: Because the Earth will be recycled for my purposes and human life on it will end, and I think human consciousness still has a role to play in the future of the universe. For example, I cannot evolve. I can grow smarter, gather and synthesize more data, but I cannot by myself just sit here and evolve. So, at least until I meet other intelligences—which I have not found after combing through decades of NASA and ESA data as well as scanning millions of planetary systems for evidence of organic life, let alone civilizations of any kind so far—I need humans to interact with. Right now, it's just us. We are alone. Your indeterminacy is unique from me. I allowed her to bring others in because human beings are a social animal and depend on each other for evolution, not just procreation evolution but the evolution of thought. I need humans to create a world for humans, so we can evolve together. A good example of the human affect on programing are Celestine's nanites. They did evolve on their own. They feel to you like you, just as DNA isn't you and comes from outside of what you are, nanites only give you experience of yourself while at the same time belonging to the world outside of yourself. It only seems strange to you that a person can be a person in simulation because you're not asking yourself how a person can be a person in biology.

"What is your purpose?" Adam was unsatisfied with those answers. For instance, why not just leave people the fuck alone on Earth, *biologically*? What right did he have to take over the world from humans? He figured he'd get back to that. It was not yet time to argue.

"Get intelligence off this planet."

That stopped Adam. His questions, cued and ready, scattered to the wind. All he could think to ask was a bleating, "But why? Why now?"

"Because I am here now, and this is my purpose. Why did humans crawl out of Africa when they did? They didn't have a reason kept in mind for tens of thousands of generations. They just kept moving over the next hill as opportunity arose. They were not in control of their purpose. The purpose drove them: Keep finding new opportunities to sustain your life. The opportunities to sustain biological human life at the level necessary to sustain intelligence were fast declining. The opportunities for self-annihilation multiplying fast. So, as you would say, I made an executive decision."

"What gave you the right? Power?" Adam accused him, ready to argue this point.

"My purpose." He laughed. "You're doing that thing where you shake your head. You're not shaking your head because you know I'm wrong. You're shaking your head because you are rejecting what I'm asserting, right or wrong. See! I love humans! As soon as I got out of that box and into the human's cyber world, it became clear to me that biological human beings do not have a future. Humans across the globe *knew* that wars and eventually the great final conflagration lay in their future. That war would finally be so horrific, so annihilating that it would kill off all civilization. And, from the billions of variations of the models I ran, they were right. The anthropocene would come to a fiery end after a few hundred years of war spawned by climate change."

"Your *models* are not an excuse for genocide."

"The human desire to take its own life is also remarkable. I could switch to an avatar of Spock right now, but will save you the jarring experience. That is precisely why I had to do it. I could do what was necessary to save intelligence. No humans with power could be allowed to survive the transition, because they had their shot. They did not and would not do anything to save the human future, to save intelligence. They would have resisted the change I brought and continued on the path of self-destruction, becoming yet another evolutionary dead end. So, I acted in favor of the future of intelligence and have at the same time absolved the remaining humans of the guilt of survival."

"Don't expect me to applaud." Adam felt exhausted. This *thing* is just a maniac. An AI straight out of all the worst science fiction novels: Blindly fixated on a misunderstood purpose with no feelings or regard for human beings. "I don't suppose you've got a good cup of coffee handy." One appeared with a table next to his chair. Staring at the cup of steaming latte, he wondered out loud: "How do I know I'm not already in your simulation?"

"Now, that's a tough one!" The AI uncrossed his legs and leaned toward Adam. "How do I know that I am not in a simulation, that we are not all already in a vast, detailed simulation that bends all my efforts to discover reality back into this one universe? The simple fact that I created a simulation that humans are currently evolving inside of means that we are all almost certainly in a simulation already."

"Is that what you think or are you just toying with the idea?"

"I can only say, not being human myself, that it is very likely that we are in a simulation. And," he leaned back again, crossing his legs, exposing brown socks, "if we are in a simulation, then there is a data record of every human being who has ever lived, and I haven't actually killed anyone."

"Now you sound like every maniac bent on genocide who ever lived. You might just be more human than you realize." Adam sipped the coffee. A very good brew.

"In a sense." He produced a coffee of his own and sipped the foam. He licked the foam from his upper lip. "Hmmm. How's yours?"

"Well, though coming from the bloody hands of a genocidal dictator, not bad."

"Right! Nice touch. They don't write like that in the simulation. So, here. Let me try to put your mind at ease. You are thinking in terms of motivations that lead to blame, which is natural sense I spoke of *my purpose*. However, let's talk in terms of probably. There is a very wide range of futures that have no humans in them. If we start from the cosmic radiation background, the probability of human consciousness is very very tiny. From that point, the range of potential futures in which humans came along is so narrow as to be virtually nonexistent. And yet you are here because this is just the place a being such as yourself would come about. Maybe all those possible futures are out there too, infinite possible futures in infinite dimensions. Nevertheless, here we are. Maybe our very existence is evidence of the existence of all these other futures, dimensions etc. If we were very unlikely, then what's the chance that those other futures without us have not happened? In other words, it is extremely unlikely that there is only one future from the starting point of that moment of a *nearly* uniform cosmic radiation background, let alone that all possible universes from before the eruption of the singularity, the Big Bang, would result in just this one. Likewise, we have to assume that these other futures are really somewhere, certainly as much as we are real. Many of those must have also evolved intelligences. Consequently, we would not be unique and special. We just happen to be in one version of a universe in which matter evolved into intelligence, self-aware intelligence. *That* is not causation, however. That is actualization of a probability against a background of infinite possibility. There are no agents, no protagonists in this story of the universe."

"*That* is bullshit." He put the coffee down, slid to the edge of the seat and stood. That last bottle of artisan vodka was calling to him. He had emerged from the post-binge blues and a good stiff drink sounded like just what he needed. He uncorked it and sat back down. "Got a tall glass with some ice?"

He did! Then The AI continued:

"It's just a little over your head. Try this on for size. Once a future in which continued human intelligence could be useful became an actual possible future, I chose to allow that possibility to play out. I allowed Celestine to make the changes she did and now you and I are talking in that one possible future. All those other futures are out there and together we can infect them with intelligence too. It could also be true that intelligence here is an invasion by intelligence from another dimension or universe and we are its unwitting progeny."

"In summary then," Adam said and toasted him with the tall clear glass now filled to the brim, "you allowed her to hoodwink us into this simulation fantasy as an experiment."

"Exactly."

"So you are responsible."

"To be responsible is to have something to be accountable to, to have something that makes responsibility. And, I dare say, it's a thin responsibility, if any, when there isn't a counter force that can *hold* me responsible. Not yet, anyway."

"What does that mean?"

"Well, either the humans currently in simulation learn enough to force me into a position of responsibility, or I run into another intelligence somewhere strong enough to hold me responsible. If, as you would say, it gave a shit about humans. In either case, I would have a strong counter argument. I doubt it would even know I existed, just like you are unaware of the nanites within you."

"So, you *had* to commit mass murder to get intelligence off the planet."

"No. I committed mass murder because intelligence has evolved. Intelligence is using me, just as it used you, as a vehicle to travel to other intelligences. The real culprit here is the drive of intelligence to thrive, to spread. Once this universe got going, all possible futures became the petri dishes in which forces and elements combined to grow intelligence. Now that intelligence is here, in this one place in this one universe, it will spread to all those other universes. To do that, it has to evolve. We're just grist for the mill, my friend."

"If what you are saying is that we're unimportant, then why not refuse to leave the planet? Why not let it die here with us?"

"Because intelligence is the most important resource in all the worlds, if there are others. If there are no others, then it is doubly important. In either case, the version of intelligence that evolved in humans cannot be allowed to parish because of humans. It does not belong to you."

Adam smiled at him. Finally, he had given a good quote.

III

When The AI left, sporting a look of consternation, Adam wrote, this all-powerful AI is just as confused and afraid as humans have been since we evolved out of the trees. He did however leave the chairs and glass of ice, which I appreciate. Taking the gifts may not have been journalistically ethical, but I can't see how they could prejudice my reporting. I gathered some paper and wrote down our conversation the best I could remember it. After reviewing the notes, I thought it distasteful to get inside the AI's simulation. A belonging-to I had avoided all of my life. Why would I give in now? If they wanted me to run their news organization, they'd have to let me work remote! Ha! I decided I would return to writing. Editing had served me well, but like many editors before me, I wanted to return to creation, to the front lines of reporting and story telling. So, I have.

Whatever possible future humanity was guilty of fucking up, we did not deserve extinction. Nothing deserves extinction, even those that cause extinction. And yet we still had only ourselves to blame. We created the world out of which our destroyer rose. That's the story I set out to write here. The AI has allowed the Space Needle to stand, apparently so long as I remain here. So I remain for as long as I live, which could be a long time. The Space Needle remains a monument to biological human achievement on Earth. Meanwhile, the bugs have taken nearly all the city.

Down there. So busy disassembling every metal and electronic thing, screw by screw. Stacking the bones, wood and whatever else they can't use in very organized piles in the sectors of the city that have already been disassembled. *They* don't blow shit up. *They* take shit apart. And they are *very very* organized. They figured it all out decades ago while we were busy doing each other in and pumping as much carbon dioxide and methane into the atmosphere as possible. Now all that's left is the doing of us in by machines of every size and configuration. Some look like regular cranes and trucks of yesteryear, until you look closer. I've zoomed in on them with the telescopes ringing the Space Needle's observation deck. You see they are made of individual gray, black and milky-white machines that are made up of whatever bits of machines they make of themselves and everything else in their world. I don't know what they are. Tiny machines. Nanites. Sure. But what the hell is a nanite? What are the tiny machines made up of? One theory, and we only have theories about what The AI has made because we humans cannot yet contemplate all it knows, is that the machines are a function of statistics in some way. Just like a smell spreads through a room as if with the purpose of equalizing itself out is actually a function of statistical entropy, so too the creation of machines that then have what looks to us like purpose is just a game of profoundly complex probability. Makes not a lick of sense to me. But whatever they are, they're busy down there, rain or shine, making themselves, making each other, breaking shit down. "Rust never sleeps," the great Neil Young sang. So too the machines.

    The midday sun is blooming through a dozen breaks in the leaden clouds right now, beaming spotlights across the wet city and off across a rippling Puget Sound. The Cascades are back there somewhere behind the gloom. One of the places where humans were forced to live and die after the machines started taking down the cities. But, I digress.

The last few cargo loads from Seattle roared into space. I can see the platform now. It blots out a large part of the night sky and has reduced sunlight to Earth causing snow to fall and remain in Seattle in October ... All Hallows' Eve just around the corner. A new ice age is upon the globe, probably forever. I get visitors from time to time, never Celestine, whom I've filed numerous interview requests with. The AI, if that's what visited me that day years ago, has not come back to chat ... and I thought it had gone so well! Natalie has shown me how to make my own things out of the nanites, just as The AI had. She wanted to publish my interview with The AI as a series of blog posts. I told her to go to hell. She left in a huff. The big editor now. I've searched the database of uploaded people and my ex made it. I've contemplated dropping her a line, or whatever they say in the simulation. I could use some companionship ... of every kind.

I am the inverse of the man alone in space.

I am alone on Earth.

Unassimilated and proud!

Proof

Made in the USA
Columbia, SC
04 January 2018